CHASING ELEANOR

KERRY CHAPUT

Black Rose Writing | Texas

The author grants the final approval for this literary material.

First printing

This is a work of fiction. Names, characters, businesses, places, events, and incidents are either the products of the author's imagination or used in a fictitious manner. Any resemblance to actual persons, living or dead, or actual events is purely coincidental.

ISBN: 978-1-68513-210-1
PUBLISHED BY BLACK ROSE WRITING
www.blackrosewriting.com

Printed in the United States of America
Suggested Retail Price (SRP) $21.95

Chasing Eleanor is printed in Garamond Premier Pro

*As a planet-friendly publisher, Black Rose Writing does its best to eliminate unnecessary waste to reduce paper usage and energy costs, while never compromising the reading experience. As a result, the final word count vs. page count may not meet common expectations.

Cover design Asya Blue asyablue.com.

CHASING
ELEANOR

CHAPTER ONE

Bend, Oregon
1935

Leaves fluttered as a sage rat scampered across the forest floor. City people called them squirrels. When he stopped, his long silvery tail curved like a question mark, and he twitched his cute button nose. I waited for the right moment, aimed for the head, and blasted his poor face to bits. Couldn't eat the brains, anyhow.

I wiped my dress clean of the moth I had unknowingly smashed and left my cool spot on the earth to inspect our would-be supper. Lifting the critter by the feet, I examined his gray fur dappled with blood spatter. I felt bad for the poor thing—but not so bad I wouldn't eat it.

Deep in the forest, coyote pups howled. There were often only a few, but their yips sounded like a thousand wild dogs hanging from the trees. It was an illusion, Papa taught me. "Magnolia," he used to say, "never let the fear break you."

Two years ago, Papa disappeared without so much as a whisper, and Mama couldn't see a reason to get out of bed. I threw that image aside and slung the shotgun over my shoulder. The boys had to eat. Thank goodness for today's kill. I hated when I had to resort to possum, or worse, bullfrog.

Woodpeckers paused their drumming as I stomped through the forest toward home. If you could call it that. As usual, nausea rolled through me at the sight of our ramshackle cabin. The stifling summer heat rippled up from the sandy dirt and wrapped around me like a straitjacket.

"Maggie!" Johnny smiled, paper airplane in hand, as beads of sweat trailed down his cheeks even under the shade of the porch.

"Hi, Pilot Parker."

He fluttered his long eyelashes. Seven years old, sweet, and cute as a bug's ear. His legs began to twist last summer, every day like the turn of a corkscrew. Today, they flamed red. That was new.

"Are you in pain?"

"I'm okay." He rubbed his swollen knees and forced a smile. "I just need a rest."

Johnny needed a doctor. But doctors cost money and that was something the Parker brood could never get their hands on. Things would change once I took charge.

"Where's your brother?"

Johnny motioned with his thumb. "Around back."

"How was Mama while I was gone?" I asked.

"Fine. She didn't even throw anything."

Relieved, I slung the bloody animal onto the porch and went to find Oscar. Crouched low, he stared down the dirt road. For a twelve-year-old, he sure had difficulty with the world. While most of us breathed air, Oscar breathed feelings.

"Hey, what're you doing?"

"Shh!" He held out his trembling hand, motioning for me to lower to the ground. "They're gonna come tonight."

"No one's coming for us."

"Yes, they are." He nibbled on his fingernails, then looked at me with glittering copper eyes, wet from the threat of tears. "The wind feels different. Something's going to happen."

I knelt to face him. His eyes were so dark, I could see my blond braid reflected in them. "I'll protect you. Now please, come on. Your brother's having trouble walking."

Reluctantly, he stood and glanced over his shoulder while nibbling his thumbnail down to the quick. Without a flinch, he sucked the drop of blood from his raw fingertip.

I walked to the dilapidated front door. Hanging heavy on its hinges, the lower corner scraped like rake tines on the wood porch.

I licked my lips and stared at the black hole inside our shack as my mouth went dry. Labored breathing, but no moans or cries, no mumbling or screaming. Safe to enter.

Light snuck through the cracks in the walls, illuminating dust particles as they floated through slivers of sunlight.

Mama didn't say a word. The only sound was a subtle whistle of forced air through her nose.

This sage rat had to be skinned.

I stepped into the dark cavity of the crumbling wood cabin and waited.

"Where..." Mama paused. "Were you?"

"I had to catch dinner." My pale eyes struggled to adjust to the dark. An outline formed in the shape of my mother. Long and lean, she looked like a pile of sticks on that lumpy mattress.

"You left me," she said.

I turned from her, unable to tolerate the sight of her frail body, her hollow eyes. I flopped the carcass onto the corner table, over a ripped flour sack for easy cleanup. The skin peeled from the pink flesh of its belly like old wallpaper.

"I'm getting worse. Sicker," Mama said.

A sharp tug released the rest of the hide, leaving a bit of fur on the feet like shoes.

"And you leave me alone for hours."

Crack. The joints split at the ankles.

"You promised me," Mama said, her voice quivering.

"I'm here," I said. "I won't let you die alone."

The head snapped from the squirrel's spine with ease. Innards covered my hands, so I let the sweat from my hair run a cold trail down my back.

Rattling coughs turned Mama's breathing to tight wheezes. "And the boys?"

"Johnny's legs are growing worse." I hesitated. "He needs a doctor."

"No," she said. "They'll take them away. You don't want to lose another one, do you?"

I swallowed the fear that felt like a shard of walnut shell scraping down my throat. An outsider might think she was referring to the multiple stillborn babies, but we both knew the truth, that Emily died because of me.

Losing her two-year-old and her husband sent Mama to a place she couldn't come back from. The ugliness of life broke her years ago, but I'd be damned if I let it break me.

After wiping my hands clean, I walked to her bedside. "Time to lift your feet." I pulled back the sheet and stifled a gasp. Swollen and weeping, they looked like the slugs the boys collected from the riverbed. Mottled and purple, shiny as eggplant skin.

Mama sat in silence, letting me grow wiggly and uncomfortable.

"You need a doctor too," I said.

"No doctors," she hissed. "You can't trust anyone, Magnolia."

My name caused her to flinch.

"I need Aspirin," she said.

"Aspirin costs a dollar. A dollar we don't have." My body went rigid as her claw-like fingers grabbed the sleeve of my dress. I pulled my arm back an inch so she was touching the fabric and not my skin underneath.

"If your father was sick, you'd find a way." She sucked wet gulps of air into her blue mouth. "A lousy drunk. That's all he ever was. And then he left you."

She stopped to cough, releasing me from her grip.

I moved my toes around to trace a knot on the wood floor. Sure, my father was a drunk, but he loved me.

"Don't go feeling sorry for yourself." She tried to lean forward but didn't have the strength. "Sit me up."

Tightness gripped my chest. Touching her felt like climbing into a mine shaft, all dark and suffocating. I pulled her shoulders forward and placed a pillow behind her back.

"Not so rough." Her clammy hands grabbed my wrist. "Someday, you'll see. I taught you the truth."

"That I'm worthless?" I yanked my arm away.

Her eyes flattened. "That you're ungrateful." She glanced through the open door at the boys sitting on the porch. "Without me, they'll take them away. Do you want them to suffer for your mistakes?"

Her words. Like an arrow shot through its target.

"I can manage the boys just fine," I said.

"When I die, you'll do it better, is that right? Don't be stupid. You're a minor without a job. Nobody cares what you want."

"I'll be eighteen in six months."

"It will be the same misery in six months as it is now."

Unable to speak, I held back what should have been said. That I couldn't get a job because of my promise to her. Aspirin wouldn't fix her. Nothing would.

"Go to the store and get me what I need. And hurry back."

Every muscle in my neck tightened. "Yes, ma'am."

The boys stumbled in with a cloud of dust. Oscar held his arm around his brother's waist to help him walk, and when they came to a stop, Oscar plucked pine needles from his hair. Faces covered in dirt, their white eyeballs glared through the filth.

"Oh, boys. Look at you." Mama stifled her cough and tucked her water-laden legs under the sheet so they wouldn't see.

"We were playing airplanes," Johnny said.

Poor kid would never fly planes with those twisted legs. Head always in the clouds, he looked up at the sky more than the world around him. I couldn't blame him.

"Johnny, let me see that face." Mama held his chin in her hand like it was a golden egg. "Darling as ever."

"I'm gonna run faster than Oscar someday," Johnny said with a smile.

"Sure you are, baby."

Oscar pulled Johnny closer. "When you fly planes all over the world, who will play with me?"

"You'll always have me," I said.

Mama laughed in between gurgling coughs. The menacing snicker flew right past the boys but landed straight in my center. Right where she intended.

"Go wash up," I told them.

Squirrel soup simmered over the wood stove while I chopped the last mealy potato and tore dandelion greens gathered from the forest. The only thing left in the cupboard was a tin with one measly sardine. It would have to do.

Mama picked at the skin on her arm until it bled. Her demons worsened as the day marched on, fever heightening her agitation. I shuddered thinking about leaving the boys but tamped down the fear, compressing it like gunpowder.

***

An hour later as I hurried to the grocery store, the sun blared high in the sky, singeing my exposed skin at the part in my hair. Soft, powdery dirt settled in the damp creases of my neck. Nothing but a lonely nickel in my pocket, it would take a miracle to return home with a bottle of Aspirin.

A loud bang shot into the air, sending my heart thumping against my chest. Crows fluttered from the pine trees at the blast of the gunshot. I turned to see the neighbor killing off his last cow. Too expensive to feed the poor animals. Too dry to maintain a farm.

By noon, I stood rigid at the threshold of the grocery store, feet stuck to the concrete like tar, while the buttery scent of popcorn wafted from the doorway. The hole in my gut felt as big as a crater, and I was thirsty for all sorts of things that were out of my reach.

I forced myself to march straight up to the groceryman. Slapped my hand on the counter and squared my shoulders at Mr. Johnson. "I need a bottle of Aspirin."

He stared at me with raised eyebrows and not a stitch of sympathy.

"Please." I practically had to spit out the word.

"You know the rules, Magnolia. You got money?"

"Yeah, I've got money." I felt around for my one lonely coin and slid the nickel across the countertop. "I've got five cents." The way the heat climbed up my cheeks, I just knew my freckles glowed bright as a neon sign.

"Aspirin is eighty cents."

"You know I don't have that much," I whispered. "Please. My mother's sick."

"You can get it in that line over there." He nodded to the desk in the back for folks who couldn't pay. They put their food on credit, hopelessly looking toward a brighter tomorrow. No one could ever pay up and eventually, old man Johnson would make them settle their debt by handing over their houses. The grocery man owned half the town.

In that dark corner, a young woman shuffled toward the desk and the scowling grocery worker. Sunken eyes, down-turned mouth, pregnant belly under her faded dress, doing what she must to save her family.

Our crumbling house wasn't worth a thing, but it was all we had.

"Well?" said Mr. Johnson.

I shook my head no.

He slid the coin back to me. "Your choice, kid."

I stared at the shoppers as they stacked food in their baskets. The women who lived in town looked foreign to me—their dresses were all one color! Smelling like powder and not like stale sweat? Now that was living. Every day I washed up just to get dirty again. Filth stuck to me, like a memory.

A woman elbowed past me to buy a carton of eggs. "I'm in a rush."

Her eyes seemed to shoo me back to my crumbling cabin, to the secrecy of the pine trees where I belonged. I held back a snarl. What a stupid idea this was. I grabbed my tears by the tail and stomped out of her way.

Mama used to sew and mend to make ends meet. This nickel was all that remained. We kept a couple dollars in an empty Hills Bros tin, to buy a coffin after Mama died. I suppose some things were just too sad to imagine.

After the woman left, I slapped that nickel on the counter and grabbed two sticks of Beeman's Chewing Gum. "Thanks for nothing."

He handed me three pennies. "Miss Parker, everyone's struggling. I can't hand out free food. I wouldn't have a business."

"But you'd have plenty of houses, wouldn't you, Mr. Johnson?"

He tightened his lips and turned from me.

Back into the blinding summer sun. The air smelled of pine dust and whistles screamed into the air, marking shift change at the timber mills. The heavy afternoon carried on toward night, and I had to face Mama with empty hands. Aspirin wouldn't make her get out of bed, or heal her skin sores, or help her forget about all she's lost.

I never could fix her, didn't matter how hard I tried.

Down at Mirror Pond, I lingered for a moment under the shade of a black cottonwood. Families picnicked with sandwiches and Coca-Cola. Mothers read magazines and fathers napped in the grass. Sweethearts held hands while kids splashed each other with the cool water of the Deschutes River.

The scene made my heart hurt, and I couldn't stand to look any longer, so I carried on to the edge of town. The grocery store incident still made me fume, and I picked up speed, gritting my teeth. By the time I neared the bread line, I had to bite back a scream.

Men dragged themselves around the corner, their hats low over their eyes, tattered suits hanging loose on their thin bodies.

My father never took a handout, told us charity was for the lazy. But there I stood, defying the unspoken rule that women weren't allowed, because I was desperate to take something home to the boys.

At the edge of the crowd, a man with a white straw hat tottered forward. He often stood on the corner with signs, demanding the community find us jobs, share food. Surely, he'd stand up for what's right. If I took a place with the others, forced them to see me, maybe I could silence that anger that burned in my throat.

I hesitated, preparing for the men to hurl insults, convinced I could take it if I had just one person to side with me.

I stepped behind him, head held high and shoulders back. No room for fear.

His eyes widened with a glance over his shoulder. His fingers fidgeted with his jacket pocket, and I could tell I overestimated his commitment to doing what was right.

"Hey kid, get outta here, would ya?" a man barked.

"This place is for men. Now get," another said.

The entire line turned to face me.

"You wanna help your family? Go home and grow some vegetables. Wash some clothes. But don't take up a man's place in the bread line."

I crossed my arms. "I have a family to feed, just like you."

The man in the white hat stared forward, silent.

One of them leaned toward me. "You don't know the first thing about what we go through. We're out here dripping with shame, begging for scraps, and we don't need some girl reminding us how we failed."

I steadied my feet. "I know a thing or two about begging for scraps."

Grown men all staring at a seventeen-year-old, about to pounce. Angry. Intimidating. Except the man with the white hat. He ignored me, like a coward.

They were probably good men deep down, but poverty does something to people. Fighting and wanting and hoping for things you could never have. This life was damn near impossible. It broke all our hearts in different ways.

I elbowed my way in front of the man I'd put my faith in and forced him to look at me. "You gonna say something?"

He stared through me like I was invisible.

"All your preaching and fighting, that only applies to men, huh?" Anger spit inside me, hot as a grease fire.

He looked down and in a thready voice said, "That's not how things work, and you know it."

Those grown men pushed me. I stumbled, thudding my backside on the concrete, staring at their faded shoes as they snickered. I couldn't look at the man with the straw hat. If I did, I would've burst into tears.

A moment of weakness. Never again.

I ducked around the corner of an alley and fixed my braid tight enough to make my head throb. *Focus, Magnolia.*

A slight breeze picked up, cooling the anger that sat hot on my skin. I exhaled. In a world like ours, these moments kept you breathing. Kept you holding on for one more day.

A newspaper fluttered at my feet, so I picked it up and leaned against the cool brick wall. On the front page, an image of Mrs. Eleanor Roosevelt driving a convertible Packard. A note at the bottom said she refused secret service but always kept a loaded pistol in her glove box.

The article detailed her driving trips through the Great Plains, New England, and everything in between. She traveled the country and reported back to her husband. My head set to spinning. This woman didn't take to her bed when life broke her down. She came out fighting.

I turned the page, hooked on every word of the article. The First Lady had hosted some fifty young women, mostly Black, at the White House. She served lemonade, cake, and ice cream, and demanded their reform school improve living conditions.

At the end, a thought from Mrs. Roosevelt. *"We do not have to become heroes overnight. Just a step at a time, meeting each thing that comes up, seeing it as not as dreadful as it appears, discovering that we have the strength to stare it down."*

The Roosevelts were a different kind of people. Hopeful people. I guess you could be that way when you had money.

A door banged open, and a kitchen worker threw a bucket of vegetable cuttings into a trash bin. That breeze picked up the odor and sent it wafting into the air. I scrunched my face and brought my hand to my nose.

"Old cauliflower and cabbage," he said. "Stinks to high heaven when they rot."

He shut the door and it was just me and Eleanor Roosevelt and a stash of rotting vegetables.

With all the strength I could muster, I stuck both my hands into that moldy pile of filth until I struck gold. Half a head of cabbage with only a few black leaves. I yanked myself out and gasped for air, choking on the stench.

When I turned the corner at the other end of the alley, I passed a group of women trading desperation pie recipes—pastry made with vinegar because there was nothing else to fill it with.

They turned from me, hands to their noses, coughing away the smell of rotting cabbage.

We do not need to become heroes overnight.

With that cabbage under my arm and two sticks of gum in my pocket, I held my head high and walked straight through the center of their little circle. "Afternoon, ladies."

My tough girl act slid away as I neared the forest outside town, just as it always did. My heart pounded when I neared the house, but I kept moving. I stomped through the door and stood firm.

"Where's my Aspirin?" Mama asked.

"I don't have any. I couldn't steal."

"Fine," she said. "I'll just suffer." She hissed a long sigh. "Do fevers cause your heart to stop?"

I didn't answer.

We ate our supper in silence. Soup of moldy cabbage, squirrel flesh, and a fish the size of my pinky. And some people called pie desperate.

Mama refused to eat until Oscar handed her a bowl and she smiled through tears. She choked down a few sips while he watched. I shooed the boys outside, knowing how hard it was for Mama to eat when she couldn't catch her breath. But she'd never let them see that.

I slid the gum into the boys' hands. Told them to chew until it lost all its flavor and spit it out before Mama saw. While I cleaned the kitchen, Mama watched me and snarled. Sometimes her silence bothered me more than her screaming.

When it was time to tuck in the boys, I cracked my knuckles to stop my hands from shaking. Darkness filled me with a specific terror, the kind you could ignore during daylight when there were other things to look at. But in the paralyzing silence of night, all my fear seemed to snake through the cracks.

Johnny lifted his arms for a hug. "Night, night, Maggie."

"Goodnight, Pilot Parker." I kissed his forehead and tucked the blanket under his sides nice and tight the way he liked it, then walked to the other side and sat next to Oscar.

"She's pretty bad, isn't she?" he whispered.

"Yeah, she is."

He rubbed his eyes. "She said she's sick with a broken heart."

"I know she believes that. Truth is, she's sick from all sorts of things." I didn't know what stole Mama's breath, but her leg sores and blue lips showed me she wasn't long for this earth. When Papa left, he took Mama's heart with him, leaving us with her wasted body.

Oscar's bottom lip trembled. "Mama says my heart's fragile as glass. Am I gonna die?"

I looked at his wide, shining eyes and I wanted to scream at the world for being so miserable, and at my father for leaving us, and my mother for putting this idea in his head. Seems like that's all I ever did, muffle my screams until they hurt.

"You know something, Oscar?"

His lips curled inward, holding tight so he didn't loosen into a mess of tears. He blinked a few times, his eyelashes wet and stuck together. "What?"

"I wish I had your tender heart."

His shoulders softened. "Why would you want that? I cry all the time, and other kids make fun of me."

"No. You're perfect."

"But you're so strong, Maggie. I want to be like you."

I wanted to shake him and tell him never to be like me. But I swallowed the thought and let it burn a trail down my throat. "Being full of fight makes it hard to breathe."

He furrowed his brow. "Is she gonna leave us like Papa did?"

I searched for an answer that would make sense to him. But who was I kidding? Nothing made sense to me. So, I pulled him tight into a hug and breathed in the sweaty musk of his dark hair. His skinny arms squeezed a little of my fear out too.

"I don't want that nightmare again," he said.

"Is it the same one, where monsters climb through the windows?"

He nodded and held back tears that rested just at the surface. "Their black shadows smother me and take me away."

The boys kept a rock collection in the corner. I stood, picked one up, and rested it on the window, balancing it halfway off the wood ledge. "Okay, I'll place this here. If the monsters come in, it will tumble the rock to the floor. I'll hear it and come save you." It was all I could think of.

His face broke into a smile, his eyes red and glassy.

I kissed his cheek and tucked him in. "Snug as a bug in a rug." As I closed the door, I said, "Sweet dreams," which was possibly the biggest lie I had ever told them.

I settled into my spot on the floor, on a sheet stuffed with straw, just at the foot of Mama's bed. In the months after Papa left, she filled the nights with screams and thrashes, sometimes banging her head against the wall. Lately, it took everything in her just to breathe.

Last year, she made me promise not to let her die alone. Our lives grew very small, shuttered in this shack in the woods, all of us with different reasons to fear the world. Someday soon, I'd fight for a job and give these boys the life they deserved. One with doctors and school and all the hugs their little hearts desired.

Then she broke the silence. "You're no better than me. I'll be gone soon, but everywhere you go, I'll be there, watching you fail."

I tightened my braid through cramped hands, the tight pull settling my thumping heartbeat. Crows screeched into the black sky as the fire roared in the wood stove. Stifling hot now, but needed once the early morning crept in. Mrs. Roosevelt's words floated to me like a feather in the wind. *Do not see things as dreadful as they appear.*

In times of distress, it didn't matter how dark I tumbled down that hole, my mind still grasped around for the light. No choice but to look fear in the face, just as I'd always done.

CHAPTER TWO

Her death took three days. She died at seven in the morning, best I could tell from the angle of the sunlight. I'd like to say she gave us a sentimental speech about saying goodbye, being tough, and how much she would miss her babies. But that wouldn't be truthful.

A late summer wind swept through the woods, rustling the pine trees and kicking up the dust. It grabbed hold of Mama and took her away as quick as a blink.

Her weak heart couldn't take any more.

The strangest feeling washed over me right after she died. The moment slashed me open, my raw, beating heart one with the world. All my fight, all my toughness fell away and all that rested between me and death was a moment—a breath. Problem was, I patched myself up with thickened skin, leaving my heart begging for love all alone inside of me.

Johnny stared at her ashen face. "When's she gonna wake up?"

It's a funny thing what a kid's mind can do, hold on to hope when everything in front of him says it's useless. I wrapped him in a hug and sang in his ear, "No Depression in Heaven."

Oscar fell to the floor and rocked in place, his long, bony legs curled into his chest. Before I knew it, we all swayed slowly, soothing ourselves with a vision that Mama had escaped to a better place.

I lowered to the floor and held the boys in my arms as they trembled. All I had to give was a kiss on their foreheads, a whispering tune, and a hope that

I could do better than our parents. So, I lied and told them we would be just fine.

The boys cradled each other, whimpering as I reached for Mama. My body could move and hurt, but Mama's couldn't. My knuckle grazed the sharpness of her cheekbone when I moved her stringy silver hair from her face.

Her cheeks used to flush pink when she'd sing. The night we realized Papa wasn't coming home, she rocked on the porch singing "America, the Beautiful" in such a haunting whisper. Mama told me it was my fault he left. I put too much pressure on him. I loved him too much. When she saw my tears, she smacked me and said, "Toughen up. He's gone."

Hidden under the window that night, I closed my eyes to listen to her angelic voice floating on the summer night. Amber waves of grain. Whenever I felt scared, I'd picture myself alone in a wheat field, golden stalks as far as the eye can see. I'd imagine that out there somewhere, outside our broken family, waited a country where hope lived.

I caught one last glimpse as I covered her with the sheet. As it crested her face, a chill shot through my fingers and landed straight in my heart. Her unmoving body under the yellowed sheet took up all the air in the room.

I was in charge now.

The three of us dug a hole for hours. Twenty steps away from the house, under the shade of a cluster of ponderosa pines. I dug hard with a shovel and Oscar with a bucket. Even Johnny scooped the dirt with his hands. We all wanted to do our part to send her off.

Beads of sweat dripped down my temples. The sun's sharp sting snapped at my face for hours, each wipe on my brow grainy from dirt.

Chunks of black lava rock made it difficult to dig. Bumpy masses with flecks of shining crystal at every turn. When we finished, we stood over the hole, staring down into the dark cave we were about to lower her in to.

"I need a minute with her," I said.

They nodded and Oscar said, "I'll fetch the box." I reckon he didn't want to use the word coffin.

The hot, thick air carried the slightest scent of pine and the river whispered from beyond the trees. Cicadas rattled and chirped, life pulsing along like a heartbeat. But in the cabin, the suffocating air taunted me as I summoned the courage to say goodbye.

"Now that you don't need me, I'll find a job," I told Mama. "Take care of the boys. Make enough money to send Johnny to a doctor and get them both back in school. Give them the life we should have had."

I scanned the outline of her body under the sheet, scared witless to look at her again, and terrified that the sight of her would crumble my resolve. I would never again tell her about the town gossip, which I used to do to keep her mind off her tight breathing.

"I'm going to be like Eleanor Roosevelt. She says that courage is more exhilarating than fear." My throat tightened. "I wanted you to teach me that." I expected her to come back to life and smack me, but she didn't.

"The Bend Water Pageant is next weekend. I've always wanted to watch all the fancy women in lace floating on wooden swans down the river. There'll even be a royal court and princesses. I know you wouldn't have gone, but it's still nice to think about."

I kept talking nonsense, anything to keep me believing she was sleeping under that sheet and that the dream of a loving mother wasn't gone forever. She was just sleeping off the blues, that's all. Since Papa left, that's all we ever saw, a world of muted blues and hungry bellies.

Relief washed over me. I wouldn't have to clean the sores that developed over the last month on her heels. If I never again saw what's under a person's skin, it would be all right with me.

"I won't fail," I said. "I won't take to my bed or blame the boys for my terrible life." Guilt ripped its way through me. "And I won't leave them."

Oscar stepped inside and placed his hand on my shoulder. "I don't wanna do this."

"Me either. But here we are."

We rolled her in a blanket. Touching her rigid body sent shivers up my arms. We lowered her to the floor and Oscar recoiled. Hands to his face, he wailed.

I choked back tears, knowing Johnny watched everything from the doorway. "Go ahead and cry," I said. "Nothing to be ashamed of."

Oscar turned his face to the wall, silently heaving into the corner. I pulled the blanket across the warped floorboards, hands cramped and sweaty. Didn't matter how carefully I tugged, Mama's bones still rattled and clunked as her body slid down the steps into the dirt.

I stopped to catch my breath. Johnny stood frozen, mouth tightened into a frown.

"Do you want to say something to her?" I asked.

He shook his head no.

"Are you scared?"

His eyes swelled into puffy orbs. "A little." He turned his face to the sky, squinting into the blaring sun.

I waited for my hands to steady and my chest to stop aching.

We lowered her into the ground as the sun splashed pink streaks across the sky. We'd been dealing with her death as many hours as it took for the sun to move over us like a rainbow, setting behind Bachelor Butte. Our skin glowed in the evening light as Mama came to rest with the lava rock and the black beetles in the low, cold earth.

We sang her favorite hymn, "Morning Has Broken," and each of us threw dirt on the box. I hammered in a cross, and we said our goodbyes.

"It's just the three of us now," Oscar said.

I held them by the hands and squeezed tight. "Things will be better. I can find a job and once summer's over, you can go back to school. We're going to get through this... together. I promise."

Johnny started collecting rocks in his little arms, wincing as he bent to the ground. He placed them over Mama's grave in the shape of a star. A circle in the middle with points on all sides.

"What are you doing, Johnny?"

He dusted his hands off on his threadbare pants. "The star will bring her home."

"What's he talking about?" I asked Oscar.

Oscar looked at it and sighed. "The neighbor girl. When her sister died, her Mama told her that as long as she sees the stars, she'll always be able to find her. The light will bring her home."

Oscar sat on his heels and placed his hand over Johnny's on the star. They looked up at me, hopeful eyes pleading, so I knelt next to them and slid my quivering hand over theirs.

We said our farewells to Mama, now buried next to my baby sister, Emily. I looked over at her weathered cross. Two years old when she drowned in the river. Every time I looked at her grave, I was certain my heart would stop beating.

Now there were two Parkers in the ground.

We quietly grieved over Mama's grave and touched the light that would bring her home. The warm radiance of sunset faded to a black night. That was the closest we ever were. To her and to each other.

Soon enough, we would splinter apart, none of us knowing where the light was.

***

A week later, I stared defiantly at the grocery store window. The last few pennies were gone, and neighbors with empty tables didn't have a crumb to spare. So that left us with a whole lot of nothing. I'd knocked on every door looking for a job, but so had every other person in town.

When I stepped into the store, Mr. Johnson tipped his head. "Afternoon, Magnolia."

I swiped a basket without so much as a smirk.

So, there I stood, in front of the credit line with the rest of the hopeless fools. I just couldn't look into the boys' eyes and make fake promises anymore. The boys were sick of eating dandelion leaves, and Johnny complained of stomachaches. Critters from the forest weren't enough for these growing boys. So, I bit my lip until it hurt, gripped the basket handle as hard as my sweaty hands would allow, and I jumped into a brand-new world.

Oh, the thrill of filling a basket with flour, and shortening, and crackers, and eggs. Apple cider vinegar and sacks of potatoes and onions. I scoured every shelf, my fingers grazing bumpy melon rinds and waxy red apples.

"This stuff is awful expensive," Mr. Johnson said. "You haven't found a job yet, have you?"

"Don't worry about me. I'll figure it out."

"Young and naive. I reckon you'll learn your lesson right quick."

Heat rolled up my arms and neck, and I wanted to punch that smug look off his face. I grabbed a sack of sugar and threw it on the counter. "Add this. I'm gonna make myself a desperation pie."

"I'll start you a tab." He pulled out a piece of paper and wrote the date at the top. He turned it to face me. "I need your name right here." He pointed. "And your address right there. Can you write, sweetheart?"

"I can write the poems of Emily Dickinson if I damn well want to." I swiped his pen and wrote my name and address, then signed the bottom.

"I need half payment by the end of every month," he said. "Full payment by month two."

Borrowed money and borrowed time—this was nothing new for us.

"Best of luck to you, Miss Parker."

"I don't need luck." No such thing, I wanted to say.

With my wagon full of groceries, I started toward home. I passed Bend High School, remembering the safety of being inside those walls. The cold milk we would drink and the crusts I'd steal from my schoolmate's sandwiches. My chest tightened like steel around the pain inside, hardening it until it stopped aching.

Head up. Move forward.

Across the bridge toward downtown, the rickety wheels bounced on the uneven ground. I moved gingerly, trying not to knock out the sugar I might lose my house for.

I approached the library cart, which looked lean, as usual.

"Morning, ma'am. Anything new today?" I asked.

She scanned my dirty dress and looked down at my shoes. "Old tires do a bang-up job of fixing the soles," I said without flinching.

"Oh, no... yes." She fumbled over her words, avoiding my eyes.

She couldn't help it. When the ugliness of poverty stares you in the face, you inspect it and try to think of ways you can avoid it happening to you.

I rifled through the sad stack of torn-up paperbacks. "You have anything on the Roosevelts?"

She tilted her head to the side. "The Roosevelts? Most girls your age want fashion or beauty magazines."

"I got tires for boots. What do I need with a fashion magazine?"

"Let me see." She searched her meager piles. "Here." She handed me a *Woman's Home Companion*, a *New York Times*, and a magazine titled *Babies: Just Babies*. "Plenty of articles written by her."

"She *wrote* them?" This woman drove herself around with a pistol in her glove box and authored articles in national publications. Was there anything she couldn't do?

"She writes all sorts of things. I'll keep an eye out for more. You know," she whispered, "supposedly she's paid for her writing almost as much as her husband makes as President."

"She really is something," I said.

"She sure is. See you around, Magnolia."

Hands full of reading and a wagon full of food. What next? Shoes that didn't come from a car?

I rolled that wagon home under the heat of the sun, feeling like I held a bomb about to go off. When I'd glance back at all that food, all I saw was the ten dollars I owed that creep, Mr. Johnson. But when I rolled up, the boys about lost their minds.

Oscar's eyes sparkled. "Maggie, where'd you get all that food?"

"Are we gonna have a real supper?" Johnny's voice shot high and clear.

I looked down at their little faces and said, "Yep. We're fixing to have a feast."

I followed the vinegar pie recipe from one of the magazines and set the dough to the side to rest. Leaned against the doorway, I watched the boys play Jacks. Their playful laughs helped me forget how sick this whole thing made me.

I pored over every word of Mrs. Roosevelt's writing. She spoke about the power women have to change the world. Those words. They were like a hug and a sweet song and a soft cloud to float away on.

The New York Times interviewed her about the desperate times children had to grow up in. She said, "I have moments of real terror when I think we might be losing this generation. We have got to bring these young people into the active life of the community and make them feel they are necessary."

Necessary. Needed. Thoughts drifted to my childhood. Emily's death. How the boys needed me as much as I needed them. Papa teaching me to hunt and cook. He found joy with me, and that damn near killed Mama.

"You only have yourself to rely on in this world, you hear?" Papa would say.

I would nod and pay close attention. As long as I had him, the world didn't seem like such a scary place. The day he disappeared, I died a little inside.

I shook the thoughts from my head and returned to reading. Mrs. Roosevelt received hundreds of letters at the White House from people all across the country asking for help. I wasn't surprised. She seemed to have all the answers.

I turned to find the boys staring at Mama's bed from the doorway. I couldn't bring myself to sleep there, so it sat like a relic, haunting us.

"Mama would have liked pie," Oscar said.

I had to strangle back the pain that gripped my throat, knowing that she wouldn't have eaten a bite of food paid for by credit. "Yes, she would have."

I served up a feast set for a king. Stew with potatoes and beans. A slice of bread with a smear of butter on it. We ate until our bellies and hearts were full.

"Did you find a job, Maggie?" Johnny asked.

"Of course she did!" Oscar pushed his arm. "She ain't stupid enough to buy food without a job."

I plastered a smile on my face, realizing what I'd done. Oscar could see it. I had welcomed the wolf into the henhouse and offered my family up for slaughter.

Regret soured inside me, so I said the only thing I could. "Who wants desperation pie?"

Their eyes glimmered with joy, and it made me smile.

That's the funny thing about desperate times. You say your prayers and you move on to the job of living. Wallowing wouldn't make our situation any better, so I baked pie with flour I hadn't found a way to pay for and held our scrappy family together with everything I had. You let yourself feel joy, even if there really wasn't any.

CHAPTER THREE

It wasn't persistence that landed me the job at Pilot Butte Inn, it was dumb luck. After knocking on every door to a sea of downcast eyes and no ma'am's, I marched into the mayor's office for the fifth time.

"I told you, Magnolia, I want to help you. There's just nothing. All the jobs go to men with families."

"I'm a girl with a family. What's the difference?"

"You're right, it's not fair. It's just the way it is. Pride and all that." He put his hand on my back to guide me out, but I planted my feet, looked back at his hand and then up at his eyes. He stepped back with a sigh. "Go on, now."

He pushed me out the door as I yelled, "I need a job. You can't ignore me!" When he did just that—and slammed the door in my face.

Fists tight and temples throbbing, I fought off tears. Then, an angelic voice as sweet as honey dripped through the air. "I might know of something."

I turned on my heel to see Mrs. Baxter, the doctor's wife. She worked at the hospital, always holding fundraisers for sick children. Prim and proper with her long plaid skirt and ivory button-up blouse without a wrinkle in sight. Too pretty for words, and there I was spittin' fire like Little Orphan Annie.

"What kind of job?" She either pitied me or wanted something. I didn't care.

"The Pilot Butte Inn. I know the manager from church."

"Okay."

"He's looking for some nice young ladies as housekeepers. Ones who can stay quiet and demure and not bother the guests."

"What's demure?"

"Modest. Shy."

"I know you don't know me, but those words have never been used to describe the Parker kids."

"You seem determined. I bet you can do it." Her smile beamed with confidence, shining a light on my dimming pride.

"How do I get him to hire me?"

"Well, let's see now." She scanned my dirty clothes as she stepped around me in a circle, as if I was a cow at an auction yard. "Come with me."

She walked at a fast clip, hands folded in front of her. I scurried behind like a mouse waiting for crumbs.

I'd never stepped foot on the church grounds, and the office by the graveyard smelled musty. A lamp chain bounced against the glass for a long while after Mrs. Baxter pulled it. Even rifling through a box of old clothes, she looked like a movie star.

"Here we are." She held up a lovely navy-blue sweater completely devoid of holes. "Try this on."

When she stepped forward, I flinched. "It's all right," she said. "I'll just slip it on."

A shiver skittered up my back at how good the fabric felt on my neck.

"Now." She reached into her bag and came out with something shiny. She clipped my bangs back with a barrette near my temple, into the pale blond hair slicked into my braid. She unclasped a gold compact and rubbed something pink on my cheeks.

Her soft curls caught my attention as they bounced against her shoulder. I bet she didn't have headaches. Her nails shined red, lacquered like a candy apple.

"There. Now you look the part."

Turning to the mirror, I gasped. My eyes didn't look tired and the blush in my cheeks looked... *pretty*. I even looked older. Less like a wild thing and more like a woman. "What happens when I have to speak?"

"Just look down. Peek through the top of your eyes and never speak above a whisper."

Barely lifting my eyes, I said softly, "Like this?"

"That's it. Now, go see about getting yourself a job."

"I'll bring the sweater back right after."

"This box is for the needy. It's yours now."

My pink cheeks turned crimson as heat climbed up my neck. "Why are you helping me?" I asked through the mirror.

"Us gals have a responsibility to help each other."

I blinked a few times. Searched her face for the real reason for her kindness. Everyone had an angle.

She stepped to the side and leaned on the edge of the desk. "We must look to each other for help. So little to go around."

"That's nothing new for us."

"You come back when you need something. It pains me to see children hurting."

"I'm not a child." The soft cotton sweater grazed my neck as I straightened my back.

"Of course you aren't, dear. You're a grown woman without a m-"

"Go ahead, say it." It was either man or mother, and either was going to make me scream.

Her eyes narrowed, hesitant. "I'd like to help you where I can, is all."

"Why? You've got your husband and your church, and all the kids at the hospital."

"Magnolia..." My skin set to crawling when she placed her hand on my shoulder. "Use what you have and take the help from people along the way, you understand?"

"Sure." Straightening the sweater gave me an excuse to pull away from her touch.

She let out a deep sigh. "Those boys don't need their life any harder than it's already been."

There it was. The Baxters never had children. She fixed up other kids on account of not having her own. Well, the boys didn't need her help, and after this job, neither would I.

"If you ever find yourself in need of something," she said. "For them I mean. You know where to find me."

Help meant interfering. It meant doing things the way they wanted. Besides, maybe Mama was right. You couldn't trust anyone. "We'll be fine. We've got each other."

"All right, then." She gave a firm nod. "Tell Mr. Hanover Betty will see him at church on Sunday."

My hand clutched the loose doorknob. I didn't open it, just stood there. As I searched for the words to say thank you, she simply said, "You're welcome."

I didn't want to walk outside, but I couldn't stand to be near her. Trust is dangerous. The thought was like a loose yarn on a sweater. It hadn't torn yet but give it time and everything would rip to pieces.

***

Mr. Hanover hired me, but it was obvious he didn't want to. What a shock, seeing what life was like for those who could afford indoor plumbing and floors without holes. The crisp new uniform came with soap to wash it in. Soap! If you used it too much, your skin turned to scales, but I didn't care. The air in my house smelled like a stew of rotting wood and sweat. But that little white bar smelled bright and new. I resisted the urge to eat it, but I might have licked it once or twice.

Problem was, the stress of pretending to be demure made me feel like a volcano about to erupt. I had to watch the other girls and mimic their movements to learn how to be a lady. I kept my eyes down, remembered my brothers, and bit my tongue so much I nearly chewed the damn thing off.

Evening, Mr. Hanover. *Morning*, Mr. Hanover. When my boss neared, it was nothing but salutations and examining the tip of my shoes, terrified I'd say or do the wrong thing. That barrette might as well have been a gold coin for how I protected it. I pinched my cheeks so much that sometimes, little bruises appeared.

I kept sneaking newspapers out of the trash bin whenever they wrote about Eleanor Roosevelt, which was nearly every day.

After two weeks, I anxiously awaited payday, my stomach twisting in knots.

"Magnolia! Stop your daydreaming." The head housekeeper whipped my leg with a towel.

"Sorry." I tossed the paper back in the trash and carried on scrubbing the floor on my hands and knees. Knuckles rubbed raw from the lye and the old brush, I wondered if I'd have any money left for hand cream.

Ten dollars in groceries sure didn't last long. I heard the boys from the bar talking about twenty dollars a paycheck, and I worked twice as hard as them.

We lined up in the kitchen as Mr. Hanover handed out envelopes. I reached for mine, but he pulled away just as my fingers grazed the white corner. "Uh-uh, Miss Parker," he said with a pop of his tongue. "I hear you've been sneaking food from the kitchen."

I shot a glance at the chef, wide-eyed. "The chef let me take a batch of burnt rolls from the trash the other day, but I didn't steal."

"I didn't want to hire an orphan," he said, "but the church is on me like white on rice."

He didn't even lower his voice.

"Orphans are angry and desperate. They're like feral cats, happy to bite the hand that feeds them."

I held back the overwhelming desire to stab him with a fork. "I don't bite, sir. Not unless you bite me first."

A few snickers led Mr. Hanover to cough until they quieted. He handed me the envelope. "I'll be watching you, Miss Parker. No handouts here, you understand?"

I slid the envelope out of his hand and slunk out to the back patio. My fingers shook as they tore open the corner of the bright white paper. Lovely green money stared back at me, and I about fainted with relief. Maybe I could afford candy for the boys. And a new pair of shoes. I stifled a smile, pulling out the pile of money. It even smelled green.

I slid my fingers against my thumb to fan out the bills. "Eight dollars?" I counted again. Surely, I'm missing something. Two weeks scrubbing my hands raw and I couldn't even pay my grocery bill.

"What's the matter, Magnolia? Thought you were gonna be rich?" The head housekeeper asked with a laugh.

"But the bartenders, they said they get twenty dollars every two weeks."

"That's the boys, darling. The faces in front of the wealthy patrons."

Another maid added, "We're just the dirty hands behind closed doors."

"Eight dollars. I'm grateful, it's just… I don't understand why we're paid less."

"That's the kicker, honey. It's never enough." She placed her hand on my shoulder. "But it's still a job."

I turned away and wiped tears with the back of my hand. They continued talking as I stepped away.

"Poor girl, she's still hoping for a miracle."

Lightheaded, I leaned my temple against the rough wood of the porch. This job was supposed to be the answer to all my problems. Right now, it only seemed to dig me deeper.

The girls carried on, blowing off steam about the job.

"All these rich folks traipse through here on vacation, pretending the country hasn't fallen apart and all the banks haven't closed. And here we are, scrubbing their toilets and begging for crumbs."

"Tell me about it. I'll be dusting the First Lady's gilded handbag next week."

I whipped around. "What did you say?"

"Mrs. Eleanor Roosevelt. I bet she's got a gold-plated handbag and shoes to match."

"Eleanor Roosevelt? In Bend?"

"Yes, you didn't hear? She'll be through here next week. On a tour of the great Northwest. The entire town will roll out the red carpet, I'm sure."

The most fascinating woman in America will be at the Pilot Butte Inn. The one who speaks her mind and fights for those of us in the shadows. The woman who has the power to fix our broken world.

Maybe things were looking up.

CHAPTER FOUR

The moment Mr. Hanover handed me my first paycheck, I hurried down the street to Newport Market, paid the groceryman, and put another twelve dollars of food on credit. In the span of thirty minutes, my money had disappeared, and I'd dug myself fourteen dollars in the hole.

The woman at the library cart gathered all the magazines with articles written by Eleanor Roosevelt and kept them for me in a special bag that I picked up every day after work. I devoured everything she wrote.

Today was the day she would arrive at the inn. I woke with the moon, as usual. All the worry rumbled around inside my head, so loud I couldn't sleep more than a few hours. Oscar still woke with nightmares, and it seemed like every night I just waited for the next scream. The terror hadn't ended with Mama's death, like I thought it would.

I sat on our porch and enjoyed the quiet twilight of a summer morning. Crickets chirped, and the gentle rush of the river strummed along in the distance. The mountains were beautiful peeking through the darkness... when you could push your worry aside long enough to enjoy them.

The sun announced itself. Orange and red glowed in the distance. The hope of the day rested on my heart while the sky turned the light on. And then, in a flash, the light show disappeared into the gray morning. Ten minutes of glory for those up early enough to witness it.

"Maggie," Oscar said as he shuffled out, scratching his head. "I don't want you to go."

"I have to work." I extended my arm, and he curled up next to me on the step.

"I get lonely here all by myself."

"But, Oscar, you've got an important job to do. Johnny is just a little boy. He needs his big brother to watch over him."

"I get scared." He buried his head in his palms, but I could still see his cheeks flush red. "My nightmares. They won't stop."

I swallowed against the biting pain in my throat.

"The river swells up," he said. "It comes tearing through our house with the monsters and washes everyone away. Except me. I'm hanging from a pine branch, looking down at everyone's dead bodies."

"Oh, Oscar." I pulled him in tighter. He rested his cheek on my leg as I rubbed his hair.

"Papa left us," he whimpered. "And Mama died of a weak heart. I'm afraid you'll leave next."

I kept making promises to be the sister they needed me to be. "I'll never leave you."

"That's what Mama said, too."

Tears rolled off his cheeks and soaked the black cotton of my work dress. We were all hanging on like a loose tooth, clinging to thready edges, about to expose the soft nerve inside.

"Well, I'm not Mama. I'll fight for you."

"Johnny's got big dreams. He's gonna be a pilot and fly away from this life. And I'll still be stuck here all by myself."

This kid sure had a clear way of seeing the world. "I know how you feel."

"Promise you'll never leave us?"

I steadied my shaking hands and tried to wash away the image of the river swallowing us whole. "I promise."

***

The inn buzzed, a flurry of activity with electric energy. We wiped every speck of dust and buffed every surface to a high shine, hoping to impress the

First Lady. Mrs. Roosevelt was the hope everyone needed. The reminder that maybe it was all right to look forward.

I stood in the dining room looking out the window when her car arrived. The sleek, black convertible rolled up around noon. Its enormous wheels and long, curved hood reminded me of an eagle grazing the water. I pressed against the glass to glimpse her driving, just like the papers said she did. I wondered if she had her loaded pistol with her. She wore a giant emerald hat and stepped out of the car with confidence. No security, just a companion and a photographer. I craned my neck, but the glare of the sun kept me from seeing much more.

"You're not missing anything."

I turned to see one of the male servers.

"She's the First Lady," I said.

"With the biggest buck teeth I've ever seen," he said with a laugh. "Nothing special about that old lady. I don't know why everyone fusses over her."

"She wants to make things better for us."

"She wants to give handouts to a bunch of people that don't work hard. Nothing admirable about that." He reached up to check his hair, black and thick with pomade.

I imagined grabbing a fistful of his greasy hair and slamming his face into the glass.

"Damn socialists want to ruin everything."

I turned to look outside again, but she had gone.

"Women don't need jobs," he said. "They should be home having babies and cooking for their men."

Every part of my body tensed. He stood so close I could smell his terrible cologne. Like allspice and cigarette smoke.

Then he winked at me.

I shoved him. Both hands to his chest. He stumbled back and caught himself on the wall. His lip snarled and his eyes grew large as he straightened his shirt. "Careful, little girl."

My breath thundered through my nose. He could treat me however he wanted. He hated the poor ones, just like Mr. Hanover, and I needed this job.

Once I gathered myself, I crept down to the maid's quarters to help fold laundry. The ladies gossiped feverishly about the First Lady.

"Did you see her pearls? That string hangs clear down to her hips! And her dress. She looks just as fresh as a daisy."

"She ordered the planked trout for lunch. Can you believe it? She could have anything on the menu, and she chose trout."

"She's resting in her room right now. Isn't it wild? The President's wife lying on sheets I washed."

I crept up the service stairway and peeked down the hall. I hoped to hear some important conversation or camera flashes popping, but it was silent. After a while, I sighed and turned to walk downstairs again.

As I stepped down, I smacked right into the head maid. I watched in horror as her tray flipped into the air. Cookie crumbs dusted her hair and tea and ice sloshed all over her chest.

"Oh, no!" I reached down to pick up the mess, my hands fumbling to wipe her clean. "I'm so sorry."

"Dammit, Magnolia," she whispered as she looked down. "Just look at me."

"I'll... I'll get you a fresh tray."

I ran down the stairs as fast as my feet would carry me. I begged the chef to hurry, my heart thumping in my chest. He handed me a fresh silver tray with a white linen napkin, a plate of butter cookies, a tall glass pitcher with sweet tea and lemons slices, and two little glasses. "Be careful this time."

I carried it upstairs like I would hold a butterfly by its wings. "Here." I handed it to the maid, hoping her crimson face would calm down a few shades.

"I can't go in there like this!" She gestured to her soiled dress.

"What do you want me to do?"

"You go," she said.

"Me? No way. I'll do something stupid."

"She asked for a woman to deliver her tea, and if she has to call again, Hanover will fire us both. Now, go on." She nudged me, so I reluctantly shuffled toward the door.

I perched the tray on one arm and raised my other to knock. My fist hovered over the wood for a while and I closed my eyes, telling myself to calm down. Two hard knocks and an exhale later, I had taken a step I couldn't turn back from.

"Come in," she said with a voice like liquid velvet. It sounded like she did on the radio, only without the scratchy noise from a microphone.

The knob shook in my hand as I turned it, and I quietly cursed the ice as it jingled against the glass. Elbows braced to my side, I stepped into the room, more nervous than I'd ever been. "Tea, ma'am," I said into the void.

"In here. You may place it on the table."

As I turned the corner, there she was. The one and only Eleanor Roosevelt read a paper by the fireplace I had scrubbed that morning. She looked up and smiled widely. I had only seen her through black newspaper ink or flat and staged in a magazine photo. She'd come to life in front of my eyes. Her pale pink dress flowed to the floor, and her simple face needed only a smile to fill it with beauty. There was something warm about her. Gracious.

She gestured to the round table under the window. I nodded and set down the tray, noting the rattle of the glasses when I pulled my arm away from the relative stability of my torso.

When she stood, I tried not to gawk at her height. So tall and regal. I must have looked like a child staring at the Titanic — mouth open, eyes wide.

She tilted her head and gave me a questioning look. "Are you from here?"

"Yes, ma'am."

"Good." She folded her hands and nodded to the vase of flowers on the table. "I'd rather hoped to meet someone who could tell me what this wonderful flower is. I've never seen it before."

"Mountain Cat's Ear," I said against a dry mouth. "A lily that grows wild in the high desert."

"Lovely." She cupped the cream flower and examined it in the light.

After an uncomfortable moment of silence, I asked, "Will there be anything else?"

She looked at me and I straightened my shoulders, suddenly very aware of my slumped posture.

She poured her tea as I contemplated seeing my way out.

"If that's all, I'll be leaving now." I turned to the door.

"Will you be serving me again?" she asked.

I turned on my heels. "The maids don't usually do this." I gestured to her tray. "Work with the guests, I mean."

"I asked that a woman assist me while I'm here. I assume that will be you."

I nodded, unsure of what to say. I kept my answers short and my mouth shut as much as possible. Less chance of sticking my foot in it.

The ice clanked against the glass, and all I could think about was the sticky sweat on my neck. It was already hotter than lava in here, and now I had the nerves to boot. I could've melted like candle wax.

"I always request a private audience with an all-women press." She smiled, waiting.

It was obvious I was to respond. "Why is that, ma'am?"

"Proves to the boss that women are needed. Encourages them to hire more."

Her words came to me from an article I'd read that day. "Only where they are organized do women get equal pay for equal work." It came shooting out of me like a Jack-in-the-box, wound up and waiting to bust open.

She smiled. "You are a smart girl, aren't you?"

"I don't know about that. I'm just trying to survive." What with my clumsiness and shoving that server, I could very well be fired as soon as I left this room. I decided this might be my one chance to say how much I admired her.

"Your speeches inspire me," I said.

"What's your name?"

"Magnolia." I shook my head like I could pull the words back out of the air. "Magnolia Parker, ma'am."

"Well, Magnolia. Most young women aren't interested in the speeches of the First Lady. I fear my message of fortitude might be lost on the younger generation."

"It's not." I tipped my head down, then found the strength to look her in the eyes. "I hear every word you say."

Before she could respond, I walked out without looking back. When the door clicked shut, a wave of nausea washed through me. All it would have taken is one slip. One mistake. I exhaled to steady my heartbeat and checked the clock in the hallway.

Two hours until quitting time.

***

The last hours of the day dripped slow as honey. Mrs. Eleanor Roosevelt— America's bravest woman—called *me* a smart girl.

When the clock struck five, I untied my lace apron and folded it neatly into my bag. Just as I stepped into the blazing sun, Mr. Hanover barreled out behind me.

"Miss Parker. Where do you think you're going?"

"Home, sir?" It came out as more of a question than a fact. Like I needed his permission to leave.

"Oh, no you're not." He removed a handkerchief from his pocket and wiped his swollen, pink face. Like a little piglet. "The First Lady has requested you."

"Me?"

"Yes. She said Miss Magnolia Parker provided such fine service that she requested your presence on the patio after dinner. Lord knows for what." His voice bit, like it had fangs. "If she wants to speak with you, then that's what she's gonna get."

"But I need to go home. My brothers worry if I'm late."

"I don't care about your family, Miss Parker. Look around. We all have problems." He rubbed his rotund belly and popped his bright red suspenders. "When Mrs. Roosevelt retires to the porch, you offer her an after-dinner liquor and stay with her as long as she wants, you hear?"

"What does she want with me?"

"Hell, if I know. Some nonsense about speaking with the help. Give the silly woman what she wants. She's married to the President, for Christ's sake."

"I've already worked ten hours."

"I told her you work the night shift. So don't go whining about your hours. Keep her happy, or you're fired."

He waddled back into the kitchen and barked orders at the chef before slamming the door.

I dropped my bag to my feet and thumped my rear onto the steps. A chance to sit with the most interesting woman in the world, and all I could see were Oscar's teary eyes, begging me not to leave him this morning.

The sun set late this time of year. If I could give Mrs. Roosevelt a bit of my time, then run the entire way home, I might make it before dark. A bead of sweat dripped down my chest, right on past my thumping heart.

Guests strolled next to the river, their faces shaded by pink parasols and their giant skirts dusting the dirt. The sun made its way low in the sky, casting an orange flood of light over the pine trees, reflecting on the water, slick as glass.

I wondered if the boys were splashing each other in the river, and if they would wait for me to make them dinner. We still had half a jar of peanut butter left. They would be all right, wouldn't they?

Forty minutes passed when I heard pointed heels click on the wood boards of the back porch. I wiped the sweat that slicked back my hair, then fanned out the wrinkles of my skirt. Mr. Hanover eyed me from the window with a grimace, so I shrugged and walked up behind Mrs. Roosevelt, who waited in a rocking chair.

"Good evening, ma'am," I said to the back of her head. Her brown hair rippled in perfect finger waves, the long sections pinned back in a low bun. Everything about her pristine appearance gleamed, and she smelled like lilacs.

She turned, propping her elbow on the back of the rocking chair. "Hello, Miss Parker. Thank you for joining me." She gestured to the other chair.

I stared at it, thinking that Mr. Hanover must be fit to be tied. The help sitting with the most important guest the inn had ever seen? He'd never forgive me for this.

"I've let your employer know you are my guest. Please, sit."

I lowered to the other rocking chair like it was an eggshell about to crack. I folded my hands as softly as I could in my lap, remembering what Mrs. Baxter taught me about being demure. "Can I offer you an after-dinner liquor? A digestif, I think they call it."

"No, thank you. I don't drink."

I knew that. Her father drank so much that when Eleanor was nine, he threw himself out a window and died the next day. When I read that, I thought about how one of the wealthiest families in America couldn't protect themselves from the ugly monsters that crawled through windows. What chance did the rest of us have?

I nodded and looked out to the river, determined not to speak unless spoken to.

"You might be wondering why I asked for time with you?"

I shrugged, then nodded.

"Washington is a difficult place. I prefer to be out in the cotton fields and the coal mines. At the table of a needy family, or the tent of a young migrant couple. I can't fix anything if I don't understand America's needs. And no one understands those struggles better than women."

"Yes, ma'am."

"Is Mr. Hanover still watching?" she asked.

I glanced over her shoulder at his puffed cheeks pressed against the wavy glass, his eyeballs bulging and red. I nodded.

She turned and gave him a controlled wave, staring straight at him until he huffed and walked away. "I assure you, your position here is not in any danger. I've demanded that he protect your job, or he will have *me* to deal with."

The tips of my shoes were wearing thin. Fine white lines had settled into the black leather. I didn't want to tell her that under these fine clothes lived a bony girl without a mother, eating tinned fish to survive, and sleeping on the floor because her mother's bed filled her with terror.

"I'm very lucky to have this job."

"I've been working tirelessly for years to improve working conditions for women," she said.

"With the Women's Trade Union League," I said without skipping a beat.

"That's right." Her voice lifted like a flute. "You've read a fair amount on me, haven't you?"

"Yes, I have." I let my eyes flick up to her, afraid this was a dream and that I'd wake any minute to a screaming Oscar in the throes of a nightmare. I rubbed my fingers together until they ached.

"Legs are meant to move," she said. "Come along."

I opened my mouth to protest, but before I could speak, her fancy boots had hit the dirt. I ran to catch up with those long legs.

"I received a letter recently." She slowed to a stroll when we stepped onto the path along the river. "A woman who had lost her only child to typhoid. She found work as a maid, but she didn't earn enough to cover rent."

"So that's why you want to speak with me? You want to understand the life of a maid?"

"I receive hundreds of letters every month. Everyone needs help. But this one..." She inhaled and steadied her shoulders, turning to watch the meandering water.

"Was it a boy?" I asked.

"Was what a boy?"

"The child she lost."

She swallowed the lump that I was certain had settled in her throat. She didn't strike me as an emotional woman. No tears. But the painful memories tinted her face like a watercolor. She lost her son, Franklin Jr. at seven months old. Influenza and a heart murmur.

I couldn't help but feel sorry for her. Everyone loses someone. But she kept a brave face, hands folded in front of her, the muscles in her neck tight like guitar strings.

In silence, we watched the ducks search for food. They flopped upside down, sticking their faces in the water and their butts up in the air.

"It's not so bad here," I said.

She turned to me, softened a bit. "I meant what I said. If Mr. Hanover fires you, I want to know about it. I'll put that man in his place."

"That's kind of you. But I don't have many complaints about the job." I hesitated and felt the ache in my chest start to wiggle its way in, like a worm through soft dirt.

"What does concern you, Miss Parker?" she asked.

I closed my eyes, unable to tolerate her stare. This was the First Lady. *Act demure.*

In the long moments of silence where I searched for the right words, she said, "I see the struggle of young women in the country right now and I want to help. In any way I can. That is the job of a politician's wife."

I blurted out, "I'm not allowed in the bread line."

"The bread line?"

"Yes. They tell us it's only for men, and it makes me so fuming mad. I have brothers to feed, and I can't get a handout because it makes the men uncomfortable. Makes them feel shameful having a woman's eyes around them. What about *my* shame? I'm wrapped up in it like a blanket and it's so tight I can hardly breathe."

She had opened a door, and I went tumbling through it.

"I'm raising two of the sweetest boys on earth, and I have to look in their eyes every day and lie to them. Tell them I know how to keep them sweet. How to keep this life from devouring them and turning them sour." I grabbed my skirt with a balled fist. "These clothes are the nicest things I own. At home, I've got tires for shoes and two dresses, yellowed with time and bad memories. I've run up a credit with the grocery man so we can eat. I don't know how to fix it because my father left us, and my mother died. And I'm so spittin' angry!"

Tears rolled down my cheeks. "I have to do better for my brothers. I just have to."

She looked at me with such sorrow. It looked like she wanted to hug me, and it made the shame even more suffocating.

"Sorry." I looked away and wiped my eyes with my sleeve. "I shouldn't have said all that."

"It's all right. You aren't the first to cry to me."

Log remnants from the sawmills floated past, softening as they fishtailed along the water.

She sighed. A long, pronounced breath that filled up the silence. "I know a thing or two about people letting you down."

Someone understood me. Her words soothed me like a balm to a burn mark.

"The bread line might fill your belly for a moment, but what happens next?"

"I don't have the luxury of thinking about what's next. I'm full up with what's happening right now."

"No, I suppose you don't. That's what I want to change. A young woman shouldn't work to fatigue, raising her siblings while they survive on food scraps. This country must do more to help you find your place in the world."

"If there is such a thing."

"You'd be surprised how many women feel the same."

Neither of us wanted to say what we both understood. Fathers who drank. Mothers who died. Eleanor Roosevelt was an orphan by the time she was ten. The women in her family called her ugly, broken. Not an ounce of love in her mother's eyes. That part I didn't have to read, I just knew.

"Truth is," she said, "My life has been a string of people I love disappointing me."

"I know that string," I said. "It's long and twisted and thorny."

"Yes, it is." A closed-mouth smile broke free on her otherwise serious face. "And I have used all of that like fuel. I will do better than what they taught me."

I wasn't making speeches or serving luncheons to influential people. "I don't have any power."

"You have more than you think. My greatest power is this. Right here. Listening to your words, your struggles. Reminding each one of you we don't belong in the shadows."

"I'm afraid I'm running out of fight," I said.

"That's the thing about women. We're like tea bags. You never know how strong we are until you put us in hot water."

No one had ever called me strong. Or capable. "I'm past hot," I said. "The water around me is already boiling."

"I bet you always find a way to land on your feet," she said.

"Yeah, but I wish I didn't keep landing in quicksand."

She released a deep, rolling laugh. "It will get easier." She lowered her voice. "Start small. Think big."

I let those words fill me up. Then I found the courage to speak.

"Mrs. Roosevelt?"

"Yes, Magnolia?"

"I need to get home to my brothers."

She pulled her shoulders back. She smiled, and her entire face brightened like a summer sunrise. "You get on home. It's been a pleasure speaking with you."

"Enjoy your trip to Oregon, ma'am."

I left her and ran at top speed toward home. The sun kissed the mountain tops in the west, low in a pink sky. I had about twenty minutes before nightfall, and it would take me an hour to reach home. I imagined Oscar and Johnny and another broken promise.

The monsters were creeping in.

CHAPTER FIVE

I had never run as fast as I did that night. I raced the sun as it sank behind the mountains. My legs burned, my chest ached, and my mind spun with what I might find at home. It's strange, the little things we tell ourselves. I whispered *they're all right* so many times the words meant nothing. But I kept on saying it, pulling a cloak over the part of me that said, *you stupid failure.*

By the time the sky went black, I still had ten minutes of country road between me and the boys. The moonlight cast a silver shine over the trail. My feet kicked the dirt so hard I had to cough through clouds of dust. I skidded into place to catch my breath at the edge of our property and stared at our deathly silent shack. No fire inside and no gas lamps in the windows. Not a sound to crack the eerie stillness.

Up the steps. The door creaked with the wind. I cracked it open wider as it scraped the wood underneath. "Boys?" I said hesitantly into the blackness.

My heart thumped in my ears so loud my eyeballs shook. I waited, hoping they were playing a trick on me. *Please be hiding. Please prove me wrong.* The boards creaked and popped under my weight. "Johnny? Oscar?" My voice rattled. "This game isn't funny!"

I fumbled for the gas lantern and a pack of matches. Last one. Will have to add to the grocery list. I looked around the boys' room. Nothing. The front room, nothing. Just shadows and ghosts and horrible memories bumping around the emptiness.

I built a fire in the stove, so they didn't return to a dark house. Once that set to blazing, I stepped outside, lantern in hand, to check their favorite hiding spots. In the juniper branches overlooking the river. A tree fort near the outhouse. Logs stacked out back to resemble a bunker. All empty.

"Oscar! Johnny!" Where the hell were they?

Oscar's nightmare was that the river drowned us, so I figured he moved away from the water. Into the depths of the forest where the snakes and the bobcats and the giant spiders waited for any human stupid enough to venture out at night.

They could have gone in any direction. I picked one and started walking.

Movement rustled around me. Was the noise just the wind quivering the pine branches, or were hidden critters watching me? The boys could be hurt, thinking I left just like Papa did.

The lantern lit a path under the shaded canopy of treetops. Every ten feet I called their names, my voice sending birds fluttering from tree branches. Pine needles crunched under my feet, and I realized I still wore my work clothes. I needed to find the boys and scrub these shoes before heading back to the inn tomorrow.

Every flicker of a shadow sent my heart racing. "Boys? Please come out."

My mind started to see things. Flashes of light and tree trunks moving. I tightened my arms at my sides and told myself to get it together. I kept blinking, but my heart's constant thumping wore on my nerves.

Don't let the fear break you.

Still no sign of them. What if I was going in the wrong direction? I couldn't use the sunlight to guide me. I couldn't see Bachelor Butte, or the Sisters Mountains. Nothing to show me the way. Just my fear with me every step. Every breath.

Why hadn't I taught them what I learned from Papa? How to hunt and track paw prints. To hit a tall stick on the ground as you walk. The vibration warns predators and clears a safe path. How to listen to your instincts. That feeling that something is watching you. How to control fear and how to shoot the eyeball out of a critter from one hundred yards.

Too late for regrets.

I slid to the ground, against a trunk, and listened to the coyotes scream. I couldn't focus while they carried on, so I closed my eyes, buried my head in my arms, and remembered Eleanor Roosevelt. Had that been a dream? She didn't need to tell me about her baby that died or her father that hung the moon, then jumped from a window. She didn't have to say that the women in her life taught her how to hate herself. I understood everything.

The balmy air of the summer night flowed over my legs as the back of my neck prickled like bee stings. Something felt off. The warm wind flooded me with a buzzing heat. Was something watching me?

I stood and looked around. I'd lost direction when I sat down. Fear— it's the most dangerous thing in the forest. I turned left and right, not sure which direction I came from. My head spun and something electric fizzled in my hair and at my fingertips. "Calm down. Think."

The towering pines blocked out the moonlight and everything took on the same charcoal-colored hue.

My legs are longer than theirs, I thought. They wouldn't make up this much ground, not with Johnny's twisted knees. They're tired. I yelled out for them again. Silence. Time to head back.

Mama flashed into my mind. Images of her dead body didn't make my skin crawl near as much as remembering her face when she was alive. That look in her eyes still burned in my memory, and I resolved to prove her wrong. I would not fail. My feet stomped over the dirt and rocks and chunks of black lava, the air still hot and humming.

A crack in the forest yanked me from my memories. Purple lightning flashed across the sky, so bright I put my hand to my eyes. A summer storm was no good. All that heat and no rain to put it out.

In-between lightning claps, the air fizzled. The musty, bitter smell of poison hemlock wafted through the air. Drums of thunder. Without a second to breathe, lightning spread across the sky like veins in a body, slithering into every corner.

A faint cry somewhere in the distance. "Help!"

"Boys?" The screams seemed to fly from every direction like the coyotes' howls. "Oscar, Johnny?"

"Magnolia!"

My feet raced so fast toward that sound, it felt like my ears did the running.

Another bolt sliced through the air, turning orange as it screeched across the inky sky. A loud crack landed on a tree less than five feet from me. The whole damn thing lit up like a match strike. Pine needles smoked, and singed branches cracked from the trunk, landing in a fiery ball across my path.

I stumbled back, then made my way down a hill toward their voices. They yelled my name and just as I opened my mouth to yell back, the ground gave way. A river of dirt had broken loose. It took out my feet and smashed my hip into a rock. A stinging pain spread through my body as I slid into boulders and scraped my arms along dried weeds.

I slid down the bank and came to an abrupt stop. A trickle of loose dirt and rocks hit the bottom of the ravine around my head.

A gunshot rang out.

Through tightened breaths, I waited for another bolt to crack light over the earth and scanned the ravine before it went black again.

On the second shot of lightning, I saw them. Huddled together under a fallen branch, shotgun pointed straight at me. In the intense purple light, one round barrel and four giant eyes stared back at me.

I threw myself to the ground, flat on my stomach. "Oscar! It's me. Magnolia. I'm here."

"Maggie?" Johnny's tiny voice.

The fragile break sent tears straight into my eyes. "Yes. It's me. Tell Oscar to put the gun down."

My arm ached.

"It's okay, Maggie. He put it down."

Pushing up, my elbow gave way, knocking my chin on a rock. Feeling my way in the dark, I followed their voices. I kept talking to them, but only heard Johnny.

When I reached their outline, I had to squint to make them out in the dark. Lightning hit again. In that flash, I saw Oscar, frozen—his face flat, his eyes dead. The gun next to him in the dirt.

"Oscar." I kneeled in front of him. "I'm here. Let's go home."

He stared straight through me.

"Magnolia, what's wrong with your arm?" Johnny asked.

"What?" I looked down and waited for the next flash. When it flickered, I saw my white sleeve torn in two. The fleshy part of my shoulder had split open, bumpy and bloody. "I must've hit it on a rock."

"I think Oscar shot you."

My numb shoulder couldn't feel a thing. Like the arm wasn't even mine. I reached around with my left hand and found a depression that ran from front to back. The inside reminded me of hamburger meat.

Oscar did shoot me. "I'm all right. Let's get you out of here."

I inspected Johnny. "Are you okay?"

"Yeah. Just scared."

I hugged him best as I could with one arm. He smelled of sweat and his chest thumped as fast as a rabbit's foot. "Stay right with me."

Oscar hadn't moved a twitch, so I let go of Johnny and moved my hand to Oscar's shoulder and shook, wanting to rattle the life back into him. I held his quivering chin and looked him straight in the eyes. "I told you I would always come for you."

Johnny fell back when he tried to straighten his knees.

I helped them both to standing. "Can you walk?"

Johnny grunted. "Yeah, but my legs hurt."

"I know. But let's try. I can't carry you." My right arm dangled at my side like a dead animal.

I slung the shotgun over my shoulder and reached for Oscar's hand. He didn't grasp back, so I grabbed his wrist. Johnny stumbled along next to me. He said he was holding my right hand, but I couldn't feel it.

"I had a lantern, but I lost it when I slid down the hill," I said. "We'll be all right. We'll find the river and follow it home."

I stopped and closed my eyes, listening for the rush of the water, but hearing a menacing crackle.

"What's that smell?" Johnny said.

"I don't know." I squeezed Oscar's wrist tighter.

Not a word escaped Oscar's mouth, but at least he moved his feet. I kept looking at Johnny to make sure he was still holding me. I hurried, faster and faster. The rocks made it difficult, and we couldn't see the ground, so we kept tripping, and poor Johnny stumbled like a toddler. We kept moving. No words. A faint glow rested in the distance. Maybe it was almost sunrise? Couldn't be. It was too early.

I noticed a path out of the ravine. We turned and climbed as the sky illuminated orange. It grew brighter and brighter. As we crested the hill, my eyes focused. It wasn't the sun.

The tree line was on fire.

All the times I'd imagined running through the forest, it was to outrun a wild animal. I never dreamed it would be to escape a forest fire. The trees crackled, and the smoke filled the air with brown clouds.

We ran away from the heat. Away from the glowing ball of fiery trees as sparks flicked onto our hair. One burned a hole in Johnny's shirt. But we kept stumbling forward. What if I couldn't get them out of here?

No. I shook my head at the thought. "We need to find the river."

My mind crept towards images of the boys screaming. On fire. Burned in the forest's belly. But I caught hold of that image. Threw it to the ground and stomped it out with every step.

My breathing tightened as my vision narrowed. Black and wobbly, danger lurked all around me. This was the fear Papa told me to fight.

The wood popped, and branches plummeted to the ground. Huge, tall pines engulfed in flames. Fire rolled along the ground, catching the duff and dry pine needles that carpeted the forest floor. The smoke thickened.

You will fail.

No. I held those little boys with everything I had, and we ran.

I fell into a tree, right into my damaged shoulder. I reached to remove the bark. Close to my bone, lodged in exposed muscle. But I didn't feel pain.

My feet ran along the rocky earth, but I seemed to float, carried away by smoke. A cool rush of wind hit my face. I gasped for fresh air like I'd just escaped from the depths of the ocean. I collapsed and looked at my scraped knees. My torn uniform. The blood dripping down my arm like grease.

I looked up to see Oscar and Johnny, their eyeballs glowing white. They stared at me, ash falling like snowflakes into their dark hair.

"Found the river." Johnny said.

I crawled to the water and stuck my face in the cold, glacial runoff as bubbles brushed along my cheeks.

They're alive. We're still here.

I yanked my head up with a gasp. The fire had climbed a tree and skittered across the sky to one across the river. The orange flames grew on either side of us. I rubbed my face clean. Papa prepared me for this.

I grabbed a log stuck into the river's edge. Rough and split down the middle, but it would do. I led them into the frigid water and told them to hold on. They looked so small draped over the log, floating in the dark river. "Don't let go, no matter what."

Johnny limped to us. "We're riding the river?"

"You can't run, and the fire's closing in. The water is gentle and not too deep. We can ride it home."

I moved in close to them, wrapped my left arm around the rear of the log, and pushed with my feet.

"Maggie, we're headed toward the fire," Johnny said.

"We aren't gonna swim upstream. It's the only way out."

Oscar buried his head in Johnny's shoulder. The fire sizzled hot enough to blister skin, but this cold water took our breath away. We trembled, but we hung on.

We glided through the arch of fiery trees, ash and broken branches dropping around us. I remembered Papa telling me about the lava tubes deep under the black water. How the river wasn't as peaceful as it appeared. The boys winced every once in a while, their shins knocking into a boulder or a briar patch, scraping the skin on their arms. But we glided past the fire into the calm, clear air.

Finally able to collect my thoughts, I asked, "What were you doing all the way out here?"

"We didn't want to be in the house," Johnny said. "There are ghosts."

"No, there aren't." There were ghosts. Everywhere. But I didn't want them to know that.

"Oscar wanted to hide out in our fort."

"You were nowhere near your fort."

Oscar's skin grew pale as skim milk.

"We heard an animal," Johnny said. "We thought it was a cougar. So, we ran into the forest and lost our way. Oscar held the gun out for hours until you found us."

The water lapped around my lifeless arm as the fire crackled in the distance. "I'm sorry I didn't make it home by nightfall."

No one said anything. The freezing water turned our bodies rigid. A sudden whoosh of cold hit my foot. Dammit. A rock pulled off my right shoe.

Oscar rested his face on the log, so still it appeared he wasn't breathing.

I steadied my feet on the river's bottom and trudged through the waist high water. "We made it home."

I'd never been so happy to see that shithole of a house.

I dragged them out with my good arm. Oscar's skin glowed so white he shined blue, and Johnny's legs looked like they could snap like old twigs.

I fell to my knees and took a moment to breathe. Wiped the wet ash that stuck to my forehead like a paste.

"Come on. Let's dry up."

I carried Johnny by my left arm. Tears puddled in his eyes as he tried to hide the pain in his joints. We changed into dry clothes, all of us trembling and pale.

We lay by the fire, the boys wrapped in Mama's quilt, silent.

Oscar's head rested in my lap as I fingered his rust-colored hair. I hoped to rub some life back into him. I leaned my head back and waited for daybreak. My body began to ache. And man, did it hurt.

A smoky haze crept through the walls. Floated in through the cracks and hovered below the ceiling.

We were home, but we were nowhere near safe.

CHAPTER SIX

Without a minute of sleep, I arrived at work in my house dress and clunky shoes, brothers in tow. I set Johnny in the wagon, his knees swollen and flaming red. Oscar hadn't spoken. He just stared at his feet and kicked rocks. My arm throbbed, shooting pain into my neck and temples.

"What are we gonna do all day?" Johnny asked.

I looked back at his little body curled up in that wagon. He looked like a stuffed animal. A pale one with broken limbs. "You'll watch the ducks swim, and the geese fly, and the fancy people stroll on the river."

"It's more fun to throw rocks at home."

"I can't leave you at home." My eyes scurried over to Oscar's blank face, his milky skin. "Besides, I can sneak you some food from the kitchen."

"Oh. That's okay then," Johnny said.

I settled them under the shade of a giant willow near the water. "Just rest in the grass and take a nap. Don't go anywhere."

I had to trust the little one because his older brother stared at the sky in a trance. "Come find me if anything happens."

"Maggie?"

I tried not to look at Johnny's legs. I kneeled, focused on his eyes.

"Are we going to be okay?" Johnny asked.

"I'm doing everything I can to keep us together." Johnny's knees, Oscar's flattened eyes, a forest fire circling our house. The images closed in, but I held a firm smile.

Johnny nodded and leaned back with closed eyes.

Every blink scratched at my eyeballs like grainy sand. My hair smelled like a campfire. This house dress was meant for the dirty tasks of managing the Parker brood, not scrubbing the toilets of rich hotel guests. Weakness gripped my legs.

I snuck into the laundry room where the maids gathered for gossip as they folded linens, my ripped and stained uniform dangling from my good hand.

"Magnolia?" The head maid's eyes bulged. "What the hell happened to you?"

"Nothing." I grunted as I straightened my shoulders. "There was a fire near our house. Probably still is."

She reached for me, but I pulled away. No time for weakness.

"I'm glad you're safe." She examined my bruised chin, then narrowed in on my shoulder. "That doesn't look good."

I noticed a wet, oozy patch of dress stuck to my skin and that trail of blood that wouldn't stop sliding down to my wrist. "No, it doesn't."

The look of concern on her face made me squirm.

"Maybe you should go home," she said.

"Mr. Hanover is looking for a reason to fire me. I can't lose this job."

She tilted her head. "Well, he'll fire you on the spot if he sees you like this."

"Find me another uniform, please?" I begged.

"All right. But after your shift today, I'm taking you to see a doctor." She led me to a back room and searched her stash of folded laundry.

She handed me the clothes, and I waited for her to step out so I could change, but she stood in front of me.

"What?"

"Can I take a look at that shoulder?" she asked.

"No." I pulled away, then realized she was trying to be kind. "No, thank you. I'll be fine."

"It doesn't look fine."

I stared at her the way I imagined facing off with a cougar. They tell you to be fierce. Unintimidated. Grow tall and make them think you're the scary one.

"I'll see the doctor after work, okay?"

"I'm holding you to that." She shut the door.

I folded my body over, hung my head, and used my good arm to throw the dress off me. Feeling over the gunshot wound, I traced the path of the bullet through my muscle and out the back. Mangled and messy. Touching the wound felt like pressing glass shards into my flesh.

"How am I gonna scrub floors with this useless thing?" I said to myself. Maybe if I put in a few hours, I could duck out early. Beads of sweat broke out on my neck.

I'd found a clean white sheet and tore off an edge with my teeth, wrapped it around the wound a few times and hoped it would last all day. After a labored attempt with plenty of rest breaks, I was dressed.

By the time I started my workday, I felt ready to collapse.

Four torturous hours went by while I used my left arm to dust and scrub. The pain grew so intense I had trouble breathing.

The chef caught me pilfering a couple of bruised apples and an old block of cheese. He handed me a basket. "Here." A few slices of bread and a bottle of lemonade. "Those boys look like they could use a meal."

"Oh, you saw them?"

"Yeah. I don't mind. They aren't bothering anyone. Keep them out of sight of the boss man if you care about keeping your job."

"Thanks." I doubled over, my heart pounding against my chest.

"Magnolia, you all right? You're looking awful peaked," the chef said.

"I'll be okay." I rubbed my scratchy eyes and stood tall. "Thank you."

I snuck out the back and ran the food out to them. Johnny lay on his stomach, chin in his hands. Opening and closing his jaw to keep himself entertained. Oscar remained frozen in place. Eyes closed. Pale skin drained of life. But his eyelashes still looked like butterflies about to take flight.

I collapsed in the grass next to him. "I brought food."

Johnny grabbed the bread. Oscar lay there like a block of ice.

I placed my shaking hand on his forehead. "Oscar, please. You're scaring me."

He turned away. I wanted to hold him. Rock him and sing to him and wrap him in all the love he deserved. I wanted to carry us all away on a swan boat on the river.

"I'm here," I said.

Oscar curled in a ball like a pill bug.

"Johnny, slow down. You'll give yourself a tummy ache." He stuffed his face so fast, he couldn't possibly be enjoying it. But he smiled through every bite.

"I need to get back." I touched Oscar's shoulder. He flinched.

I wondered if his heart would stop beating. The fear and the pain, it was enough to squeeze the life out of anybody. I looked back at the inn. Then at Oscar. He needed me. But I needed this job.

With the slightest roll of nausea, I did what I always had. I made the hard choices.

"I love you boys," I said. Neither spoke.

Once down in the maid's quarters, I tucked into a corner behind the washing tubs. I slid to the floor and buried my face in my arm until my heart settled. Worry was always with me. Like the wind or a heartbeat. This was worse. Immediate and threatening. The sweat covered me now, dripping down my temples. Fluid soaked the arm of my shirt. It wasn't bright red like you'd think it would be. Rust-colored. Tinged with yellow.

Back to work.

I scrubbed and folded, wiping my dripping wet skin with scrap linen. My head spun, my skin hot as lava. The thought of my brothers kept me going. Just get through the next few hours.

By the time my shift was over, I could hardly breathe. I stumbled on the bottom step and caught myself on the wall. In the kitchen, Mr. Hanover glowered, hands on hips, red cheeks puffed out like blisters.

"I said, whose children are they?" he barked. A handful of workers exchanged glances. "I hear you gave them food?" he asked the chef.

"They look hungry and sick."

"Handouts make those little rats multiply, don't you know that? More orphans will infest this place, begging for food."

The chef looked down, careful not to make eye contact with me. He had three daughters and an ailing wife. He needed this job.

Drops of sweat rolled down the back of my clammy knees.

"We can't have this here. Understand?"

"Yes, sir," the chef said.

"Get your things. You're fired."

It's moments like this where you decide there's a bottom line to your soul. His family or mine. Those were the stakes. Maybe it was the weakness taking over, but I did what I had to do—be both brave and stupid.

"It was me. They're my brothers, and I stole the food." I said it plainly. I didn't have it in me to beg.

My eyelids heavy, I had to raise my eyebrows to see Mr. Hanover's reaction. He didn't say a word. Just pointed to the back door. I shuffled past him, not able to look at the chef.

"Don't come back here again. Good day, Miss Parker."

I blinked my eyes to focus. Nodded and tried not to cry. I didn't look at anyone as I left. My legs wobbled to the tree where I'd left them.

They were gone. Wagon and all.

***

My heart begged to find them, but my body had trouble moving. Every step tortured and shaky. I wouldn't let my mind wander to bad places. They couldn't have gone far. I tried to call for them, but all that snuck out was a strained whisper.

Horns honked in the center of town. Chatter and screams from women. I followed them, worried the commotion had something to do with my boys.

Less than a block. That's all I had to walk, and it might as well have been a mile. By the time I found them, a crowd had gathered. Oscar stood in the middle of the street, rifle in one hand, wagon handle in the other. His lips glowed a deep purple like summer blackberries. Johnny's swollen legs hung out of the wagon. He reminded me of the willows near the river, limbs dangling towards earth.

The sheriff stood by, hands up, like taming a wild horse. "Now, son. Just let me help you."

Oscar's hand trembled, the rifle flying all over the place. His giant eyes shone like full moons, static and bright.

By this time, I had to drag my right leg.

"Magnolia, be careful," the sheriff said. "He's not well."

I didn't even look at him. "None of us are well, haven't you noticed?"

Oscar pointed the gun at my face as the crowd gasped. He'd already shot me once. I had no doubt this stranger—this ghost of a kid that snatched my brother—would blow that bullet through my skull. I didn't care.

"I'm here, Oscar." The hot sun did nothing to warm me. The icy core inside reminded me of those long icicles that grow off roofs in the winter. I limped toward him until that barrel jammed into my chest. "Put the gun down."

"He stole it from the store," Johnny whispered. "Right in front of the owner."

"Shh, it'll be all right." I flashed him a forced smile then looked back to Oscar, the gun still pressed to my ribcage.

"Let's go home," I said.

"They'll come for us. Just like Mama always said they would. The bad men will come through the windows."

"No, Oscar. I'm here."

The sheriff took a few steps forward, but I lifted my trembling hand to stop him. "There are no bad men. I'm here to take you home."

"There's nowhere to go," Oscar said. He might as well have been looking at the sun, the way he squinted.

"The house is gone," Johnny said. "Forest fire burned it this morning. We heard people talking."

"No. No way," I stuttered, my legs about to buckle.

"It's true, Miss Parker," the sheriff said. "The fire swept through the west side of the river. It's been so hot and dry. I'm sorry."

The only thought in my head was that Oscar was about to shoot me, and Johnny couldn't walk. My legs turned wobbly, about to give out. But I couldn't pass out, not here.

I rested my hand on the barrel. Gently lowered it then eased the rifle out of his tight fingers, stripping them back like a banana peel. He let go. And when tears sprang to his eyes, I wrapped my arms around him. My body felt like a feather frozen in ice. "I'm here. Let's get you out of the street."

He buried his head in my shoulder and cried. And as he did, his skin started to pink up. "What are we going to do?" His giant, copper eyes tore a hole straight through me.

I had no answers.

I handed the gun to the sheriff. Everyone stood still and watched us limp and roll out of the street. Bloody, mangled, crying. They wanted to help us, but no one had anything to give.

By the time we made it to Mrs. Baxter's little green house, a thick coat of sweat covered my skin. Oscar tried to steady my hand, but I jerked and jolted. I knocked on her door, then fell to my knees, out of options. I had to trust her.

Mrs. Baxter opened her door, mouth open.

"Help us," I said.

Then everything went black.

CHAPTER SEVEN

My vision faded in and out. Flashes of Mrs. Baxter, her doctor husband. Searing pain. Were the screams from me or someone else? Couldn't be sure. I muttered, "The boys." But no one answered.

Light blared into my eyes, so bright I couldn't open them. I kept my head to the side so much my neck cramped. Sharp little blades lined up on a tray near my face. Bloody rags. A metal bin that hands kept plopping something red and yellow into. Flushes of water hit my arm, as if shooting through pipes inside my body.

Did I hear Oscar scream? I tried to sit up, but they held me, arms and feet pinned, while they cut into my flesh.

So many lights.

Their masks looked like duckbills poking around a meal. I closed my eyes and thought about the ducks gliding across Mirror Pond. How it's not really a pond, it's just a part where the river slows. In the right light, the trees reflect on the still water like a mirror, looking like pine and larch trees grow out of the water and down into it. It's still because of the dam next to it. The water becomes dangerous rapids after that. Just a pretty body of water with ducks giving the illusion of calm.

That vision floated me away to a dream. The trees became limbs. Feet and hands dangled down. They were all Johnny's, and they swayed in the breeze. A group of hands held on to Oscar by one arm. I reached my arms out to catch him, but a hard smack to my head knocked me out and the river washed me away.

Blackness again.

By the time I opened my eyes, I was certain I had died. But my body hurt too much to be dead. It even hurt when I blinked. I managed a grunt, but my mouth felt dry as volcanic sand. A foggy view focused.

Hospital room. White everything. Mrs. Baxter in a chair.

"Oh, hello dear. You're awake."

I tried to talk, but strange sounds sputtered out, like a dying horse.

"It's all right, don't speak." She wrapped her arms around me and pulled my body upright to fix a pillow, but it felt like a hug, so I closed my eyes and leaned my cheek against her shoulder. The cool pink silk sleeve of her dress slid against my skin.

When she pulled away, I felt the urge to bury myself under the covers. Stupid girl. She wasn't hugging you.

She brought a cup and straw to my mouth. My lips stuck together as I forced the dry, cracked skin apart. I sipped the cold water and winced, wondering if the doctors had taken those blades to my throat.

"It'll get better. You're just dehydrated." She placed the cup at the bedside table and scraped the chair along the linoleum to sit next to me. "You had a terrible wound in your arm, Magnolia. Clear to the bone."

"Ugh," I said.

"Besides inhaling smoke, you lost a lot of blood, an infection was setting in, and your body went into shock. You're lucky to be alive." She straightened the foot of my blanket. "They had to cut out a lot of flesh. Your arm will look different, but you'll be fine."

Craning my neck to see my arm, I willed my fingers to wiggle, and they did. White bandages snaked around my elbow up to my neck.

"I've learned it's best to tell people the hard truth. Just get it out and let them grieve a bit."

"Okay." A smile crept to my face at being able to form a word. "Water."

"Yes, of course." Her voice dripped like molasses. Thick and sweet. What was it like to sound and look so pretty? I'll never know. The next sip wasn't much better. Little cuts bathed in cold water. By the fourth, my voice felt stronger.

"Brothers."

"Yes. Your brothers." She straightened her skirt, avoiding my eyes. "They're in good hands."

My body stopped hurting. A soft boil of rage rolled through me.

"Little Johnny. His bones are soft. You know that, right?"

I managed one firm nod of my head. My eyelids felt so heavy.

"It's called rickets," Betty said. "It happens quite a lot. They're treating it and you know what? He's going to run and walk like every healthy boy his age."

It's funny how the words can be good, but you can tell when something ugly lurks behind them.

"He was malnourished," she said.

A jab. I didn't feed him enough. No one had enough food. She couldn't fault me for that.

"What with being alone all the time and not being treated properly…"

Hook. Punch. Like a ballerina with a boxing arm.

She smoothed the curls of her hair. "But he's going to be just fine."

"Oscar," I muttered.

"Yes. Oscar." Her eyes instantly shot to the window. "He'll be fine, too," she said. "He's a troubled boy."

"Not troubled. Scared."

"He stole a gun and threatened women and children. Including his little brother."

I wanted to take back my cheek resting on her shoulder. Take it back and replace it with a flinch.

"He needs help. For his brain."

"His brain is fine," I said. "He needs me."

"Of course. But he also needs doctors and nurses and medications that can help him with his anger."

"Not angry." My voice found its volume. "He was afraid. Of the monsters."

"Yes, the people coming to get him. That's what I mean. He has..." She wrung her hands together. "Worrisome delusions."

His nightmares. His unending tears. He's crazy. Was that what she was trying to say?

"I need to see them." I used my good arm to swing the covers off, but when I sat up everything spun, and I couldn't see straight.

She lowered me down. *Get your filthy, lying hands off me.* That's what I wanted to say. But she would use it against me. Prove I wasn't fit to mother them. I probably wasn't. But that wasn't her call to make.

"Relax, it's just the ether. You need to rest. The boys are taken care of. The doctors will make sure they have everything they need."

I dropped my head back only because I had to. Nothing in me worked.

"There's no house," she said. "You know that, right?"

Oh, the house. I'd forgotten about the fire. *Gone.* That crumbling, horrid shack in the pine trees where Papa drank and Mama held us prisoners. Good riddance.

"We still have the land," I said. "We'll live in a tent. I'll make another home."

She swallowed, like something bitter offended her mouth. "You see, sweetheart, the grocery man has taken it. Your debt finally caught up with you."

The only thing my brain could hear out of that sentence was sweetheart. Pouring sugar over a pile of garbage doesn't make it any more edible. My temples throbbed. My body flailed without an ounce of strength, but my mind felt ready to take on the world. Sling fists at everyone, knock down walls, rescue my brothers.

"You enjoying this?" I asked.

"Of course not. Someone had to tell you. I wanted it to be me. I know you don't have anyone else." She looked around the room, all sad and pious.

"I have my brothers. I don't need you."

She flinched. And it wasn't my insult. There was something more she wasn't telling me.

"You just rest. You can see them when everyone is strong and healed, all right?" There dripped that molasses again.

She touched my hand, but I grabbed her wrist and pulled her toward me. The look of fear in her eyes didn't bother me. "This is my family. Not yours. You understand?"

She nodded, worming her way out of my grip. I held tighter until that pretty face twisted with worry. Then I let go. I felt like I'd run twenty miles, all thirsty and exhausted.

"Rest up, darling." Her perfect curls bounced as she walked out.

My body fell limp. I would go find the boys and scoop them in my arms. I would protect them.

Just as soon as I could move.

***

Day after day, the nurses fussed over me and when I asked about my brothers, they just smiled and told me to rest. I needed my strength. So, I drank water and ate all the food. Oh, dear lord, the food. Chicken and biscuits. Warm tea with milk. Peanut butter cookies. I scooped up every crumb and after a week, my throat stopped hurting. I recognized my arm as my own and took a few steps. Almost there.

One nurse caught my attention. It seemed like she lived at the hospital. Gray hair in a bun. Thin but sturdy. Wrinkled as old laundry.

"Franny's the name." She said it without me asking. "I'm going to change the bandage. You can watch, but it won't be pretty."

She unwrapped quickly, my arm propped on a pillow. As the last of the wrap slipped off, I wondered where my shoulder had gone. The once round flesh now looked sunken and puny. Covered in yellowed gauze.

"It looks atrocious," she said. "But trust me, you'll be fine."

"How do you know?"

"It's something in the eyes. Some shrink away. Others come out swinging... even when they can't."

"I've swung at many people in my mind," I said.

"You and me both." She smiled. "You were pretty sick for a few days there, but you fought hard."

"I have things to do. I can't die now."

She wrapped my arm in clean white gauze. "Can't stitch it yet. We need to keep the wound open until it stops oozing. You'll be here a bit longer."

"I need to find my brothers."

"They're well taken care of," she said.

"I'll believe it when I see it."

She placed her hands on her hips and cocked her head to the side. "You don't trust much, do you?"

"Nope."

"Like I said. You've got fight." She winked and cleaned up her supplies, her nurse's uniform swinging in time to her purposeful walk.

I stood at the bedside and held onto the nightstand. Bend and lower. Over and over until I couldn't take it anymore. Twenty knee bends today. Progress.

I collapsed back, sweat drenching my forehead.

"I almost forgot," Franny said. She picked up her clipboard. "Someone brought you a letter."

"What? Why?"

"The chef at the inn said to hand this to you. Said it was the least he could do." She handed me an envelope.

On the front, my name in rolling cursive. I would know that writing anywhere—I'd seen it enough times in her printed letters. Mrs. Eleanor Roosevelt wrote me a note.

"Sounds important," Franny said.

"Yeah, it is."

"Rest up, Magnolia." Franny winked and left me alone with Eleanor Roosevelt's words.

I sat in the warmth of it, the feeling that someone cared what happened to me. But I couldn't open it. Not yet.

CHAPTER EIGHT

Two days I stared at that envelope. So few good things in my world, I wanted to savor this one. As soon as I ripped that paper open, there would be nothing to be excited about. I tucked it away, hidden under the Bible in my nightstand.

I walked to the end of the hall and back three times a day. The musty, damp smell disappeared from my shoulder, and a small bandage replaced the giant wrap. They finally stitched the wound. Mottled blue and yellow bruises dotted my arm from my wrist to my earlobe.

Nurse Franny took her breaks with me. She wheeled me to the window to sit with her while she read her paper. "More of the same. Every day, more of the same." She said it all the time. She'd sip her coffee as we stared into the tips of the pine trees and listened for the mill whistles.

"Why won't anyone let me see my brothers?" I asked.

She didn't look at me, just slurped her hot coffee and placed it on the tray table ever so gently. "They believe you need to focus on healing. Just like your brothers."

"And you, what do you believe?"

"Now that's an interesting question." She spun her wedding ring around her finger. A thin gold band too big for her bony fingers. "What I believe doesn't mean much around here."

"I know the feeling."

"At some point in life, you'll decide for yourself what's right. You'll risk everything because you know in your heart what you feel."

"I've always done that."

"Maybe." She leaned back and stretched her long arms. "But there's a difference between reacting to life and fighting for it."

"I don't understand."

"No, but I presume you will someday." She flicked her eyes to the wall clock. "Lunch break's over."

"Wait."

She crossed her arms and waited for me to speak.

"Bring me to the boys. Pretend you're taking me for a walk. Let me see them. Hug them." My voice trembled, but I rolled it back in. "Please," I said calmly.

"And get fired?"

"You understand, I know you do. The way you fuss with that band when you need strength. There's someone you fight for. These boys are my someone."

She sighed and then scrunched up her face, eyes shut tight, as if willing her mind to stop thinking. The tip of her shoe tapped the linoleum floor.

I reached back to unlock the brakes and stared at her, hopeful.

"Damn those sad blue eyes." She grunted and grabbed the wheelchair handles.

Stride after stride, her rubber soles squeaked across the linoleum. Her stockings rubbed together, and the whole thing had a musicality to it. *Squeak, squeak, swoosh.* She strode with purpose. Down the hall, around the corner. She slid open a metal door and rolled me into the elevator. Up we went.

On the top floor, the view from Hospital Hill held a peek of the river, as yellow sunshine kissed the rolling landscape of trees.

"Stay here." She crept through a door and muffled voices slipped through the crack. A baby cried, then stopped. She re-emerged and backed us into the room, swinging the door open with her backside.

Past a nurse's desk and down the hall, around a corner. Johnny sat on the edge of a bed, swinging his bowed legs and licking a lollipop. Looking like a normal, carefree kid.

"Maggie!" He jumped up and hobbled over to me.

"Careful, Johnny."

He wrapped his little arms around my neck and squeezed. He smelled clean. Medicinal. "My legs don't hurt." he said.

"What? Really?"

"They're treating his rickets," Nurse Franny said. "Lots of milk and eggs for this young man."

"Scrambled eggs with every meal," Johnny said with a smile.

"Where'd you get the lollipop?"

"Mrs. Baxter brought it."

A twinge shot through my heart. She visited while keeping me from him. Wicked witch.

"She told me I'm almost all better. And she's gonna help us find a new home!"

"She is?"

He nodded with a smile and sucked on his lollipop. "Can I have my own room?"

"We'll see." Thoughts rolled around my mind like loose pebbles. How would I pay for it? Why would she do that? Maybe she found me a job. Maybe I misjudged her. But my instincts were never wrong.

"He's going to be just fine," Franny said. "So will you." She smiled, and my body relaxed.

I grabbed Johnny with my good arm and kissed his cheek enough times that he pushed me off him. He wiped his skin and said, "Maggie, stop!"

"I'm just so happy you're okay. I'll visit you again soon, all right?"

He nodded and jumped back into bed and buried his face in a comic book.

I turned to face Franny. "Oscar?"

"Right." Franny lowered herself to my eye level. "Oscar is in a locked room. They're worried for his safety. And others."

"That's ridiculous. He's the kindest kid in the world. He refuses to hunt because he would rather starve than kill an animal."

"They're keeping him under observation. He's in good hands."

"That's what everyone keeps saying. I want to see him." I stood and grabbed the wall to steady myself.

"Okay, sit down. I don't need any emergencies while I'm breaking the rules."

She wheeled me through the doors to the other end of the hall and parked me by a window. Waiting for a group of nurses to walk past, she snuck me through another set of doors that required a key to enter.

She wheeled me to a thick metal door. A faint brown diamond pattern colored the small window at the top. I stood and peered through. Oscar sat on the edge of the bed, staring at his feet.

I tapped my finger on the window, soft at first, then used my knuckles to knock. He lifted his head. He stared at me without a hint of a smile.

"Open the door, Franny."

"I can't. I don't have a key."

"Look at him. He's terrified. Let me in."

"I can't, Magnolia. I wish I could. But we only have two minutes. Say what you need to say and let's go."

Two minutes. We could waste that staring at each other through the glass. "Oscar, come here, please."

His chest rose and fell, his breathing rapid. He shook his head.

"Please, Oscar. I don't have much time. I need you to come to the door."

Tears escaped his closed lids and rolled down his cheeks.

I clawed at the door, shook the knob. "I need you. Please."

He exhaled and shuffled toward the door. The little window framed his sweet face. Enormous eyes and long eyelashes, like a puppy in a cage.

"Oscar. Are you okay? Are they treating you well?"

He nodded.

"Then why do you look so sad?"

His lip quivered. Rimmed red, his copper eyes looked like glass marbles. "I hurt us."

"What? No. We're fine."

"I shot you. You almost died. I stole a rifle and rolled Johnny to the middle of the street." His trembling fingers scratched at his temples. "I'm a bad kid."

"No." Heat climbed my neck. "Don't listen to those words. Please." Both hands wrapped around the knob, trying to shake it loose. "No such thing as bad kids. Only terrible adults who aren't strong enough to love them."

"Mrs. Baxter says I can leave here when they're certain I won't hurt anyone. What if I try to hurt another kid? It'll happen again."

"No. You're a good person. You hear me?" My throat tightened. Sweat drenched my neck.

"Please, I need to hug him. He's so scared," I said to Franny.

She closed her eyes and turned away. Shook her head slightly. "It's time to go."

"No. I'm not leaving him."

"If they find him agitated, they'll medicate him. Put him in restraints. You don't want that."

Restraints. Like a crazy person. Like a damaged member of society.

"Oscar. Listen to me."

He stepped a little closer and so did I and we were only a few inches from each other, a thick metal slab and sheet of glass between us. I placed my hand on the window. "You're perfect, and kind. You're a good person. I know your heart, and it's pure love. We don't listen to them, okay? We listen to us."

He raised his hand to the window and placed his palm to mine. This was the moment. The moment the world broke him. All I could say was, "I know you. I love you."

Franny lowered me to the chair, my legs fighting to stay standing. My hand slid down that glass and I watched his face in the window until the doors shut and the only thing left was a memory. And a cold, empty crater eating its way through me.

Back in my room, I climbed under the covers and buried my head in the dark space warmed by my shaking breath. The tears fell so hard my throat stung. I let the hate climb up and devour me.

"Maggie, you're going to be all right," Franny said.

I pulled the sheet down. Stared at her with my puffy face. "But Oscar won't be fine."

She looked down. No words could make this better.

I cried so much that tears drifted me to sleep. Before I knew it, the morning sun had tumbled through my window and pulled me out of the dark place of nightmares.

Morning exercise. Leg work. Arm work. Breathing. Walking. Marching. Maybe it was the anger, but I felt stronger. I brushed my teeth with my damaged arm, even though it hurt like hell. If I had to burn this place to the ground, I was going to bust us out.

I needed a tight braid, pulling the fine hairs on my neck until I winced. But I couldn't do it with one arm. Under the bandage a scab had formed, a jagged line of sewed skin like a quilt. The flesh scooped out like a spoon to mashed potatoes.

I shoved the wheelchair across the room with a kick. Only walking now.

My chest ached. Pulling the envelope from under the Bible, I ran my fingers along its edge and traced Mrs. Roosevelt's handwriting.

Miss Magnolia Parker.

Just as I tucked my finger under the flap to open it, Franny arrived to clean my wound. I slid it back before she could see.

Franny set up her tray with strips of linen and water and ointment.

"Franny, how do people stay here? Do they pay, I mean?"

"Yes. Everything costs money. The community cooks and donates food so the patients can eat."

"How am I going to pay for us to be here? We don't have any money."

"Well, your care is covered."

"By who?"

She dabbed around my shrinking wound. Examined it and pulled back for a better look. "Betty Baxter."

"Why would she do that?"

"She collects donations. Her job is to work with the children. She makes sure they have what they need."

"Do you really think she'll find us a place to live?"

Franny secured a fresh bandage. "I sure hope so, Magnolia."

A shot of doubt ripped through me. Hope. It's all I'd ever had. When life disappoints you enough times, even that dwindles to a trickle.

"Coffee break?" Franny said with a smile.

"Sure. I'll meet you at our window."

After Franny left, I slid out the envelope. A splash of warm sunlight warmed my face. The heavy paper shined in the window's reflection, embossed with a seal of the First Lady of the United States.

Miss Parker,

I was delighted to meet you and greatly appreciate your honesty. I know how difficult this life can be, but we mustn't give up hope, and we must never give up on people. The ultimate strength comes from learning to love. People in your life have let you down. I understand the pain of that. Really, I do. The only way through it is by loving bigger and harder.

It is in ourselves that we find the most glorious gifts. Ones we hadn't known were there. Your childhood does not define you, and your past does not determine your future. Of that, I am certain.

I wish to hold you to the light so you may see how capable you truly are. How much this country and your brothers need you. It is in our home where we change the world.

If I may ever be of help to you, please write to me. I would like to be more than a politician's wife. I wish to be a good person who listens to the women she has met, and helps make the world safe for all its children.

Best wishes,

Mrs. Eleanor Roosevelt

In our home is where we change the world. Her words hit me straight in the heart. Somehow, magically, my terrible parents turned out two lovely little boys and one angry but capable girl. The children want to be loved so badly, they rise above the hate and the neglect. They find smiles and laughter. They look past the mistakes and beg for love. That's really all they need for the world to make sense—someone to love them.

Franny returned with the coffee. "You weren't at the window."

"Franny, will you braid my hair?"

She smiled. Placed the coffee on the tray. "Of course, I will."

She sat behind me on the bed and combed through my stringy blond locks. It felt so different to have someone brush my hair. She weaved the sections softly at my neck.

"As tight as you can manage."

"Won't that hurt?" she asked.

"Yes, if you do it right."

CHAPTER NINE

I laced up the donated shoes and smoothed out the thin cotton dress, determined to take the boys home today.

Franny walked in, hands on her hips. "What do you think you're doing?"

"Time to get out of this place. We're going home." I caught myself. "Well, not home. I'll figure it out."

"But... your arm. You need a few more days to heal."

"What I need is to hold my brothers and let them know we'll figure this out together."

"Johnny sounds like he's ready, but... Oscar," she said. "They're worried about releasing him."

"Nonsense. I'm his sister. I'm going to take him home."

"You'll have a fight on your hands, Magnolia."

"Good thing I'm used to that." I slung my bag over my shoulder, filled with a bar of soap, a toothbrush and toothpaste, a comb, and, of course, my letter. I didn't know if I was allowed to take them, but I figured no one else would want my used toiletries.

I threw open the door, and Franny rushed after me.

In the children's ward, I found nothing but an empty bed. I turned to a nurse. "Where is he? Johnny Parker."

She shook her head and walked off.

"Where is he, Franny?"

"I don't know." She looked around and found Mrs. Baxter. Franny exhaled and stormed up to her.

"Oh, hello Nurse Fran," Mrs. Baxter said with a smile.

"Where's the Parker boy?"

Mrs. Baxter glanced at me, then quickly back at Franny. "Don't you worry. He's well taken care of." She hugged her clipboard to her chest.

I pushed past and squared my shoulders. "Where is he? I want my brother."

"Magnolia, please calm down," Betty said. "You need to heal."

With my damaged arm, I swiped the clipboard from Mrs. Baxter, sent it banging to the floor at her feet. "My arm is fine. Tell me where he is."

Her cheeks flushed. "I, um..." She loosened her collar from her neck. "We took care of him. Him and Oscar. They'll be fine now."

"You took care of them? Like they're rodents that need cleared from a barn?"

Her lips tightened. "I always do what's right for the children. I care about them."

"The hell you do."

Franny pulled me away. "Tell us where you sent them, Betty. Magnolia has a right to know. They're her family."

"They're leaving right now. For a facility that will better suit their needs."

Much as I wanted to shove my fist into her face, my legs carried me downstairs and out to the driveway, hoping I'd catch them.

I threw the door open, the sun brighter than expected. A car that looked like a bread truck idled. I ran to it, my throat stinging. A man situated himself in the driver's seat, elbow propped on the open window.

"Stop," I said. "My brothers are in there. I need them."

"Sorry, miss. Orders to follow."

He put the shift in drive, and the wheels started rolling. I banged on the window with my fist, screaming their names. "No, I'm here. I'm here. Please, boys!"

I lost my footing and fell to the ground. When I stood, both their faces stared out the back window, wide-eyed and confused.

I ran towards them, throwing rocks at the wheels, begging them to stop, but the van picked up speed. It rolled down Hospital Hill, disappearing into the pine trees.

"No, I'm here." I looked at my shoulder, now soaked in blood. "I'm here." Tears burned behind my eyes, but nothing came out. Dry as dust. Hands balled into fists, arms trembling, I collapsed.

A voice from behind me. "I know you think me a monster."

I turned to face Mrs. Baxter. The wind bounced her curls. Not a hair out of place.

"You told Johnny you were buying us a house."

"I told him I found a home where he could be safe. He heard what he wanted to hear. I did what's right for them. In time, you'll see."

"What I see is a woman who destroyed a family to make herself feel like a hero." I rose, willing myself to stand straight when all I wanted was to wither in silence in the blistering sun.

"Think about this, Magnolia. Where were you going to live? How would you find food? They need clothes, shelter. Medical care."

"Nothing I have enough money for. That's what it comes down to, right? We're so poor we don't deserve to stay together."

"I collected donations and found a place they can both get the care they need. If you want to keep them from that, then you are the monster."

A stray maple leaf rocked back and forth in the wind with big, swaying motions. When the air stilled, the leaf hovered near me, close enough I could see the veins through its thin amber skin.

"You didn't even let me say goodbye."

"Would that make this any easier?"

"I know you've never had children, Mrs. Baxter. No one to protect and love. I suppose you'll never feel the pain I do because you can't."

It was a nasty thing to say, but I didn't care. I wanted to slash open her heart and make it bleed. My legs trembled and then gave way. Franny rushed to my side. Arm around me, she whispered, "It's quitting time. Come home with me."

Franny's white cottage sat near Mirror Pond. A willow swayed its feathery branches in the wind, fluttering bright yellow leaves from the approaching autumn.

Inside, a woman sat at the fire, reading.

"Magnolia, this is my roommate, Bernadette."

She stood, eyes wide. She fiddled with her dress and placed her book on the chair. "Well, welcome, Magnolia. I'll grab you a snack."

I sat by the fire, remembering those scared faces in the window, and it was all I could do not to burst into tears.

Franny removed her coat, slipped into the kitchen where she whispered to the woman, then emerged with a tray of gauze. "Come on, let's fix up that arm."

"How could she take them from me? It doesn't seem right."

"It isn't right. But it's legal." She cleaned my wound, focused. "Since you have no parents and you're a minor, the state takes over rights."

"I'm almost eighteen."

"Almost isn't enough," Franny said.

"Can I get them back? After they're better?"

She finished the bandage, securing it in place. "They've sent them to an orphanage. Then they'll put them up for adoption."

I shook my head, not sure why she would say something so awful without offering a way to help. "What?"

"Mrs. Baxter thinks she's saving children from poverty," Franny said.

Bernadette returned with a tray of milk and sugar cookies. "Magnolia, we have a spare room. You're welcome to stay as long as you like."

"Thank you. But I need to go... I don't know where. Where are they?" I asked.

"Portland," Franny said. "I peeked at the paperwork."

"How will you get there?" Bernadette asked.

I shrugged. "Train, I suppose."

Franny nodded. "You should know that they won't let you in to see them."

"So, I'll break the door down."

"And they might arrest you," she said.

"Whose side are you on?"

"Yours, of course. I want to see you all reunited. I just know what a battle you're up against." She handed me a glass of cold milk, which I gulped down. "There's something else."

"What?" I said with a grimace.

She glanced at Bernadette. "Oscar. They've determined him to be unstable. He'll stay at the hospital in Portland until they find him another place."

"What kind of place?"

She lowered her eyes. "An orphan asylum. A mental facility for troubled children."

Troubled. Unstable. Wrong.

"He doesn't need that. He needs his family."

Her eyes shut. "I know he does."

"It's not his fault his mother convinced him bad men would steal him. He never asked to be stuck with me."

I buried my face in my hands while the pain rose like a fever.

"You can try to get him back. Plead your case. If you're lucky, you'll find someone who believes love is more important than anything."

"And if I'm not lucky?" I asked.

"You'll have to find a miracle."

I reached into my bag, holding Eleanor Roosevelt's letter. Our encounter was the closest to a miracle I could imagine.

Bernadette lifted the phone and spoke to the operator.

I couldn't breathe.

After a muffled conversation, she hung up. "Okay," Bernadette said. "My brother works at the rail yard and does night trips to Portland on the freight cars. He said a passenger train leaves tomorrow afternoon. We can scrounge up a few coins, right?"

Franny nodded.

"That's very kind. But I can't wait. Can't I get on the freight car?" I asked.

"He says kids sneak on there all the time and hide in empty cars," Bernadette said.

"I can do that." A glimmer of possibility seemed like enough just then.

"That's awful dangerous, Magnolia." Franny placed her hand on my wrist.

"Franny, you should know by now that nothing's going to stop me."

She tightened her lips, took a pause. "Fine. You'll need your rest," Franny said. "Take our spare room and sleep. We'll find out when the freight leaves and wake you when it's time."

She led me to the small bedroom near the front of the house. I climbed into cool cotton sheets and pulled a blanket over me. The day still hung around the window, bleeding color into the autumn sky. I placed Mrs. Roosevelt's letter under the pillow. I fell asleep, knowing I had something to hold on to, and it looked a little something like hope.

I woke to a dark, cool night. I rubbed my scratchy eyes and walked to the living room. Empty. But the radio hummed a soft tune into the night.

An orchestra played "Old Susanna." A subtle breeze blew through the kitchen, the back door ajar. As the music faded, a woman's voice began, "When I was young..." Her words floated in the air, welcoming and soft like a hug.

Eleanor Roosevelt on the Simmons Program. She spoke of her life as a child, the pressures on women. Her voice settled my nerves and sent my mind drifting to images of breezy summer days and picnics with lemonade, fields of waving wheat. Children without fear.

I was no longer the homeless orphan who let her brothers slip away. I was free in a world where good things happen and families stay together. A place where mothers try, and soothe, and care.

America's mother. She did what mothers do. What they're supposed to do.

By the time the National Broadcasting Company bid me goodnight, my sleepy eyes had focused. I went to shut the back door but noticed Franny and Bernadette sitting together on a swing. They swayed back and forth, their feet dangling like children. Bernadette lowered her head to Franny's shoulder and Franny reached across to grab her hand. Their gold bands reflected the moonlight.

I didn't understand what I was looking at, but it didn't frighten me. The way they trusted each other left me hopeful for the world. I leaned my body against the doorframe and watched them stare at the harvest moon as it dusted orange light over the treetops.

"Do you think she can get them back?" Bernadette asked.

Franny, with a sigh, laced her fingers through Bernadette's. "I think that love makes ordinary people do extraordinary things."

Bernadette smiled. "Magnolia reminds me of you at that age. All fire, wit, and balled up anger."

"With a dark past she isn't ready to deal with."

"Like I said, reminds me of you."

I snuck back to the living room to listen to the radio. When they announced that Eleanor Roosevelt was enjoying her tour through the Northwest, I watched the embers flicker in the fire. "She has visited a boy's home in Portland, Oregon, and will tour the Bonneville Dam construction site before heading back to Washington," the announcer said.

Franny and Bernadette walked in holding hands. When they saw me, they let go of each other. Bernadette smiled and said, "You two have a chat while I clean up."

Franny sat next to me with a hesitant smile.

"Franny, why are some people hateful? My mother. She was awful."

"Some things in life just don't make any sense," she said.

"She told me I would fail. Not just before she died, either. She said it every day in glances and whispers. That look that told me I was never supposed to be here."

"She was ill, if that's what she told you."

"She didn't have to. That's the genius of her. She buried it so deep in my brain that I can never run from it. It's just something I know. A hard truth in the world, like seasons or death."

"You learned love from somewhere. Your father?"

"My father drank too much and taught me that life was a fight. And then he abandoned us."

She tilted her head. "How did you learn to love your brothers so fiercely?"

Memories crept into my mind like spiders. "By rocking them to sleep and telling them stories when the nightmares set in. By watching their faces melt into shame at another kid's teasing, and Johnny's bones twisting from not enough food. Then you see a five-year-old steal a can of milk, so his brother won't complain of belly aches. When something tears you up enough, you can't help but find a way to make it stop."

"Who took care of *you*?"

"Nobody. I wake every day fighting. And I'll keep swinging until my arms give out."

"What if I told you that your mother was wrong," Franny said. "That you were never broken."

I closed my eyes, focusing on the darkness to get away from words I didn't want to hear. Tears burst to my eyes and my bad shoulder gnawed like a toothache. Suddenly, Franny's arms enveloped me in a hug.

A real hug.

She pulled me in, the way I've seen mothers do. Close to her chest, her bony hands webbed out around my back. Her hair smelled of baby powder and castor oil. She exhaled, and I lowered my cheek to her shoulder. When I opened my eyes, the tears fell hard, and I leaned into her.

She pulled me up and looked into my eyes, her own shining with tears. "In this life, you'll meet people who will heal you. All the ugly this world has put in your heart will turn beautiful if you give yourself a chance."

"But I'm a worthless sister and daughter."

"No." She wiped her finger along the puffy area under her eye. "You're worthy. Of everything."

"I don't know how to accept that."

"One step. One choice, then another. That's how you fight for your life. A moment at a time."

"I'm not worried about my life right now."

"I know. But I hope you will be someday."

Bernadette came in holding a rolled-up paper bag. "Here's some food. A bit of money."

"You don't have to…"

"We *want* to," Franny said. "It's only a few coins. Wish it could be more."

"Why are you so nice to me?" I asked.

"I was young and brave once," Franny said. "I wish someone would have told me how much I had to offer the world."

"Did people finally heal the cracks in your heart?"

"Yes." She glanced at Bernadette. "Mostly."

I took the bag and stared at Franny. "Bernadette isn't your roommate, is she?"

She paused. Rolled her eyes to the ceiling. Then she looked down and fiddled with her ring. "You don't have to understand something to know it's right. It's the stuff of magic, really. Some people feel like home."

I smiled and placed the paper sack in my shoulder bag. "I suppose it's time to hop a freight train."

"Want us to walk you?" Franny said.

"No. I can manage." A warm ache settled in my stomach at the thought of leaving them. "Thank you."

Franny nodded slowly. "The boys are at the hospital for crippled children."

"Crippled children," I said with a laugh. "Aren't we all?"

"Yes. Until we aren't."

***

The freight yard hopped with lights and whistles and men moving crates through air thickened with steam and grease. No time for fear.

Only two freight trains this time of night, and the men were loading into the largest of the two. I snuck behind a bitterbrush plant and eyed an open car. Blinking lights flooded the night in red mist. A man swinging a flashlight walked past me and when he moved out of sight, I pushed past the biting pain in my shoulder to race up the ladder into the dark corner of the metal car. A whistle screamed, and the floor vibrated under my feet.

The train rattled, and, with a lurch, rolled forward. My heart thumped so fast it was hard to catch my breath. The moonlight lit the trees. Even in the dark, I could see the warm colors kissing the leaves. They whooshed past me as the train gained speed, clacking over the rails as we sped into the forest.

I opened the bag Franny gave me. Inside was a small knife. I slid it into the side of my boot.

I stepped forward, legs wide, and grabbed the rail at the doorway to steady myself. The tree-lined tracks flicked past me in tones of warm amber and copper, like streaks of finger paint. Like the color of Oscar's eyes.

The wind smacked my cheeks as Bend faded from view. My home, a slice of Oregon forest where sawmills are king and the river glides through its belly. A place with a burned house under the pines and two graves with rocks in the shape of stars. Memories of a family who never knew how to love each other.

The train carved a path toward the only thing I had to hold on to. Two little boys with fragile hearts. And a hope that maybe, I could save us all.

CHAPTER TEN

The train's quake pulled me from sleep in the dark corner of the freight car. Brakes screeched as two boots landed with a thud and I shot up to the cold wall against my back.

A boy my age. He leaned his hand against the doorway, unmoving, but staring at me. A mop of black, wavy hair fell over his mahogany eyes. The early morning light turned on his shining olive skin. His lean arms bulged in all the places that made a boy look like a man. Shoulders. Chest.

Papa used to say to never trust an Italian.

I didn't budge. Alone in a car with a boy. No one could hear me scream. My hand slid to my boot, touching the hilt of Franny's knife.

He retreated to the corner opposite me, sliding to the floor. Sifting through remnants of gravel from a previous haul, he threw pebbles at the metal wall for fifteen straight minutes, not a word mumbled between us.

We stayed alert for the next two hours, eyes across the freight car on each other. We rolled past camps with cardboard houses and shacks of tin and tires. Smoke curled from garbage can fires as children ran in circles, waving at the train.

As we slowed, the boy jumped past me and out of the car. He glanced back over his shoulder. Took a piece of hay from his mouth and flicked it to the ground. Hands in his pockets, he sauntered into the steamy morning and disappeared.

Portland. The air no longer carried the woodsy comfort of freshly milled timber. No crosscut saws grinding their teeth through Ponderosas, no river with a mouthful of softening trunks. Here, the trains belched thick sulfurous smoke, choking out the lingering scent of pine from the cut logs on the open freight cars.

I walked into the city, clutching my bag to my chest. People rushed past me in all directions, shoes clicking the pavement, while men gathered behind newspapers, yelling and laughing. Life in motion.

Nobody here was kicking rocks or watching clouds. I bobbed and weaved and jumped over grates in the street. Buildings grew tall like beanstalks while frantic noise bounced around the cool, wet air.

"Excuse me, where is the hospital for crippled children?" I asked a man reading his paper.

"Across the bridge. Just take the railcar up the hill."

I nodded and made my way toward the river.

Men lined up outside a diner, offering a cup of coffee and donut for ten cents. Little boys held signs asking for work for their dads while tall men in smooth suits sauntered by. Carts of apples, five cents apiece. Steaming bowls of soup in the hands of shuffling fathers and grandfathers and brothers and sons. Not a woman to be found. Window washers with curved backs and knotted knuckles. A sea of jackets and fedoras and honking Fords and Cadillacs.

I found the railcar and paid with a coin, thankful to Franny and Bernadette. Out the open window, I watched another homeless camp near the water. A cluster of shacks under the bridge. A boy touched up a painted sign that read "Mayor" and a makeshift toilet floated on the river.

"Hooverville," a woman said.

I turned and noticed a tall, slender woman wearing a scarlet hat. "What?"

"Shantytown, some call it." She clutched her handbag. "A bunch of families living in squalor, hoping to find a bit of work."

I leaned out to see a family. The father drank coffee as the mother swept the doorstep of their tin shack. Their two boys kicked a can back and forth.

"Isn't it just the saddest thing you've ever seen?" the woman said.

"No. I think it's hopeful."

"Hopeful? What sort of woman are you?" The disgust in her eyes was all too familiar.

All I saw was a family where the mother hadn't died, the father hadn't left, and the kids played with each other. "They're together."

"But love alone isn't enough," she said.

"It should be."

"How do you think those parents feel? Losing everything, unable to feed their children. It's heartbreaking."

I leaned my head against the window. "At least those kids will know that someone cared enough to build a tin house."

"Good luck to you, miss. I hope you never find yourself in that situation." She turned, laying her hand against her pearls.

These hard times were all so shocking to women with pearls and handbags. It was people like me, the always poor and forgotten, that didn't feel betrayed by the current state of things. To us, this was just life. More of the same.

I jumped off when the trolley arrived at the Hospital for Crippled Children. Vines with shiny leaves climbed the brick walls, the building set in a vibrant field of grass like a green rippling lake. A flash of gratitude shot through me. Maybe my boys had a nice meal and a comfortable room last night.

Through the doors, a heavyset woman greeted me. Her pointy white hat didn't fit over her frizzy hair.

"How can I help you?" she said without a smile.

"I'm here to see my brothers. Johnny and Oscar Parker."

She flipped pages in a book and furrowed her brow. She pointed at her oversized glasses and pushed them back up, only to have them slide down again. "Parker, you say?"

"Yes."

"I don't see them listed. Could you have the wrong hospital?"

"This is the hospital for crippled children, yes? I'm certain this is where they took them. From Bend."

"Oh, I see." She closed the book.

"I'm their older sister. I'm here to take them home."

She tilted her head. "You came here from Bend? To find them?"

"Yes." A sigh escaped before I could stop it. "They took them from me. Johnny has rickets and Oscar has... well, he has a nervous disposition."

She removed her glasses and placed them on the counter. "They aren't here."

She might as well have punched me in the gut. It would have hurt less. "They arrived yesterday. How could they be gone already?"

"A team of doctors evaluated the boys. Determined the best place to send them."

"And where is that?"

She bristled. "I'm afraid I can't tell you that."

I shut my eyes and grabbed hold of the anger that was about to explode into my fists. "I'm the only family they have. Now tell me where they are."

"They'll fire me."

"Or maybe I'll bust your lip open."

She straightened up. Placed her glasses back on. "Threatening me will get you nowhere."

My fingers gripped the counter. "Why did they take them? They need me."

"Rickets, you say? That's from malnutrition. Maybe they needed more than you could give."

"Why does everyone think that food is a substitute for family? No one knows how to hold Oscar so he stops screaming during a nightmare. Or the story I tell Johnny to make him giggle at bedtime."

"A story and a hug won't feed them."

I gritted my teeth so tight my jaw ached. A young nurse nearby pretended to look through files but glanced over at us. Franny's voice came back to me. I can't save them if I'm arrested.

I stepped back, glaring at my reflection in her giant glasses, and willed myself to walk away.

I slammed the doors open, back into the now wet afternoon as raindrops dripped down my temples. The air was so thick I couldn't see past the hospital grounds—all I saw were treetops peeking above clouds, the faraway sounds of the city humming through the fog.

On a bench under a tree, I stared into the mist.

Behind me I heard, "What are you going to do now?"

The young nurse approached. She sat next to me, tightening her sweater around her shoulders.

"I don't know."

"I can tell you won't stop looking for your family," she said.

"Would you?"

She grinned. "No. I wouldn't."

The birds cried around us. I couldn't see them, but they were there.

"Our specialists evaluate each child. Then they send them to the best facility for their needs." Her voice trailed off.

"The best place for the boys is with me."

"They keep them with family when they can," she said. "Are you a minor?"

"I'll be eighteen in a few months."

"Yeah." She shook her head. "Sometimes they'll look past that, if you have a job and a stable home."

My cheeks burned hot. "I had both of those. I couldn't hold on to either."

"Seems to be the story of our times."

"How do you do it?" I asked. "Work here and let them take kids away from people who love them."

She flinched, then turned away and wiped her eyes with the edge of her sweater. "Your brothers are in Denver. Oscar's in the wing for troubled kids."

Elbows locked to hold myself up, I blinked to hold the words at a distance. I wouldn't let them in. I couldn't.

She rested her hand on my shoulder. "They'll try to keep the boys together, if they can."

We let the silence settle around us for a good, long while. "You could get fired for helping me," I said.

"Yes."

"So why?"

"Because I understand you," she said.

"You've been where I am?"

"Sort of." She bit her lip. "I was in love at fifteen. So, I thought. He left when he found out I was pregnant, so my family sent me to a Catholic hospital for unwed girls." She wiped her red-rimmed eyes. "They drugged me and told me he died. Still born. But I remember—they pulled him away as I brushed my hand against his clubfoot."

"Why would they do that?"

"People think he's better with another family. If I think he died, I won't come looking for him. It's just easier."

"How can that be easier?"

"Easier for *them*." Her mouth tightened.

"I'm sorry."

"I work here hoping that someday, a child with clubfoot comes in for treatment and that I will see him again," she said.

"How would you know it's him?"

"I hope that my heart remembers."

We watched the mist roll past, the sun breaking into fragments of light through the rain.

"It's so unfair." I rubbed my eyes until they ached. "I had a plan. After our mother died, I could finally secure a job and food, and the boys could see a doctor. They were supposed to start school this month."

"What happened?" she asked.

"Everything fell apart. Our house burned down, and I lost my job." I didn't talk about Oscar's gun mishap, though she probably already knew. "What am I supposed to do without a family?"

"There's no easy answer to that." The nurse sighed deep and slow.

"Where do I find the Bonneville Dam?"

The nurse cocked her head. "What do you need that for?"

"I hear the Roosevelts will be there."

"That's right." She fastened the top button on her sweater. "I heard on the radio they toured it this morning. The President gave a broadcast before they left for Spokane."

"Oh, they're gone already?" Disappointment hammered through me like a stampede.

"Would be nice to meet the First Lady," she said. "She seems to really care about families and all the lost kids."

"Yes. All the lost kids."

"Enjoy Denver. I hear it's lovely this time of year." The nurse winked before heading back to work.

Fog hovered around me. I removed my letter from Eleanor Roosevelt. A bit crinkled now, but her words still rang clear, her message sharp in my mind. Home is where we change the world.

Looks like I was Denver-bound.

CHAPTER ELEVEN

Climbing into an empty freight was one thing. Launching myself onto the ladder of a moving train was entirely another. The cars flicked past, kids hanging out the doorways and staring down from the rooftops.

"Is this train heading east?" I asked a kid walking toward me.

"Yep. Better hop on. If you can't count the bolts on the wheel, it's going too fast. Another twenty seconds and you'll have to wait till tomorrow."

I counted the nubs on the rolling steel. Running alongside the train and building speed, I met the open car as it approached. For just a moment, my mind caught on the thought of losing my chance... and possibly a limb.

My left arm swung up, hand grabbing a ladder rung as I leapt, my body swinging into the metal door. I clung to the ladder and tried to catch my breath as my heart thumped against my chest.

I climbed in, my bad arm dangling at my side and throbbing with pain. This car wasn't empty. Must have been a dozen kids scattered around. The country's forgotten children huddled in the shadows, hurling toward unknown dangers.

I stepped into the dark, gazing over dirty faces and wide eyes. On alert. We all stared at each other, a knowing in the air.

A girl emerged from the dark, falling to her knees when the train lurched. Bright orange hair chopped ragged at her chin, the remnants balled into a matted mess. I had the urge to reach out and untangle it with my fingers.

A boy stared down at her, stance wide, arms crossed, his round freckled face doughy and flushed.

She stood slowly, her thin arms dangling at her hips. She looked to be about fourteen, but with purple hollows under her eyes, and an expression flat as death. Boy's overalls and a torn button-up shirt hung on her frail body while her bare toes dug into the floor to steady herself.

Her eyes flitted around, searching and desperate. I rose to standing and slid my feet a little closer. I wanted to wrap my arm around her and hug that desperate look off her face. Whatever this kid had seen, it had scared the life right out of her.

"Hey, you got any money?" the boy said to the girl in overalls.

She stared him down, steady eyes boring right through him.

"You heard me. It'll cost ya if you wanna ride this train."

The gnawing ache in my belly returned, and I crept toward them.

"What, are you mute or something?" the boy scoffed. "Or just plain dumb?"

Her nostrils flared, eyes narrowed like a bull staring down a matador. Her body looked about as strong as a pussywillow, but her ferocious eyes warned that she didn't care about her skinny arms. Something in her ate away all the fear.

The boy shoved her. Two hands straight on the shoulders. "Don't ignore me." He pushed her closer to the edge, but she caught herself. "Pay up," he said.

I lunged forward without a thought. Grabbed the strap of his overalls and yanked until his backside hit the floor with a bang.

"Leave her alone," I said.

He looked up at me, then stood slowly. "What's it to you, little girl?"

I rubbed my hands on the sides of my dress, knowing I had just entered an unwinnable fight. I took one shot with my good arm. Fist hammered straight to his chin.

After a stumble, he rubbed his face. "You're gonna pay for that."

I didn't see his hands but, in a blink, I flew backward, punched into the metal wall. A blinding pain shot through me as I crumbled to the ground.

Silently, I cupped my hand around my injured shoulder and waited for the air to return to my chest. I couldn't even scream.

The freckled boy grabbed the girl by her bright red hair. She flailed, arms smacking him as weak as a kitten's paws. A deep rolling anger grew inside me, and I wanted to cry.

A voice bellowed from the dark corner. "Let her go."

The train rumbled and whistled as it tore through the forest.

Out of the corner shadow, a boy emerged. The Italian who threw rocks at the wall on the ride into Portland. He walked over to the scrapper like he was strolling by the river on a summer's day. "You a coward or something?" he said.

The fat-faced boy loosened his grip on the girl's ragged hair. "You just call me a coward?"

A whistle rang into the sky, and the train jerked and bumped, a force building under me. "Only cowards beat up girls. You wanna fight someone, fight me."

The fat one hesitated. Looked over the Italian's arms and his unwavering stare. "Hey, just trying to make a buck."

"Find a better way to do it."

Something released, and the bouncing took on a forward pull. We sped up, and all three of them widened their feet. My belly jumped, the pain fading with the exhilaration of chugging and shaking across the earth.

The Italian grabbed the fat one by the shirt, and with a balled fist, brought his face close.

"Let go of me, will ya?" The boy's voice raised into a whine.

The train rumbled faster and louder, screeching across the rails and building speed, trees flicking past as quick as a flash. The Italian dangled the boy by his arm over the edge of the train—I assumed to teach him a lesson—but without an ounce of hesitation, the Italian let go. His screams evaporated into the hollow blackness where the ground rushed below.

The Italian swiped his palms together a few times. He glanced back at me with eyes like black pools, his stare enough to hold me frozen in place. My good hand cupped my shoulder, the pain throbbing into my neck.

He led the girl away from the edge and lowered her to the corner with both hands so she wouldn't hit with a bang and sat next to her, his head leaned back against the wall. His skin glinted like a sheen of gold over his sharp cheekbones.

When I removed my hand, the blood had soaked onto my palm. I curled into a ball the shape of a fox's tail and watched the boy look into the dark, a slight smile cast across his face.

My body shook with the train bound for Boise, the Italian boy's shining profile leaving an imprint in my eyes, even after I shut my eyelids. I wondered if he smiled about the life he lived, or the one he wished he did.

***

As morning light flooded the car, my scratchy eyes blinked open. I sat up, seeing only the frail redhead and the boy who'd saved her. The rest of the kids had jumped off.

I stood, my back against the wall and eyes on him.

"Plenty of people you should be afraid of out here," he said. "But I'm not one of them."

"Did you kill that boy?" I asked.

"Nah, he'll live. But a twisted ankle or a broken bone ought to teach him." His messy dark hair fell into his eyes, and he ran his fingers through it with the softness of a feather.

He looked at the girl, asleep, coiled into a ball. "She shouldn't be out here."

"And we should?" I asked.

His lip pulled into a smile on one side. "I know *I* belong out here. You seem tough enough. You took on that ugly kid without the strength to do it. I like your gumption."

"I would rather go out swinging than be helpless." I pulled my hand away from my shoulder with a flinch.

"I know the feeling," he said. "But you need to fix up that arm. It'll mark you as weak, and that's a dangerous thing out here."

"I will." Blood had dried into the cracks of my palm. "You helped her."

"You did too."

"The other night we rode the same train to Portland," I said.

He pulled his knees up and leaned his chin on them. "Yeah, I followed word of a job. Found nothing, so I'm headed east."

"You sat in the dark and threw rocks the whole time."

"I saw you touch your boot," he said. "You've got a knife in there, right?"

I looked away.

"Everyone on the train is dangerous until proven otherwise. Including soft looking girls."

"I'm not soft." I stood tall.

"I meant gentle," he said.

I let out a laugh. "You're a terrible judge of character."

"Nah, I meet all kinds out here. You can't hide a big heart."

I leaned back hard into the wall. The girl grumbled and shifted her legs. When she did, the light hit the bottom of her feet. Bloody and bruised. I bent down to examine the purple marks on her wrists and ankles.

"Restraints," the boy said.

I stood to face him. "Restraints?"

"Yes. The institutions. They tie the unruly ones to their beds. Drug them, too."

"She was in an institution?"

"She has that same look they all get when they're coming down from the drugs. Same bruises from those thick brown straps. Same sad haircut." He shook his head. "This kid escaped an orphan asylum."

Her bruised body and her sad, childish face. It took my breath away. This is what they do to the broken kids.

"Look at her," he said. "She's terrified."

The redhead recoiled, hands balled into fists in front of her face like a boxer, but still asleep.

"Did she escape?"

"Looks like it," he said. "Tough little girl."

Tough, broken little girl. "What are we gonna do about her?"

"First thing, we find her some shoes."

CHAPTER TWELVE

We rolled into Idaho as the redhead woke with a fire in her eyes. I offered to help her up, but she simply stared at me.

"Hi. My name's Magnolia. Are you feeling all right?"

She shoved me to the side and jumped down onto the loose gravel. She crunched the raw, open skin on her feet into sharp pebbles without so much as a flinch. Not quite a teenager and definitely not a child, I could tell this girl had already experienced one hell of a life.

Hesitant, we all searched each other for clues, for reasons to trust. I glanced at her threadbare overalls and bloody feet. They looked at my deformed shoulder. The light hit the Italian as he jumped down to join us, illuminating a scarred and thin right hand.

"Just up ahead is the jungle," he said. "We can search for shoes."

The girl didn't need to say a word. Her eyes did all the talking.

"What's a jungle?" I asked.

We walked along the ridge near the train. When we broke through the trees, a valley spread out below. Hundreds of tents and broken cars. Clothes hung on the tree branches and small fires dotted the ground.

"*This* is the jungle," he said.

We scrambled down the dirt path to the camp. He reached for the girl, but she pulled away and slid on her backside.

The place stunk with every scent imaginable. Fried meat, sweaty clothes, even death. The men still held on to their pride, standing tall at their tents as their spindly wives and ragged children sat in the dirt at their feet.

"There's an unofficial mayor. He's been here for years. He keeps a stash of old clothes if someone needs them."

I stepped around muddy puddles of piss.

Two men spun tales around a fire wearing suits too big and too old. Holes and stains everywhere, and hats with bent brims. One held a curved pipe under his mustached lips and chewed on the end nervously as he looked down at a yellowed photograph. When he raised his gaze, his eyes shone in the sunlight. He wiped the tears with the back of his finger. I'd never seen a man cry before.

We approached a shack made of corrugated tin. Seemed odd to build this flimsy structure around a solid brick fireplace. A man leaned back in his chair with a mug of steaming coffee.

"Been awhile since I've seen you around, Hop," the man said to the Italian boy. "Not since last year's barley harvest." They shook hands.

"This girl needs shoes. Her feet are all torn up."

"We can't have you walking around barefoot," the man said. "Not with winter approaching. You'll lose your toes." He walked into his shack and rummaged around. He came out with a pair of boots. "It's your lucky day. The soles are a bit torn up, but they're the same size. Here ya go."

"How much?" I asked.

"We don't charge for clothes. A family left these behind, knew someone here would need them."

The man handed me the shoes, and Hop shook his hand again.

"I can fix these soles," I said. "Did it all the time at home. Got any spare tires around?"

"Down the hill. Old tires here are like Crisco in the south. We use 'em for everything."

We found the pile next to an abandoned fire. I set to work on melting down a hunk of rubber to drip onto the holes.

"I'll never get used to that smell," Hop said. "Feels wrong."

"All sorts of things I'll never get used to."

The girl sat cross-legged, throwing rocks into the holes of the tires.

"We need to find out where she's from, and if she has family," I said.

He sighed and stared at me with that gaze again, the one that made it hard to breathe. "Hard to do when she won't talk," he said.

"So, your name's Hop?"

"Sure is." He removed a bag from his pocket. Untied it and laid it flat. A shortened toothbrush, a comb, a razor, and a sliver of soap. He slid the comb through his hair and rubbed the dry soap into his armpits under his shirt.

Shaking myself from staring at him, I said, "I've never heard that name before."

"That's because it's not a name. It's a plant." He splashed a drop of oil on his hands, rubbed them together, then pat his cheeks and chin. "I was born on a hop farm. My parents were farm workers and travelled where the crops were."

He smelled like spicy vanilla. "They named you after the hop farm?"

"No, the orphanage did."

"Oh." I turned to the golden hills in the cool, dusty evening with a pain in my chest.

"Don't feel sorry for me. I'm a boxcar kid. A king of the road!" He reeled himself back in like a fishing line.

"You're homeless but smell like a freshly baked cookie."

He chuckled. "I'm a hobo. It's part of the code to stay clean and groomed. Helps us find jobs at a moment's notice." He paused. "You think I smell nice?"

My cheeks burned, and I cursed my fair skin for betraying me with flushed cheeks.

"What about you?" he said. "What's your story?"

"The name's Magnolia. I'm out here to get my brothers back."

"Noble cause." He nodded. "You know where they are?"

"Denver. I think."

"I've worked the apple crop there plenty of times. Gets mighty cold," he said.

"You work the fields a lot?"

"Field, orchards, sheep farms." He shrugged. "Wherever I can find a day's work."

"What if you don't find any?"

"That's the thing about living on the road. The kindness of people never stops surprising me."

"My parents wouldn't let me take handouts," I said. "Told me to keep my pride."

"Charity, as we call it, is not to be ashamed of. It's nothing more than an old Latin word for love." Hop half-smiled. "So the hobos tell me."

He had scars on his face and hands. Looked strong enough to fight anyone in his path but seemed to be something like a poet. Saw the beauty in the world.

The day settled as pink streaks of clouds lit up the twilight and we all stopped to watch it. I put the girl's shoes aside to harden and scanned her for clues to her identity. She closed her eyes, smiling into the light. Hop leaned back, hands behind his head. Just for a few minutes, we weren't orphans living in a world of despair.

We were three kids watching a strawberry sunset.

***

We woke in the same scattered mess we fell asleep in. Each in a spot near the fire, the sunset long gone. My stomach groaned as soon as my eyes opened. The girl still slept. Hop whittled away at a stick using his pocketknife, using that damaged hand like it was nothing.

"What happened?" I asked.

"Oh, this?" He lifted his hand and flipped it back and forth. "Rattlesnake bite."

Two holes had scarred over on the back of his hand.

"You're lucky to be alive."

"You can say that again. One of my least favorite jobs. Rattlesnake catcher." His head shook with the thought.

"You got paid to catch snakes?"

"Yep. In Arizona. The desert blacktop gets hotter than hell during the day, so the rattlers gather on the roadside. When it cools at night, they all cross. Coyote trappers pay good money for them."

I blinked a few times.

"It was two hours to the closest hospital. One of those men loaded me into his truck and drove me the whole way. Paid for my treatment, too. The doctors had to slice me open and shoot me full of anti-venom."

"He helped you? Just like that?"

"His son died in a farming accident. He would have been my age and all the old man could think about was me dying alone on the roadside surrounded by snakes. Said he never would have slept again."

The girl rose to sitting and rubbed her eyes. Her hair looked like an eagle's nest I once saw in a dead tree back home.

"Good morning." I waited for her to focus. "You know we're Hop and Magnolia. Do you want to tell us your name?"

She flinched and looked away.

"It's all right. You don't have to speak," I said. "I'll call you Red. For your hair."

She raised a finger and pointed to my braid.

"I know, mine's so light." I pulled the plait over my shoulder. "Like the sun has stripped it of all its color."

She reached out and touched it. Tilted her head.

"Your hair is pretty ratted. Will you let me brush it?"

She raised her hand to her head and ran it along the back like she had forgotten she had hair. She nodded once.

Down at the creek, I instructed her to sit near the water. "It's gonna be cold, so don't be afraid." I scooped up handfuls and dripped them over her head, letting her lean back into my good hand so the water didn't soak her clothes.

Red looked up at me, eyes puffy and cheeks flushed. Her shoulder blades jutted out, sharp and thin.

I sat her up and pulled a comb from my dress pocket. "I'm going to brush out these tangles."

I laid my hand on the top of her head, her skull prominent under the thinned orange hair. I started at the bottom, working those little knots before moving up higher, holding the hair at the scalp to lessen the pull. A trick I learned a long time ago. A faraway memory settled in my hands. Brushing my little sister's hair. Singing a song. Hugs. I pulled my trembling hands to my lap and closed my eyes until the memory returned to the dark.

When I opened my eyes, Red had turned to watch me, her head tilted, trying to understand. I couldn't speak. Emily would have been almost six by now.

Red hovered her hand over my lap, then lowered it ever so gently atop mine. Her fingers felt like chicken bones, but her touch let me know she understood.

She turned her back to me and I kept brushing. Cleared my throat.

"Do you know who Eleanor Roosevelt is?" I asked.

Red didn't respond.

"She's the First Lady. She's had a hard life, just like the rest of us. She's been abandoned, unloved, scared. She once said that we must do the thing we think we cannot do. I don't know about you, but every day feels like I'm facing something I'm not sure I can do. Just getting through the day and still breathing feels impossible."

She lowered her head and examined her new shoes.

"As a child, her father would leave her on the curb while he drank the day away in a club. Her mother and grandmother called her ugly. Too timid." I ran the comb through the last of the knots, gliding the teeth through her stringy hair until it felt smooth as silk. "When I get scared or sad, I think about Mrs. Roosevelt succeeding at all she thought she couldn't do."

Red looked over her shoulder, expression still flat. She ran her hand over her smooth hair and closed her eyes as a smile twitched on one side of her mouth.

"Do you know where you're going?" I asked.

She shook her head no.

"You should clean your feet in the river. Dry them real good before you put the shoes on. I have some ointment for my shoulder. It will help heal the cuts."

She took off her shoes and waded in the cold creek water. She returned and placed her feet in my lap, wincing as I rubbed the ointment on her bruised and cut skin.

Back near the fire I whispered to Hop, "What now? I have to get to Denver, but I can't leave her."

"What happens when you get there? With your brothers, I mean."

"I don't know." I lowered my eyes.

"Are they in an orphanage?" Hop asked.

I shrugged. "The little one, I think. He's got bad bones. The ten-year-old..." I stopped to catch my breath. "He's in a place like she was." I gestured to Red.

"Oh."

"Those bruises. Do they really restrain them? Tie them up?" I shuddered with the thought.

Hop ran his hand through his mess of hair. "Some places are worse than others."

"They're just kids. Why are they so cruel?"

"Kids aren't supposed to have voices. They're supposed to swallow their fear. They're supposed to trust when all grown-ups ever do is let them down. When kids remind them of their own failures, they tie them to beds."

Hop raised his shoulders to his ears and cracked his neck sideways. "I'll go with you to Denver. We can keep an eye on the girl. Did you figure out her name?"

"I call her Red. Don't you have a harvest to get to? Why would you come with me?"

He placed his hands in his pockets and took in a long inhale of morning air. "It's a lonely life out here on the road. Believe it or not, most kids have families they can return to if they want. It's not every day I meet other kids like me without a soul to lean on."

"How do you know I have no one?"

"You get good at spotting these things."

Unnerved, I crossed my arms. "I've gotten by on my own for years."

"Like I said, we're kindred spirits."

We both glanced at Red, huddled under a tree, drawing shapes in the ground with a stick. We knew nothing about her. Where she's from, where she's going.

"Think the kid has someone who misses her?"

Hop shrugged. "I don't know, but it doesn't look like she misses them. Besides, what if we find her home and they don't want her?"

"Then I'll find one who does."

"So, it's decided," Hop said. "We go to Denver to find your brothers. Then we return the kid home. Wherever that is."

"You know, I can do this on my own," I said.

"I know. But that doesn't mean you have to."

I wondered where Eleanor Roosevelt was today.

***

We hopped on a freight train headed for Ogden, Utah. I didn't realize there were so many states between Oregon and Colorado. Hop drew the path on a map, how the railroad took us south through Idaho and across the top of Utah. We chugged past miles of wheat fields cut down and dry, hills shining a golden yellow. The wind beat against the open freight door like a hummingbird's wings. Red flinched from the noise.

A man stood from a circle of hobos in the corner, pointing at Red. "You the one they lookin' for?"

Hop shot up. "What are you talking about?"

"A young girl with red hair escaped from some crazy hospital in Salem. They say she killed a man."

Red didn't react. She didn't move a twitch from her cross-legged position. She stared him down with the same look of an angry bull she gave that nasty kid on the last train.

"Just because she has red hair?" I asked. "Look at her. How could she kill a man?"

"Gun. Blew his face clean off."

Red glared at him through the tops of her eyeballs. Her hand tapped the metal floor in a steady rhythm.

I scooted closer to her. "This is my little sister. She didn't kill anyone. Now leave us alone."

He placed his hands in his pockets. "I've got my eye on you. The last thing we need is the police bothering us. Soon as we get to Ogden, you make yourself scarce, you hear?"

Red's hand still tapped to the same steady rhythm. She looked like she could scratch his eyes out with all that hate inside her. I pulled her tighter until the tapping slowed and eventually stopped.

The men gathered on the other side of the freight car and opened a bag of peanuts and sandwiches wrapped in wax paper. Passed them around to each other. Except for one. A Black man leaned against the back wall, eyes out the door. The white men glanced at him, then went back to eating.

"Why won't they share with him?" I whispered.

"You haven't been out in the world much, have you?" Hop said.

I just shrugged and watched the man try to hide his sadness. Hop walked along the wall, shoved his hand in his pocket, and came out with a handful of sunflower seeds. The Black man took it, with a nod that looked like *thank you*. The two didn't say a word to each other as they snacked.

I kept my arm around Red for three whole hours, afraid she might explode. How could a fourteen-year-old kill a man? They must be mistaken.

"You said you were headed east. Where to?" I asked Hop.

"Arkansas. I heard there were jobs in the oil fields."

Red sat tall at the mention of it. Her head started trembling and her breathing sped up.

"What is it?" I asked. "Arkansas?"

She flinched.

"Is that where you're from?"

She curled into a ball and lowered to my lap, eyes shut tight. I lowered my hand to her head and kept a steady pressure. No quick movements or stroking her hair, nothing that could ignite her agitation.

Hop sat in front of us, protective. I didn't understand why he was helping us.

As the train lurched into Ogden, those men gathered in a circle, sneering at Red. One even pulled a newspaper out and looked at it and then to her, nodding to his friend.

The brakes squealed along the metal tracks into another dusty town, another chilly afternoon. But one day closer to Denver.

"We need to get a move on," Hop said. "They'll report her, I guarantee it."

We jumped down before the group could approach us. The lonely man Hop shared his sunflower seeds with leaned his shoulder against the doorway and tipped his hat to us.

"We need to find a bite to eat." Hop rubbed the back of his neck. "Then we get back on the next freight heading east."

"Will the next take us to Denver?" I asked.

"If we're lucky, we'll catch a long-haul train straight to Denver. If not, we'll have to settle for a local train to the Colorado border."

"Is there another jungle here?" I asked.

"Nope. Here we'll have to rely on a kind stranger who will take pity on a few hungry kids."

We ran out to the fields, expansive and golden. The sun did little to warm us against the crisp air. Down the hill away from town, along the empty roads. Red pulled her arms around her waist and hugged herself.

"You look cold." I started to remove my coat, but Hop stopped me.

"Here," he said. "Take mine. It's warmer."

She shook her head and turned to me, snatching my coat. She tightened every button and shoved her hands in the pockets. It hung down to her knees.

The world looked brown here. Different shades of dirt as far as the eye could see. Even the sky looked like cocoa. Grains of dust filled the air, sucking out the moisture and sputtering flecks into the wind.

One abandoned house after another. "What about this one?" I asked.

After examining the fence post, he said, "Nope. Keep moving."

A symbol had been scratched by a pocketknife. Like a half moon. "What does this mean?"

"Dishonest person," Hop said. "The hobos, they leave communication. These symbols describe what kind of people live here. Likely this one stole or lied."

I inched toward Red as her face grew tighter, more frightened. She pulled away every time I neared. The cold bit at my arms. My shoulder pounded and begged for a rest, but I said nothing.

The next house, a mile down the road, looked battered by time. Piles of dirt along the barn. A tattered American flag flapped in the wind.

"Here." Hop pointed to the symbol. A cross. "Religious folk. They'll probably feed us if we listen to a sermon."

We followed in line behind him.

A man came to the door. His once white shirt now a faded brown to match the land. Still buttoned up to the collar. His hair was newly trimmed and his belt shining. He looked to be holding onto his dignity by his fingernails.

"You kids searching for a handout?"

"We're hungry, sir," I said. "Do you have anything to spare?"

His eyes softened when he saw us girls. He looked back at Hop, narrowing his eyes. "You Italian?"

"I don't actually know, sir."

"How do you not know?" the man scoffed.

"I've never met my parents."

"Your skin is dark and oily," he said. "You sure look the part."

"I hear you're the praying kind," Hop said. "Might we join you for a Bible reading and a bite to eat?"

"Only the purest kind are allowed in this house."

They stared at each other. Fierce. Untrusting. "What are you girls doing with this swindler?" He motioned his thumb to Hop.

Red's entire body tightened. The man took a step closer, and she recoiled. Her breathing sped up—so fast I could hear it rush through her nose.

"We're all just trying to find our way back to family," I said.

He leaned toward Red and squinted. "You." His voice turned sharp. He walked back into his house and came out with a folded newspaper. Threw it at me. "Is this the kid they're looking for?"

I unfolded the paper. The front page with the headline, Murderer Escapes Mental Institution. Underneath, a mugshot of a young girl with dead eyes, the spitting image of Red.

Red stared at him, her hand slapping her thigh in a steady rhythm.

I stepped in front of her. "Of course it isn't. This is my sister."

"Maybe she is, and maybe she ain't. But one look in her eyes tells me she's a sinner."

Heat pounded through my neck and arms. "She's a child."

"You can come in." He nodded to me.

"Just me?"

"You're pure. I can tell."

"Just by looking at me? You can tell I'm good?"

"God speaks to me. He tells me to feed you, and I'm keen to listen."

I handed Hop the newspaper. "I don't want to eat if they have to go hungry."

"Suit yourself."

Hop leaned to my ear. "No sense in all of us missing out. You still got your knife?"

I nodded.

"Go on. I'll be right here." Hop gestured to the man. "Keep the door open. In case she needs me."

"Son, this girl is safer with me than she'll ever be with you." He creaked open the door and extended his hand.

My heart thumped. I didn't want food if they had to sit outside hungry. But Hop's eyes pleaded, so I stepped into the house. Down to a few scratched pieces of furniture, but clean as could be. I glanced over my shoulder. Four wide eyes stared at me from the porch.

"Come on, now. I've made lunch," he said.

His kitchen, once bright with yellow walls now faded and dull. Bubbles formed under the wallpaper where someone had pushed the seams back together with glue. Quarry tiles chipped and faded. I ran my hand along the bowl of fruit on the counter. Apples and oranges and a banana. In the corner, a refrigerator. I eyed it in awe.

"I'm very lucky," he said. "God provides for me. As he will for you if you stay on the right path."

"What, then, is the right path?"

He pulled out a metal chair, the plastic seat cracked to reveal carrot-colored padding underneath. "For starters, don't spend your time with trash."

My fingertips dug into my thighs. He handed me a plate. Fried bologna sandwich, half an apple, and a butter cookie.

"They aren't trash."

"A greasy Italian, and a murderer. You're turning away from the goodness of God."

"You've decided that innocent children are garbage and you're lecturing me on the ways of God?"

His eye twitched. "I know people. God grants me the wisdom to see in their soul." He pushed the plate toward me. It was ivory, with chipped edges and strawberries painted in the center.

I stared at that food and my belly rumbled deep and hard. Hunger is like that—you can ignore it somewhat, until all that hope is in front of you. All I had to do was reach out and grab it.

"You've been through hell on earth. I can see it." He scooted his chair closer to me.

My eyes shifted to the side. I swallowed the saliva that pooled in my mouth.

"You deserve this. Fill your belly and your soul. Let God fill you with his love."

"Eating this sandwich will fill me with God's love?"

"Pray with me."

The room grew hot as a bead of sweat trickled down my neck. The man stared up at me. Hopeful. Desperate. A glance back to the food. I imagined biting down on the crisp, cool apple with its shiny red skin.

"All right," I said.

He placed a Bible on the table. A maroon felt bookmark stuck out of the top, the kind I used in school. It reminded me of a simpler time. One where babies didn't die, and fathers didn't disappear. Where mothers sing.

He grabbed my hands so fiercely that I gasped and jerked away. He tightened his sweaty hands around mine and squeezed like he was juicing a lemon. His voice shook as he prayed for my soul and my protection. Asked God to change my heart, to send me home and find my way back to my parents, oblivious that I asked God for years to change my heart. He never listened.

His touch sent chills skittering up my arms. His need. The white spit that foamed in the corners of his mouth. The way he pulled his body close to mine.

He opened his eyes and reached his hand for my cheek. I swatted his hand away. "Don't touch me."

"I don't want to hurt you, child. I want to save you." His breath grew rapid, his face flushed.

The cookie had cracked in the middle, crumbling pieces onto the plate. All that fatty butter and sweet sugar.

The man stood, then lowered down behind me, his sour breath warming my ear. "Go on. Eat."

A bite wouldn't hurt anything.

"Feed yourself. Accept God into your heart."

The tart apple. The yeasty bread. I leaned toward it. I hated myself for being weak.

Then, his tongue flicked over my earlobe. I shot up and kicked the chair with the back of my legs. "What the hell!"

Hop ran in, arms out. "What did you do to her?"

The man stood and straightened his shirt. "I didn't do a thing. Just showing her the ways of the Lord." He turned to me. "What will it be, child? A meal and eternal happiness, or a life of sin?"

I stared at Hop and leaned to the side to see Red in the doorway. Their faces showed only one thing. Worry. *For me.* "I've known a life of disappointment, of God shaming me. I don't care to return to that world."

His face turned to a scowl. The redness in his cheeks dissipated. I reached for the apple, but he swiped the plate. He sauntered past me, wafting the food under my nose. He bit his sharp teeth into the apple right next to my face. Sprays of sticky juice flew onto my cheek.

"Good luck to you. May you find a way home." He walked to the garbage can and turned the plate sideways. The food slid away, and a smile crept to his face. "Should have let me save you."

"I don't need your saving. Or your food." I wiped my earlobe. Hop led me out the door, away from that house where God most certainly did not live.

Along the dirt road, Hop lowered his hand from my back. I squirmed. I wanted his touch. It was tender and kind. But something inside me wanted to spit that out. Pull back to a space where all I felt was that braid pulling on my scalp until it hurt.

"You didn't take the food," Hop said.

"No. I'd rather go hungry than let that creep touch me."

Red watched us with rapid breaths.

"Next time, eat. Eat fast then kick him in the shin," he said.

I pulled my shoulders back to stretch out the tension in my neck. "I couldn't eat while you went hungry."

He kicked a pile of gravel. The bits bounced along the road ahead that unfolded into the gray expanse of the autumn sky.

I reached into my pocket and pulled out an orange. "Here. I didn't kick him in the shin, but I did distract him for a moment."

Hop tilted his head. "You're pretty clever."

"It's not a meal, but it's something."

We found a ditch. We leaned against the dirt and split the orange three ways. Orange liquid rolled down my forearm, and I licked it before I lost a drop of that sweet, tangy juice. We sucked our dirty fingers clean and leaned our heads back to watch the sunset.

I opened the newspaper to examine the picture. Could it be Red? Sure did look like her. But I didn't see how this child could murder anyone.

At the top of page two, another headline. *Eleanor Roosevelt to Focus Efforts on Youth.* As Hop and Red got lost in the pink horizon, I pulled the paper closer. It read about how Eleanor Roosevelt worked with the American Youth Congress to provide jobs and education for young women. "It is not enough to find women a place in the bread line," Mrs. Roosevelt wrote. "We must change their future so they may find a place in the world."

I could have floated away on that moment of hope. She heard me. Once I found the boys, Eleanor's Youth Congress could find me a job.

My belly growled. The sweet syrup of a few orange slices grew the wanting. I gave up a meal for a slice of pride. Maybe I was stupid, but I would do it again. I'd had enough of grown-ups taking from me. I hoped for a miracle in Denver and kept my eyes on Hop and Red and the image of Eleanor Roosevelt as I clung to their goodness like I was drowning.

CHAPTER THIRTEEN

The next morning, we stared at the train headed for Salt Lake City. Crouched in the bushes, that newspaper image stuck to my mind. I didn't know how to protect Red. I didn't even know what her voice sounded like.

"Do you think it's safe?" I asked.

"I don't know," Hop said. "Everyone's looking for her."

I wanted to ask if she really killed a man, but one look at her face stopped me. She didn't look like a teenager. She looked like a hardened old woman, beat down with the misery of life.

Red pointed to an empty car at the front of the train. A wide-open door past the end of the bushes. Nobody wanted to be near the conductor and the hot coal spitting into the air.

"Bulls are out," Hop said.

Bulls, as I'd come to learn, were the guards that patrolled the freight yards. They carried metal clubs and pistols and thrived on torturing people who rode the cars. They were known to lock kids in a refrigerator car just to see if they lived through the night.

"It's going to be cold tonight, I can feel it," Hop said. "I don't think we have a choice." He removed his jacket and wrapped it around my shoulders.

My head had been pounding all day. No water, no food. I'd been surviving on stress and dwindling hope. "You both sure you want to come with me to Denver?"

"What else are we gonna do?" Hop said. "As long as you don't mind a greasy Italian and a murderess tagging along."

Red turned to Hop and growled.

"Okay. I guess we take a chance."

"Yeah," he said. "We take a chance."

We watched the guards stomp around in their heavy shoes and crisp jackets, clubs and guns attached to their belts.

Red's face remained still as a morning lake while her neck pulsed.

"Now," Hop said.

We ran with light feet away from the cover of bushes. I kept my eyes on the end of the train, heart thumping. Laughter spilled out as the bulls cracked their clubs against the sides of the cars.

More kids scurried out with us, like an army of ants heading for a picnic. We had to make it to the dark recess of the freight car. Gravel crunched under our shoes, so I bent my knees to lessen the sound. Ten feet away, Red tripped, so I leaned down to lift her. When I looked up, a bull rounded the corner, the sun shining right on our faces.

"Hey kids, you thinking of boarding this train?" he barked.

We shook our heads and backed away. We should have waited until dark. I turned Red to face me, pulling her into a hug.

"Hey, that kid. She's got red hair," he said with a lean forward and a glimmer in his eyes.

"Run," Hop said.

We turned and ran along the train in a pounding fury of feet.

"Get back here!" He lumbered, eager to catch a runaway murderer. A whistle screeched as the train rumbled.

A long line of open cargo freight with piles of lumber and pipes tied with rope. Nowhere to jump on. I looked back, staying behind Red in case he lunged for her. He hobbled and sputtered like an engine out of gas. Then, a trio of young rail workers came up behind him.

"Go!" I pressed my hand to Red's back.

Brakes released with a thud, sending the train rolling past in a slow chug.

"We can catch the end. Jump on it as it rolls away," I yelled.

The men neared us, practically nipping at our heels like cattle dogs. From behind the bushes, someone leapt in front of us as we all screeched to a halt. The Black man from the ride in.

He threw us back and yanked on a long rope. The white plastic pipes rolled out in a clattering wave, blocking the bulls in a steamy cloud from the train's exhaust.

"Come on," he said. "The name's Samuel.

He led us down a hillside to a ravine below. We traversed the riverbed, long dried of water, following behind him to who knows where.

Two men scrambled down the hill after us. "They're still there."

"Hurry it up," Samuel said. "My truck's just ahead."

I grabbed Hop's arm. "Can we trust him?"

"Don't have a choice."

We huddled in the truck bed under a worn tarp and rumbled off. I peeked out from underneath to see the bulls throw their hands up.

Hop's arm brushed mine, and I could hear his breath. The car shook, rattling my knee against his. Every time our bodies touched, my belly flipped. I pulled away, pretending to protect my shoulder.

"Can I see it?" he asked.

Red eyed him with a scowl.

I rolled up my sleeve. Dark brown blood saturated the bandage over my wound.

"What the hell happened to you?"

"My brother shot me." I shrugged. "It was an accident."

Hop examined the blue and yellow bruises, the scooped out flesh where my muscle should be.

"You've had a gunshot to your arm this whole time?"

"It only hurts when I lift it."

"That's a problem for an arm." A smile crept to his face. He pulled the neckline down to see how far the bruise climbed. Chills spread over my body as his soft fingers trailed along the curve of my collarbone. I instinctively closed my eyes. No one had ever touched me like that.

Red kicked Hop in the ankle, then shot him a fierce look.

"It's all right, Red," I said.

Hop pulled away, releasing my collar back over my bruise. He pulled away and placed his hands around his knees.

I felt the aching need to grab his hand and place it back on my neck. But Red's face looked so terrified, like she needed to protect me.

Voices and cars and horns boomed. The truck lurched to a stop. Metal clanged as a door rolled up, then the truck rolled slowly into the dark.

Samuel helped us out. Light filtered through a high window, and all I saw were shadows. I reached around for Red's hand.

We followed through a garage and into a kitchen with clanging pots and pans and jazz blaring on the radio. Women danced and sang. They all froze when they saw us.

One woman cocked her head, hands on her hips as she scanned our faces. "What were you thinking, bringing dirty white kids here?"

Samuel removed his hat. "You know I can't let them kids get beat, Mae. The little one is wanted for murder."

Beads of sweat instantly formed on Mae's brow. "Sweet Jesus, we gonna need to pray tonight." She threw her head back and closed her eyes. "Dear Lord, save my idiot husband. He knows not what he does."

"We won't be any trouble," Hop said.

"Samuel's heart is too big for that pea-sized brain of his," she said with a shake of her head. "If our patrons get wind of whites staying here, we'll be an empty hotel from here until eternity."

Mae threw a towel over her shoulder and mumbled to Samuel.

Suddenly, lights flickered around the windows. Samuel grabbed us and led us into the pantry. He lifted floor panels on a hinge and pointed. "Get to the crawl space and stay put. Not a sound, you here?"

We climbed down the steps and into the dark hole below. The floor closed shut, and he slid something over the top. I understood why they called it a crawl space. We settled onto our backs just as a hush came over us. Mae stepped calmly to the door. Muffled voices and a door banging open. I closed my eyes and swallowed, praying I wouldn't cough from all the dust.

Boots clopped through the room. The slats above us darkened as the men blocked the light with their bodies. Knocked free from the boards, dirt fell onto our faces as we stifled coughs. They stopped right above us. Still.

Red didn't move. She stared at her feet and started tapping in the cool dirt underneath us. Certain the police could hear my heartbeat through the floor, I held my breath, but Hop's hand slid over mine. Our faces nearly touched. He held his finger to his mouth to tell me to stay silent as he stared into my eyes.

"You all seen a redhead? This one right here." The sound of a finger smacking a newspaper. "She's wanted for murder. You don't want to house a white girl wanted by the law. All of you would be complicit. Every last one of you would be hauled away and taken care of... the proper way."

Hop pulled close enough that our noses touched. If I focused on him, I could do this. His dark eyes and his warm, sweet breath. I tightened my fingers around his.

"I'm not that stupid," Mae said. "See for yourself. You're welcome to search the place."

Silence.

A spider crawled up my arm. I tried flicking it away, but it kept marching toward my shoulder, probably wanting to feast on the nasty blood dripping from my skin. I tensed, knowing I couldn't move a muscle. It's just a spider. Don't let the fear take hold.

"Rail yard officers report seeing Mr. Williams leave with three kids. One matched the description of this redheaded bitch."

I turned to look at Red. She stared up, mouth pursed, ready to spit.

"That redhead had a knife," Samuel said. "I barely got away from her."

The spider reached my shoulder and crawled inside my neckline. I scratched and grabbed, but its little legs still pattered under my dress. My head pounded.

It burrowed under the soiled bandage. Too far back to reach. I tightened my face as tears gathered in my eyes.

"I better not hear of you having anything to do with those kids."

Red pulled down my collar. Peeled back the bandage. She lifted the spider by one leg and held it to her face. She flicked it back into the dark corner with a sneer.

I could still feel it crawling on me.

The boots stomped off, but not before they knocked something to the floor, glass shattering in pieces above us. We waited a few minutes, Hop still squeezing my hand. The trap door lifted.

"It's all right." Samuel reached his hand in. "You can come out."

We crawled up the ladder, into the light, our heads and faces covered with dirt.

"Get them the hell out of here," Mae barked to her husband.

"We can't leave them covered in mice droppings," he said.

Mae glanced at my arm and the brown stained blood on my sleeve. "Take them out back."

Samuel kissed her cheek and led us outside to a shed tucked behind the hotel. The musty smell of old liquor and stale air made us cough. He swept the floor and shook out a few blankets.

"It ain't much, but it will keep you out of sight."

"Your wife doesn't want us here," I said.

"She's just scared, is all."

"I know the feeling," I said.

Samuel rubbed his neck. "If they find out we're helping you..."

We shuddered. We knew what would happen.

Hop walked to the man. "Why are you taking such a risk?"

"Sounds ridiculous, really. Those sunflower seeds. I could tell you all don't have two pennies to rub together. Gas is so expensive, so I use the freight to visit my brother when money is tight. Those men see me all the time and still ignore me. But you didn't. It hit me in a soft spot."

Hop reached to shake Samuel's hand.

Hop built a fire while I tried to ignore the thumping in my arm. The bleeding had stopped, but it didn't feel right.

We settled in, listening to the quiet night. Red pulled a blanket over her, eyes already fluttering asleep.

Hop whispered, "Are you tired?"

"Not really."

"Let's see if these crates hold anything interesting." He rummaged around until he found a bottle of Canada Dry ginger ale. He balanced the cap on a window ledge and slammed it with his palm, popping the top. "I've slept in a lot of shacks over the years and there's usually treasure to be found."

I took a sip, the sweet, bitter bubbles tickling my mouth. I handed it back to him, our fingers brushing. "You've seen a lot."

"I work jobs as necessary. Until I grow restless and wanderlust calls. Been out here on my own since nine years old."

"You've been on the road since you were nine?"

"I couldn't take living in the orphanages anymore. They bounced me around from place to place. They kept our heads shaved near clean, and I hated it. All itchy and pale. It's why I leave it long and messy now. It was aways the same. A belt to the backside and locking me in a closet for misbehaving. Not that I knew any other way."

I winced at the thought.

I think Hop realized what he had said because he stuttered a bit. "Oh, hey...I... I was just really lost. They don't treat every kid that way."

I closed my eyes, trying not to rock to soothe myself. He gently caressed my back. I blinked my eyes open and looked at him.

"Those places, they aren't a home," he said. "Sure, there's food and clothes, but there's no one there that loves you. I used to dream of someone rescuing me. Your brothers are lucky to have you."

"I don't know what I'm gonna do once I find them."

Hop's hand slid from my back. The muscles in his jaw twitched. "I lay awake every night and I dream of a family," Hop said. "I imagine seeing my parents in a wheat field. That they recognize me."

I flashed a hesitant smile.

"You think it sounds stupid, right?" Hop said.

"No, I think it sounds perfect."

I'd moved closer, hungry to smell him. "Ignore your body," Mama used to say. "When it yearns for a boy, it means something's rotten inside of you." But the wanting grew so strong that I leaned closer, my chest toward his. Maybe I could be rotten.

His hand neared my face. I nearly gasped, need sat so close to the surface. He lay his palm on my hair and brushed back along my scalp. My neck softened.

His full lips parted. "Your freckles look like a starry night."

"They make me feel like a little girl."

"They make you beautiful," he said.

My chest heaved like my heart needed extra room. The bumps and ridges on his body were so foreign. I looked into his dark eyes. "Are you gonna hurt me?"

He pulled back. Lowered his hand from my face. I wanted to take it back, pull his body next to mine.

"I would sooner die," he said.

I knew he was good. But those thoughts were buried so deep, my mind wouldn't let my heart take over.

"Where'd you get that idea?" Hop asked.

"I'm sorry. I just don't know how we're supposed to trust anyone. Most seventeen-year-olds are going to dances and flirting with boys." I shook my head. "Not me."

"You had a family. But I think you're as lonely as I am."

Hop wrapped me in his strong arms, lowered me to the floor, and pulled a blanket over us. His body pressed into me, his chest and hips curled with the shape of mine. His hands never touched my body, but I deeply wanted them to.

In the morning, as the light tumbled through the window, I shifted, still feeling his chest pressed into my back. I cuddled into his soft, warm curves.

A tapping sound caught my attention. My foggy eyes blinked a few times, seeing only shadows of a figure over top of me. I saw Red, her hand slapping rhythmically against her leg. Her other hand gripped my knife. Knuckles white, arm trembling.

"Hey," I whispered. "I'm okay." I moved slowly. She watched me slide Hop's arm away from my waist, the skin tightening around her mouth. Hop shifted and pulled away.

I stood and stared into her eyes. "I'm fine. He was just keeping me warm."

Red's upper lip glistened with sweat, and her whole body trembled. I reached, arms out, like she was a mustang, and my touch might send her searching for open land. She stared over my shoulder at Hop, her hand beating, tap, tap, tap. I pulled her into me, squeezed tight until her arms softened. My hand slid down, removing the knife from her clammy fingers.

I held her close for a long while, but after a few more minutes, the tapping stopped. I let her feel me exhale, just as I'd done with Oscar many times. She lowered her forehead onto my shoulder, and her body softened ever so slightly.

Red stepped back and turned toward the morning light, fingers pressed against the window. Her palm left foggy streaks as she slid her hand down the cold glass.

CHAPTER FOURTEEN

Mid-morning Mae slid the door open, holding a tray and an expressionless face. She watched me, sitting on an overturned bucket, head back on the wall and hand around my injured shoulder.

Mae dropped the tray on the ground and slid it inside with her feet. "Eat up, then get a move on."

I lifted my hand to see fresh blood had soaked through the bandage.

Mae tightened her mouth, like she would do anything to avoid feeling sorry for us. Then she walked off as Hop split the stale bread and dried meat. When he leaned against the doorway to eat his sandwich, the morning light hit his profile. Smooth, tanned skin with a splash of red that never left his cheeks. He tucked a stray wave of hair behind his ear.

After lunch, Red walked out to relieve herself in the field.

"Poor kid is scared of everything," I said.

"I've seen it so many times at the orphanages. Kids shackled and beaten." Hop sat next to me. "But they never really break us, you know?"

"Hop, how did you find your way out?"

"I don't know that I did," he said. "Not completely."

He placed his hand behind his head, stared at the rafters with a wide-open chest. Like it welcomed me to curl up against its warmth.

"You follow harvests all year?" I asked.

He hesitated. "Yes."

"You go to Willamette every fall. To the same hop farm."

He sighed.

"You aren't out here for wanderlust," I said, suddenly understanding. "You're looking for your parents."

Hop watched a flock of birds fly past the window. "They're out there somewhere. Maybe they lay awake at night too and dream of finding me."

"That's a nice thought."

"I spend the season at the same hop farm where the workers found me wrapped in a blanket. My parents left a bottle of milk, so they cared a little."

Red returned, and we pulled away from each other.

Samuel came back for the tray. "Cold snap coming through. You better stay a few nights."

"But your wife..." I said.

"You let me deal with her. She's just not trusting is all." Samuel closed the door.

"That arm isn't looking good," Hop said.

"I know. It keeps weeping."

Red glared at Hop as he reached for my shoulder.

"We need to find you a doctor," Hop said.

"We don't have any money. I'll be fine."

We spent the day napping and building stacks with empty jars, trying to keep busy. Mae returned with another tray for supper. Still bread and dried meat, but also an apple to share. She lingered this time.

"Hey, you." She pointed at me. "What's going on with your arm?"

"Just a little blood."

She slid the tray toward us again and walked away. Then stopped, looked back at us with slumped shoulders and shook her head. "Dammit," she said back at the door. "Get your butt on in here."

I froze, afraid to anger her if I moved.

"Come on," she said. "Before I change my mind."

I followed her hesitantly. She slipped in through the kitchen. "Samuel, bring those kids a bucket of warm soapy water. They're starting to stink to high heaven."

He kissed her on her cheek. "You're a good egg."

Mae swatted him away. She led me to a chair in the pantry and shut the door, returning with a first aid kit. She shook her head again. "What the hell kind of trouble did you get yourself into?"

"It was an accident."

"Mm-hmm." She opened the tin box and set out supplies then reached for my sleeve. I flinched.

"I ain't gonna hurt you," she said.

"But you don't trust me."

She ripped the sleeve of my dress in two pieces and winced at the smell. "I don't trust anybody. It's the only way to keep safe."

"I know."

"Yeah, I'm sure you do." She dabbed something wet on the wound. "Samuel," Mae said with an eye roll. "That man is always bringing home strays."

"But you don't want us here."

"Life is complicated. It's not that I don't want to help you. It's that this world don't like our kinds mixing. Neither do I."

Samuel knocked on the door. "Here's one for the girl."

Mae peeked out, grabbed a pail and a towel, then slid the door shut again. "I'm gonna help you get this nasty dress off. That all right?"

I nodded.

She ripped the sleeve all the way, so I didn't have to lift my arm, and she lowered it to the ground. She unsnapped my bra then held the towel in front of me as she looked away. "Go on. Clean. And hurry it up."

I wiped the warm washcloth over me as suds tickling my skin. I scrubbed my face and all the important places. We called it a TPA bath. Tits, pits, and ass. "All done."

Mae wrapped the towel around my trunk, under my arms. "Sit down. Let's fix this wound." She pulled out a curved needle. Slid black thread through the eye and wiped it with alcohol. "This is gonna hurt."

It pierced my skin sharp as a flick from my Mama.

"Just a few stitches come loose. Hang on, now." She sliced right through, patching me up in less than thirty seconds.

She dabbed on some ointment. "There we are. Right as rain."

I glanced at the closed wound. "Thank you." I wanted to ask what to do about my nakedness.

"Hold on." She slipped out of the pantry and came back with a dress folded in her hands. "My daughters don't need it anymore. You can have it."

"You have daughters?"

"We have five. They're all grown now." She helped me fasten my bra and slip my arm through the dress.

"I bet you love them."

She tightened her brow. "Of course, I do. Don't you have a mama?"

"I guess so. She didn't love me though." I don't know why I said it. Maybe I was desperate for someone to understand that not all mothers are loving. "Mama needed someone to hate, and I was that someone."

Her face softened. "Here's the thing about women. The world can try to shove us into the dark and break our bones and steal our pride. But they can't touch our spirit. That is something we all have."

"Like a tea bag."

"Like a what?"

"Nothing, just... someone told me once that a woman is like a tea bag. You never know how strong she is until you put her in hot water."

Mae smiled. "Yeah, exactly like that."

***

I returned to the barn after dusk with a clean shoulder and a new dress. Flecks of snow hovered above me, not quite making it to the ground. Red snored, but it sounded more like a growl. Hop's eyes widened when he saw me.

I reached for him. "Come with me."

He stood and grabbed my hand, my vanilla skin glowing next to the warmth of his. We wrapped ourselves in blankets and slipped out the back door. The cool air smacked our faces as we breathed in the sharp sting. I threw down a blanket and lowered myself to my back. "Here." I patted the ground next to me.

Our arms brushed as he lowered, and my braid tickled my neck. "Lean your head back and watch the snowflakes fall on you," I said.

They fluttered around us, melting onto our noses and lips.

"I've never seen snow from this angle," he said. "It's beautiful."

"When things seem impossibly sad, the seasons remind me that life marches on. I can close my eyes and imagine the snow carrying me past the heartache, out to the sunny spring on the other side." I looked down at his big brown eyes. "I dream of standing in a field of waving wheat someday where the world's troubles rest far away."

He scooted closer and rested his head in my lap. "You dream of wheat fields. Just like me."

"Yes." I softened my stomach and released a slow breath. "We both have to find our way back to family."

"We'll start with your brothers," Hop said. "Me, well that's a near impossible feat. And who knows about Red. I have no idea how we can do this on our own."

"I know someone who might help us," I said.

"Yeah?"

"She might be the only one who can put our families back together."

"Where do we find her?"

I wiped a dusting of snow from his forehead, letting my fingers slide through his thick, black hair. "I met Eleanor Roosevelt this summer. She promised to help me."

He raised his eyebrows. "Wait, the President's wife is going to help find our families?"

"Well, yes. I know it sounds crazy."

"Wrangling rattlers was crazy. Not this."

"We've had similar lives." I shrugged. "She understood me. How much I need to keep my family together." I swallowed to wash away the bitter taste of failure, as if it wouldn't rise again a minute later. "She promised to get my job back if Mr. Hanover fired me. I think she wanted to protect me."

He rested the back of his hand on my arm. Held it there while he looked at me. "That's nice... to have someone care like that."

"It is." I looked up to watch the fluttering snow. "I can't explain it, but I trust her."

"All right then," Hop said. "Looks like we've got an adventure on our hands."

"Aren't you glad you met me, Hop? You can follow me on a wild chase after the First Lady." Realizing I was still stroking his hair, I pulled my hand away.

"I'd follow you anywhere." He held my hand and placed it on his cheek with a half-smile. "Let's enjoy the snow. For one more minute."

I ran my fingers along his soft temple and watched the snow dance in the wind. "Just one more minute," I whispered.

***

"We need a plan." Hop spread out newspapers Samuel gave him.

"We could write to the White House, but who knows how long that will take," I said. "If she's traveling, she won't get a letter for months. If it gets to her at all."

Red kneeled next to us with eyebrows raised.

"You heard right," Hop said. "We're going in search of Eleanor Roosevelt. She can help us."

Red lifted a *Pathfinder* magazine. I wondered if she could read. She opened her mouth to say something, then caught herself. Shut her lips together tight.

"We'll have to find out where she's going and meet her there," Hop said. "You say she travels a lot?"

"Yes. Alone with a pistol."

He laughed. "Not your typical rich woman."

"No, she's not. Did you know she was an orphan by age nine?" Hop shook his head. "And once, she left a state dinner to take a night flight with Amelia Earhart. They commandeered a transport plane in their evening gowns."

"She sounds like one hell of a woman." Hop flipped through newspapers.

"She really is. Sometimes it feels like she's the only one looking out for us."

"Denver-bound?" Hop said.

Red took my hand. Hop nodded with a smile.

Hesitant, I slid my hand back to my lap. "What if we can't get my brothers out?"

Hop lifted the paper. "Here's what Eleanor Roosevelt has to say about that. *The future is literally in our hands to mold as we like. But we cannot wait until tomorrow. Tomorrow is now.*"

***

Mae didn't say goodbye. But she did leave a few coats and gloves folded for us on the back porch.

Samuel loaded us into his truck, a blanket over our heads. "Keep the kid hidden. They're still looking for her. It's in the paper every day."

Crowded in the back of Samuel's rusted Ford truck, each bump knocked me into Hop, sending a shot of yearning through my body.

Along a rough mountain road, we passed a reservoir named after strawberries. I missed the rush of the wind and the clacking of the rails, that feeling of pure freedom, like you could leave the past dusting the tracks as you powered ahead.

Samuel pulled up to a gas station in the middle of nowhere, surrounded by rabbit brush. He came back and lowered the tailgate. "See that truck over there? You go get in the back. A friend of mine will take you to Colorado."

We tumbled out of the car and made our way to the truck parked under a cottonwood tree. Dry wind hit my face and I licked my lips, only to have them dry up again. We climbed in the back behind a row of boxes and Red crouched next to me. Hop extended his arm, ready to shake Samuel's hand, but Samuel opted for a hug. They held each other in the silent language of men's emotions, something I rarely see.

Hop climbed in next to me, and Red leaned her head on my shoulder. I noticed a card peeking out from under a box.

"Cartwright glass supply, Roosevelt, Utah," I said. "We're in a town called Roosevelt?"

"Named after Teddy Roosevelt," Samuel said. "Have a safe trip, kids."

"Eleanor's favorite uncle," I whispered to Hop.

He leaned his mouth to my ear, his warm lips brushing my skin. "It's a sign."

I couldn't turn to him or touch him—Red sat too close and didn't miss a thing. So I settled for shading my cheek toward his mouth while I closed my eyes. The truck jumped and rumbled as we pulled away, Samuel fading in the distance.

***

Eight hours moving east over the state line into Colorado, the wind growing thinner, my skin drier. As Hop and Red slept, I lifted the tarp to watch the farmland disappear, rolling into tangerine mountains that seemed to kiss the sky.

Sunset spilled onto the landscape like an artist's palette in a blur of orange and yellow and every shade in between. It struck me how we all look at the same sky, but each town, each state, and each home seems to see a different color.

The truck crept into a farm on the outskirts of town just as night fell and the air dropped to freezing. We tumbled out and stretched our legs. The man appeared, hat low over his eyes. "You can stay the night in the barn. I'll drop you in the city before daybreak." He looked down at Red. "Everyone's looking for you."

"The red hair doesn't help," I said.

"Samuel's a friend. I promised I would see you all to safety. I'll bring you some food and blankets. Go on." He slid the barn door open.

Hop gathered piles of hay from empty stalls to make beds. The man brought us a tin bucket of chili and a brick of cornbread wrapped in foil.

"You weren't kidding about the kindness of strangers," I said.

"It's a funny thing," Hop said. "The less people have, the more they want to give."

With full bellies, we wrapped our bodies in wool blankets. "He keeps blankets in a barn?" I asked.

Hop smiled. "We aren't the first strangers to rest in here, would be my guess. The man seems to have a good heart. I bet he's fed and housed lots of people over the years."

I ran my hand along my lower ribs. It didn't drop off to a hollow below. My stomach filled the space, softening the sharp edges of my bony torso. A grassy scent clung to the air, the slightest hint that horses once lived here.

I had more out here on the road than I ever did back home. Strangers give and give, and you realize just how similar people are. How we've all touched different shades of the same despair.

My mind shifted to the boys, with shaved heads and welts on their backsides. The image gripped me so fast I couldn't breathe. Their pleading eyes begging me to save them. Every minute they seemed to drift farther away, and I worried what would be left when I finally reached them.

Red crawled closer to me. She wiped away the hay and ran her hand over the dirt. With a stick, she drew a picture of four children.

"Is this me and my brothers?" I asked.

She drew a circle over the small one.

"Oh, you want to know about Emily."

She nodded.

Never did understand how you can push a memory down for so long and then in a moment of weakness, it forces through the cracks in your heart to find the light.

"Emily and I used to hunt for thundereggs."

She tilted her head, like a question.

"Dueling spirits on Mount Hood and Mount Jefferson hurled the eggs of thunderbirds at each other during thunderstorms. At least that's what the Central Oregon tribes believed."

She nodded, wanting more.

"They look like round, dried mud balls. Sandy and dirty pieces of earth. But when you cut them open, it's nothing but glorious color, like the sun reflecting on sea glass. I used to take Em to search for them along the river."

Hop moved closer, leaned in to listen.

"I'd heard of thundereggs all my life. I'd seen plenty of lava rock, but never those little eggs. When she was two..." The ache in my chest squeezed so hard it felt like it might bleed. "She made her way to the river alone."

"What happened?" Hop asked.

"I found her blue and swollen. Face down. Dress hooked on a branch. My baby sister drowned searching for thundereggs."

My voice caught on the last word like a fishhook. Red crawled close to me and wrapped her arms around my shoulders. Her hair appeared orange, like the center of a flame or a summer sunset. I touched it, expecting it to burn me, but it felt as cool and dry as the Colorado air. Feathery like the ornamental grass back home.

Hop moved closer and stopped just short of touching me. Red softened her tightened mouth and cast her eyes downward. Hop spread his arms out over the two of us.

We huddled together in the soft glow of moonlight.

That night, Red didn't tap her hands when Hop pulled me close to sleep next to him. He stroked my hair and nowhere inside of me worried about him hurting me. With Hop's strong arms around me and Red's almost smile bidding me goodnight, for the first time in my life, I wasn't terrified of the dark.

CHAPTER FIFTEEN

"That's the orphanage." The man slammed the car door, the bang echoing into the misty morning. "Lots of kids coming and going from this place."

"Is this the only one in Denver?" I asked.

"The only one they send the troubled kids to."

Hop slid his fingers through mine.

The man handed Red a cap. "Here, tuck that hair in. You stick out like a tomato in a cucumber patch."

Red did as he said, and she looked just like a boy. Those overalls and no hair. Maybe we could do this.

"They keep the troubled ones in that building." He pointed to the left. "I supply bottles to their kitchen."

Before I could respond, he ducked into his truck and drove off.

I exhaled into the thready, white air.

"How do you want to do this?" Hop said.

"I'm just going to walk in and ask. I'm their sister, dammit."

"Okay," Hop said. "What can we do?"

"Just wait for me."

His hand touched my shoulder. "We'll be right here."

The building towered over me. Imposing arches and a door as thick as a tree trunk. All that stood between me and the boys was a layer of bricks.

The door wouldn't budge, but I eyed a brass handle with the word "turn" on it. Even the doorbell looked haunted. The chime rang in the entryway. A slender woman opened the door. Her sleek black hair was pulled in a high bun, so tight it caused her eyebrows to arch like bridges.

"Yes?" she said.

"My name is Magnolia Parker, and I'm here for my brothers."

She pulled her shoulders back. Bony things like wire hangers under her black wool dress. "Parker, you say?"

"That's right. Johnny and Oscar Parker. I'm eighteen now and I have a job and place to live, and I'll be damned if I leave here today without them." A little lie for a large purpose.

People say you get more with honey than with vinegar, but all I knew was spittin' acid. I wanted to tear through that place and wrap them in my arms.

"Come in."

I followed her to the office, our steps echoing in the wood hallway. Distant sounds of water running and voices chattering gave the illusion of life, but I didn't see anyone.

She closed the door behind me. "Please, sit."

The morning light shined on her flat white skin, like someone had turned the light off inside her.

"Where are they?" I asked.

"So, you're their sister?"

"Yes. Our mother died a few months ago, and the hospital took the boys away. But I'm here now. Please."

She glanced at a cross on the wall. I thought of Franny, telling me that fighting for life wasn't the same as reacting to it. I wiped my palms on my thighs to dry the sweat.

"We didn't know they had family." The woman pursed her lips.

"Of course you did," I said. "You just didn't care."

"No." She slid out a drawer and flicked her knobby fingers over the folders. She opened one, as flimsy as one sheet of paper. "Their records say nothing about a sister."

"If you bothered to ask them, you would know."

"Miss Parker..."

"No. Don't tell me another reason why I can't have them back." My hands gripped the armrests tight enough to make my palms ache. "You stole them."

She paused, then shook her head. Like empathy was nothing more than a fly that needed swatted away. "I'm afraid they're gone."

"Gone?" My nervous heartbeat stopped like a dead bird falling from the sky. A hot anger filled the space inside. "What do you mean?"

"A nice family adopted Johnny. He's a sweet boy. Lots of people wanted him."

I slammed my hands on her desk. "Like he's a damn puppy? What is wrong with you people?"

She looked down her long, thin nose angled like a ski slope. "He went to a good home. His legs still have a lot of healing to do. The Benson's... uh, the parents have agreed to pay for his therapy. He even has a dog named Banjo."

"So, you yank him like a weed and throw him into a new life? A better life than he had."

"We didn't know what he had," she said.

"Why didn't you ask him?"

The muscles in her arms twitched as she removed her glasses. "We did."

I held myself in the chair, ready to launch across the desk and rip that bun off her head. "What did he say?"

"We asked if he had a family, and he said no, just his brother." Her rigid face dropped ever so slightly. "He wanted to be adopted."

The room dimmed to brown, then almost black. The light faded in and out, same as when I replaced a light bulb at the inn. As the room took shape, a clicking sound became noticeable. A metronome ticked away the seconds on top of a piano.

"I was practicing Chopin when you rang our doorbell," she said.

"He's gone."

"I'm afraid so, Miss Parker."

"And Oscar?"

"He doesn't speak much." She hesitated. "He doesn't even remember his brother."

My mouth went dry. "Where is he?"

She looked at the cross on the wall. "Adopted."

I lowered my head between my knees, feeling as if the floor could swallow me. I wished it would.

"Oscar is troubled." She sighed. "Johnny probably wanted to do the right thing."

"By pretending I never existed?"

"By taking an opportunity for a better life."

The metronome continued its rhythm in absence of fingers dancing across the piano keys. Tick, tick, tick.

"I lost another one," I mumbled.

"Pardon?"

I shook the fear right out of my head and stood. "Where are they?"

"Miss Parker, you know I can't tell you that."

"No. Wouldn't want me to take him from his family." I stared her down until she broke my gaze.

"You mustn't stay any longer." She strode to the door. "We don't want to disrupt the others."

"I hope that one day, someone steals your heart. Rips it right out of your chest and leaves a gaping hole that can never close. And I hope you bleed pain. Forever."

I left that hellhole, scratching lines along the wallpaper with my fingernails.

When I reached the bottom of the hill, out of sight from the big brick house, I fell to my knees, dug my fingers into the earth, and waited to breathe again.

"What happened?" Hop lowered next to me.

"Gone. To parents named Benson, and a dog named Banjo." I stood and kicked a pile of rocks into a tree. "I failed." I tightened my hands around a stick and swung into a tree. Bark chipped off and fell to the ground and I whacked that trunk until the skin on my palm ripped open and my shoulder bit like a snake's fangs.

"Maggie, we'll find them," Hop said.

I dropped the stick. "You've been searching for nineteen years for some invisible dream. It hasn't worked out for you."

His face twisted into an expression I had never seen before. Part horror and part broken little boy. I wanted to die. Maybe I really was rotten.

"I have nothing to hope for," I whispered.

Hop turned away and wiped his eyes. I wanted to hug him, but I couldn't move. Anger held me in place.

Red tapped my arm and pointed to the hospital.

"She told me they're gone. Both adopted."

She closed her eyes and shook her head no.

"Oscar. You think he's still here?"

"The troubled kids aren't likely to be adopted," Hop said with his back to me.

Red removed her jacket. She took off her cap and shook out her hair. She grabbed my hand and led me toward the building. Over my shoulder I saw Hop watch us, the saddest expression across his face.

We crouched in the bushes for a long while. "Red, what are we doing?"

She placed her finger to her mouth, telling me to stay silent. Twenty torturous minutes ticked by until a man that looked to be the janitor slipped out the back and propped a box in the door. Tucked around the corner behind a bush, he lit a cigarette and leaned his head against the wall.

Red grabbed my hand and led me over the box, through the door, stealthy as a cat. The janitor kept his eyes closed, not a clue we'd snuck past.

The smell of bleach burned my nose. Moans emanated from behind closed doors and wheelchairs squeaked against linoleum floors. We ducked into a dark hallway, where my eyes watered from the acrid fumes of medicine and cleaner.

"How do we find him?" I whispered.

She placed my hand on her chest, then hers over top. She looked into my eyes as if to ask, "Do you trust me?"

I nodded. She had never uttered a word that didn't come through her eyes, but I trusted her with my life.

She yanked me forward, around the corner, and down another hall. At a nurse's desk, Red flipped open a book and ran her finger down a list of names. She stopped, looked up at me with a close-mouthed smile. Her finger on the name Oscar Parker. Room nine.

Before I could think about what to do next, Red dragged me to a common area. Inside a room of zombie-like children with limp arms and shuffling feet. Nurses held clipboards and handed out tiny paper cups.

All of them children. Eyelids like umbrellas over bloodshot orbs.

"What's wrong with all of them?" I asked.

And then Red screamed. The shrillest, highest screech I'd ever heard. She grabbed the front of my jacket and threw me to the ground. Legs straddled over me, she reached into my boot and came up with my knife. Her stare hovered lifeless like the first time I met her. I shuddered, certain she'd slice me open.

She held the blade aimed at my chest. Both hands gripped the handle, arms rigid, as she howled like the coyote pups in the forest. Just as I thought she might stab me, hands flew every which way, yanking her away.

"No! What are you doing?" I scrambled to standing.

Nurses and orderlies ran from all corners. Red kicked and screamed and bucked like a wild horse. She slammed her foot into a woman's nose, sending blood trickling down her lips.

"No, wait. Don't take her!"

They held her down as Red thrashed with bared teeth. Then she shot me a look. Nodded quickly as if to say, "Now."

I raced down the hall, still in shock. I wanted to save Red. Rip her from their hands and carry her to safety.

But... Oscar.

Room five. Seven. Around a corner. Nine. A flat metal door with no window. I banged and banged. Nothing. "Dammit!" I only had a few minutes. I kicked it so hard my toe split open and I could feel blood pool in my shoe. Then, the door creaked open.

Oscar.

His sweet eyes and long black eyelashes stared at me without the slightest hint of fear.

"Oscar." My voice wavered. "I'm here."

"What do you want?" he croaked out.

"I came back for you. Just like I promised." I smiled through tears. He was really here.

"You came for me?" he stuttered.

My heart soared. "Yes. Now, we don't have much time." I reached forward to pull him into my arms, but he put out his hand to stop me.

"What is it?" I asked.

His left eye twitched. "Who are you?"

"Oscar, it's me." My voice grew thready. "Magnolia."

"Who is Magnolia?"

My legs nearly crumbled. "Oh, Buddy. Please. I'm your sister."

"I don't have a sister. Emily died." His voice hummed, like a one note harmonica. "This is my home." He gestured to his shoebox of a room.

A twin mattress on a concrete floor. A toilet no larger than a bucket stuck in the corner. No mirrors, no pictures. One wooden shelf with clothes and shoes folded neatly next to a tin cup holding a toothbrush and a black comb. Chipped white paint on the windowsill revealed a mint green underneath. The window couldn't open. It was merely the view of a world he no longer lived in. No rocks balanced to alert him to intruders.

"Remember? You shot me." I pulled back my sleeve. "We ran from a forest fire. The Deschutes River. Our shack. Bend. You're my tender heart. Please. You must remember!" I shook his shoulders.

He yanked back, started pulling his hair. "No. Don't let them take me. Please. I'm home. Don't let the monsters take me."

"No, shh. It's okay. No one is taking you." I walked closer, but he backed away. "Please, Oscar, I just want to hug you. I love you."

"No. No!"

I wrapped him in my arms. If I held him close and he felt my skin, he would remember. He pulled away whimpering, but I wouldn't let go. "Please remember."

He stopped bucking and leaned his head on my shoulder to cry.

"It's all right, Oscar. I'm here."

He raised his head. His eyes had changed so much, it seemed impossible that he was the same person, but I couldn't let go.

"I don't know you," he said. "Leave me alone."

"Please come with me. I need you."

"Help!" He screamed it over and over, swiping his hand across the shelf. His only possessions clanged on the ground. "It's the monster!"

"No." I backed away. "Please. I love you."

He kept screaming and kicking. Maybe I could throw him over my shoulder and run. Tie him to a wheelchair. And then I looked at his terror-stricken face, his eyes bulging, neck pulled taut.

I was the monster climbing through the windows.

I backed out, hid around the corner just as a man in a brown uniform ran in. "Oscar, it's all right."

I peeked through the crack of the door hinge. Oscar let this man hold him, hug him, and soothe his fear.

"Everything is all right. There are no bad men. You're home." The man hummed as he shut the door.

You're home.

My forehead pressed against the cool wall.

A voice said, "What's your name?"

I turned to see a girl. Three feet tall, her auburn hair in two braids.

"What?" I squeaked out.

"What's your name?" she repeated.

"Magnolia."

She turned her back to me. "See?" She looked over her shoulder. "I'm G25." Written on the back of her pinafore with a black marker.

"What does that mean?"

"Girl twenty-five." She swung her hips side to side to watch her dress move. "I'm five years old."

I wondered who braided her hair and if it made her cry or smile while they brushed it.

"I like your name better," she said.

"G25 isn't your real name, sweetheart." I kneeled to face her.

"Sure it is." She twirled in a circle, then skipped away.

Memories of her true self, erased forever, and replaced with a number. Girl twenty-five.

"Red."

I found the back door again, the box resting just inside the corridor. I propped it open and ran for Hop.

Breathless, I muttered, "I need you."

"Oscar?" he asked.

I shook my head. "He's gone."

"And Red?"

"They took her. She pretended to attack me, and they hauled her away." My eyelids fell heavy, the light fading to brown.

Hop shook me. "No fainting now. Let's go." He dragged me back through the propped door. The stench of human sweat and ammonia brought me back.

"They've probably tied her up by now," he said.

The realization hit me like a backhand to the cheek. "We were in the common room where they give medicine. How do we get her out?"

"Same way you got in. Distraction." We ran to the nurse's desk and Hop slid everything off the counter. Picked up the stapler and threw it at the piano.

The room became a mass of shuffling bodies bumping into each other. One boy yelled, "Danger!" Grunts and squeals hummed around us like a swarm of bees.

"Come on." He pulled me to the alcove behind a set of doors. A rush of nurses and doctors flooded the room, which made the zombies burst into hysterics. People screamed and kicked, and the workers yelled for more help as nurses came running.

"Now." He threw open the door and ran down the hall. A new wave of smells nearly knocked me over. Feces and burnt hair. We yanked on every door. Locked.

A nurse slunk out of a room and held her clipboard out, ready to swat us with it.

Hop, always the quick thinker, said, "You better get out there, it's anarchy! We were visiting family when all hell broke loose."

The muffled sounds of chaos drifted down the hall. The nurse picked up speed toward the common room and we kept running toward the rank odors of the dark hallway. One blue door at the end of a white hall. He threw it open and there sat Red, limbs strapped in place, drugged to nearly comatose.

A doctor stood, a glint in his eyes. "The police are on their way. This girl is dangerous."

"Let her free," Hop said.

The doctor straightened the lapel of his white coat. "No. Leave now, or I'll have you both arrested."

Hop punched the doctor in his nose. He stumbled, wiping blood from his upper lip.

"You can let us take her," Hop said. "Or I can break your face."

The doctor wiped his nose with the back of his hand, then shook out a handkerchief to wipe it clean. "This girl is damaged."

Damaged.

I kicked my boot into the sharp line of his shin, doubling him over. Hop grabbed a needle on the bedside tray, stabbed it into the man's arm, and pushed his thumb down to inject something. The doctor stared at us then wilted toward the floor. Hop lowered him so he wouldn't hit his head.

I reached into a pocket of the white coat and snatched a set of keys, then scrambled to unlock Red's restraints. Hop grabbed a yellow glass bottle and swiped it under her nose. She gasped, and her eyes popped open.

"It's just us," Hop said. "You're okay. We're going to get you out of here."

Red's body turned limp as she blinked over and over.

"They'll lock this place down in about two minutes," Hop said. "Come on."

He lifted Red over his shoulder as if she were a sack of flour. We stepped over the doctor, down the hall, and approached a back door. Locked.

"We have to go back through that madness," I said. "We'll never make it."

A boy strolled out of his room. "You rescuing that girl?"

"She doesn't belong here," Hop said.

"Yeah, I know the feeling."

They nodded in understanding.

"Come here." The boy led us to an empty room and slid open the window. "It's been broken for months. Too cheap to fix it."

We climbed out the window and into the dirt. Red fell back into dreamland, limp as an animal carcass. Hop looked at the boy. "You can leave any time you want. They lie to you. It's not bad out here."

"Maybe someday. Now go. I'll keep them busy." He slid the window down past his lonely face. We ran into the bushes and down a trail into the trees. Hop never stopped to rest. He kept moving as steady as a steam train.

We walked for hours. The distant sound of sirens came and went, but never closed in on us. My legs ached, but Hop marched forward.

"Hop..."

"Don't talk to me," he said.

Around nightfall, we found an abandoned church, alone in a field of rabbit brush.

Inside, Hop laid Red down and covered her with his jacket. He checked her eyes and her skin. Felt her forehead.

"Is she gonna be okay?" I asked.

"Yeah." He looked in boxes and under the pews for anything to keep us warm. He came up with a faded blanket, thinned at the edges.

"Did you kill that doctor?"

"No. They use sedatives, so the kids don't fight back. I just gave him a little taste of what he gave Red." He lay the blanket over her and stroked her forehead as she groaned.

"Hop..."

"Don't," he said.

"What I said today, about your parents..."

"Maggie, just stop. I don't care what you think."

He pulled the blanket so it covered our legs, but he wouldn't touch me.

I stared at the rafters lined with cobwebs. Unable to sleep, I turned to look at the back of Hop's head, his body not touching mine. I listened to the wind howl and the others breathe in and out and thought about Oscar's haunted eyes.

In the depths of the black night, Red came to. She stirred for a while, a tight moan escaping as a whisper. I crawled over and stroked her hair for a long while. Her eyes twitched and fluttered open.

"Hi," I whispered.

She swallowed and opened her mouth with no sound.

"Welcome back."

She nodded and rubbed her temples. A groan escaped her lips.

She propped herself up on her scrawny arms, the moon casting a silver light on her smooth, pale skin.

I waited for her eyes to focus. "You risked everything. For me."

She crossed her legs and rubbed her wrists where bruises had taken shape.

"You shouldn't have done that."

She nodded once.

"Red, I'm not gonna let anyone hurt you again. If I have to build a shack or live on the railcars, I'm going to keep you close." I rubbed my fingers along the purple rings on her wrists. "No more hurt. I won't watch one more person get taken from me."

Her neck tightened. She nodded, as if to say, "Well?"

"Oscar? He's gone." The words took my breath away. "They're all gone."

She placed her hand on her chest.

"Yes, I have you. If you have family or a home, I won't rest until I get you there. I need to do something right."

I tried to shake the tears away, but they pushed through my resistance. Rain pattered the roof and the musky smell of old wood seeped into the air.

She pulled my hands from my face and stared at me.

"My name is Gracie," she said.

Shocked, I let the sound of her husky voice settle around me. Clear and strong, and a little deep. Not what I expected.

"I'm from Little Rock," she said. "And I never want to see my home ever again."

CHAPTER SIXTEEN

Wanted for murder in Arkansas, and escaping custody in Oregon and Colorado, the Jilted Jezebel is on the run from the police. Who is the crazed killer out for next?

I read the headline and crumpled the paper before Red could see. We were headed to the next closest city, Colorado Springs. There were enough migrant kids on the road that we blended in, as long as we kept a cap on Red's hair.

A kind man took pity on three homeless kids, letting us bundle together in the back of his flatbed. He was a grandfather who should be enjoying lazy afternoons somewhere, but the times kept him working. Old and frail, his knobby fingers had trouble grasping the tailgate to close it.

"What do we do now?" Hop said.

"To find Johnny, we track down Mrs. Roosevelt and ask for her help. Who knows where the Bensons live?"

Red widened her eyes. She said nothing more after her declaration last night.

"You think we can convince Mrs. Roosevelt to protect Red too?" Hop asked.

I nodded. "I bet she could find your parents, Hop."

He rubbed the back of his neck. "Like you said, I've been chasing a stupid dream."

"No, I didn't mean that."

"I'm nineteen and still hoping for my parents to show up. The ones who never wanted me. I'm chasing ghosts."

I grasped the rough skin of his working hands, scarred by snakebites and picking fruit and beans and cotton. They were full of memories. Memories I had no right to judge. "Then we'll chase ghosts together. All three of us."

We shook with the movement of the truck, sitting cross-legged. Red slid her shaky hand out to grab Hop's. He hesitated. She turned her palm up and nodded, so he held her.

"Where do we start?" I said.

"In all those articles we read, it said that the President spends several weeks a year in Warm Springs, Georgia, including an annual Thanksgiving dinner. We have one week to get there."

"I hope she remembers her promise to me."

We were all searching for something. We thought it was about lost parents, or adopted brothers, or broken homes, but we also knew, deep down, that it was about this circle right here.

**

"We're going to have to jump again," Hop said. The air sat heavy on my chest, thick with oil, as the smell of coal burned my nose.

"Yeah," I said. "Count the bolts. Run fast alongside it, don't grab the door."

"You got it. Red, you good?"

She narrowed her vision and nodded confidently.

We crouched and readied our legs. I swung my bag across my body, held it against my back, and felt the rumble of the earth when the train rolled near. To avoid the bulls, we aimed for the train after it left the freight yard.

We jogged alongside the massive beast as it screeched across the metal rails. The horn bellowed into the night, and our hot breaths left a fog of white behind us. It chugged louder and faster, and our legs churned with the speed of the wheels. Our feet thumped and gravel spit at us. Hop leapt onto the ladder and swung inside. His hand out, he yelled for Red, who jumped as easy as a cougar.

They stood together, waving their hands for me to jump. My shoulder. It wouldn't hold me. I hesitated too long. I forced my legs to sprint, but I kept losing ground.

"Come on, Maggie!" Hop yelled. "You'll miss it."

I yanked my bag off and threw it inside. I felt lighter, but by the time I picked up speed again, their car had disappeared. I pumped my arms, but the train veered away from me on a turn.

"Stay there!" I yelled. "I'll find you."

Car after car flicked past me as their faces faded from view. I had ten seconds to jump on the last one.

I cleared my mind of everything and exhaled. Jumped and caught the ladder. A turn swung me into the wall of the boxcar. My shoulder stung like a knife wound. I pressed my cheeks to the cold metal rungs, gasping for breath.

I peered inside. A whole car of frowning men. They stared at me, arms folded and lips tight. A shudder trembled through me like an earthquake, so I climbed the ladder to the roof of the train. It was a stupid thing to do, but sometimes stupid is your only option.

The train reached top speed, sailing through the trees under a low-hanging moon. Icy wind whipped through my clothes, knocking me off balance. With the slightest jolt, I could tumble down into the abyss of tracks below.

I crawled on my stomach, arms out wide along the curve of the top. Past a few men asleep, belts tied to the rails along the edge. One of them said something to me, but the words disappeared into the whistling wind.

A boy my age crouched next to an old man, gripped the roof's edge, and mouthed something.

"What?" I yelled.

"Tunnel!" the boy said.

I looked ahead to a curved black hole and froze. The old man threw himself over me, flattened my cheek against the cold metal.

"I'm right here," said the faceless man.

I bit back tears. This man didn't leave me to fight for my life all alone, unprepared. He didn't know me at all, yet he stayed and protected me.

We clattered through the black cave, the sound echoing like drums. Like being locked in one of those washing tubs from the Pilot Butte Inn. Dark and loud and tumbling around.

"Is it almost over?" I screamed.

"Almost," he said calmly.

Smoke filled my nose. I coughed as the air turned thick and oily. Embers of red flitted through the darkness. My vision blurred and my head spun.

My ears popped just as we came into the moonlight. We coughed and wheezed, grateful for clear air. My head thumped as the silvery outline of trees took focus. I held that man's hand so tight, I nearly popped his bones. "Thank you," I sputtered.

His face took shape. A middle-aged man, face burned on one side.

I sat up and looked around. Something was amiss.

"Where is that boy?"

The man sat up. "Oh."

"What happened?"

He scratched his temple. "Well, he wasn't tied to the rails along the side like the rest of us. The fumes can knock you unconscious. He likely fell."

My throat tightened. He fell to his death. Gone like a whisper.

I gripped the cold metal rails and shook. "Why did you save me and not him?"

"I tried to tell him," he said. "He thought he could just hang on."

"I would have died without you."

"I figured you were someone's daughter. Couldn't live with that on my conscience."

"I'm no one's daughter, sir." I caught my breath. "But I am someone's sister. Thank you."

"Riding the tops is a young man's sport. I'm too old for this." He shook his head. "Crawl down between the cars to cross. Don't be a fool and try to jump. I've seen kids chopped in half doing that."

I decided to crawl. At the edge, I climbed down the ladder. Standing on a platform just wide enough for my boots, I watched the earth rush under me. One metal hook connected these two cars. I held on tight with my left arm and stepped as wide as my hips would go, reaching for that next car through the ripping sensation in my shoulder.

Through a final heave, I screamed and barely grabbed hold of the ladder on the other side. Yanking my body forward, my heart about leapt out of my mouth. After my breathing settled, I climbed to the next roof. I took it one step and one crawl at a time. Metal screeched under the open channel between cars as I hovered over that single metal hook, knowing I was merely a slip away from joining that boy, dead along the tracks.

A dozen boxcars later, I finally hopped into the right one. Hop caught me before I could collapse. He wrapped his strong arms around my aching shoulders, and I melted into him.

"Magnolia, are you all right?" His hands slid to my waist.

"Yeah. I'm fine."

"I thought we lost you." He pulled me into his chest again and cradled his hand behind my head.

His heart thumped against my cheek, the beat carrying me home. I softened for a moment, then pushed away.

Red examined me with worried eyes.

"I'm fine," I told her. "Really."

We settled into the darkness of a long ride. I imagined the boy's body. Crumpled and bloody. Gone forever.

Hop caught my eyes and wouldn't look away, even when I did. He ran his hand under my braid, laying it over my shoulder. "Don't leave me again."

Something split open inside me. Warmth flooded through the cracks and slid to all my lonely places. All the hateful, rotten, dark recesses that I never wanted to look at. And it bathed them in light.

***

Red slept curled in a ball, covered by her jacket. Hop sat wide awake, feet dangling off the edge of the boxcar as we chugged through the morning, a burst of orange lighting our world. The still waters of a clear river lit up bluer than the sky. So expansive and wild, I yearned to throw myself outside and float over it like a bird. I lowered myself next to Hop to enjoy the peaceful vision, a side of America we were lucky enough to see.

The trees held a dusting of snow, the sun reflected off pure white piles along the sides of the river. The speed of the train turned the view into a moving picture my whole body wanted to get lost in.

Something felt different. The view rushed past, Hop's dark eyes lit up with the glow of Missouri morning sunshine.

"Red spoke."

"She did?" He glanced back at her. "What did she say?"

"Her name is Gracie. She's from Little Rock, and she never wants to go back."

"Woah. I wonder what happened to her. Maybe her family was awful."

"I think you're brave, you know. To search for your parents," I said.

"It doesn't feel brave. It feels lonely."

"Seems everyone is fighting to let go of something awful. And trying to grasp onto something good."

Hop nestled his hands between his knees and shrugged. "You know what I believe?"

"What?"

"Everything that happens to us teaches us to be strong. Even the horrendous things that we never talk about."

"What if I don't want to be any stronger?"

"Then you just sit in that. For a long while. Let yourself feel it."

"How are you so much wiser than me?"

"Living on the road is an education," he said. "Everyone's in a similar fight. Afraid of loss."

I scooted closer, wanting to touch him. "Is that what you're afraid of?"

"I'm afraid," he inhaled sharply, "that I'm unlovable and forgettable."

I closed my eyes to feel that warmth that flooded my heart last night. I looked past my ugly center, where my mother held my heart in her gnarled hands, and I let that light shine until she faded.

Hop's lips brushed mine. So lightly, I couldn't tell if it really happened. I opened my eyes and scanned his perfect, strong face, and traced my finger along a faint smile line curved like a rainbow on his cheek.

His crimson lips pressed into mine, and I let my hand glide through his hair, stopping at the base of his neck. I parted my mouth as his tongue caressed mine. My body trembled with the unknown of being so close to someone.

I had no room for fear, the want was too great. Though I knew I shouldn't, I pressed my lips against his, feeling the softness and the hungry desire to touch him. Our lips drifted apart, our faces still close.

"Nothing about you is forgettable, Hop."

He smiled and pulled me into him. I leaned my head on his shoulder and we watched the morning rise. Nowhere inside me felt wicked.

Love was nothing like Mama taught me it would be.

CHAPTER SEVENTEEN

After three nights and four long days on the freight trains, we arrived in Atlanta. Just like Hop said, we survived on the kindness of strangers. A farmhouse outside St. Louis handed out half sandwiches and a grandmother in Chattanooga gave us cookies and milk when she saw us walking.

All it seemed to take was a smile and the ability to ask for help.

In Atlanta, we sat on a street corner, watching people scurry around the city like ants. "How do we find Mrs. Roosevelt once we get to Warm Springs?" I asked.

"They have a house near the hot springs," Hop said. "That's what the papers said."

Red gave him a face, a look of confusion.

"They're soaking pools. Warmed by underground volcanoes," I said.

"Mr. Roosevelt seems like an impressive man," Hop said.

"I've heard a few of his fireside chats, but I prefer her voice on the radio. She wants women to approach life with goals and desires. If I hadn't met her in person, I wouldn't believe she's real."

"What was she like?" Hop asked.

"Tall. Gracious. It's like she sees all the wrongs in the world and she's going to right every damn one of them. She sees us."

We extended our legs, happy for a bit of warmth this far south. This time of year in Bend we're sliding on ice crystals, but here, the bright yellow sun warmed our bones.

"Hey, you," a man barked at Red. "You that kid they lookin' for?"

I wrapped my arm around Red to pull her close. "Leave my sister alone."

"She looks an awful lot like the Jilted Jezebel."

"The what?" I asked.

He threw his folded newspaper at us. Not only had the papers dubbed her *The Jilted Jezebel,* but they had sensationalized her story into some sort of sick entertainment.

"I get a reward for handing her to the cops." He stepped closer. "Come here, little girl."

Hop punched him right in the face. The man's head bobbed like an apple in water. Before he could focus, Hop came at him again, and again. The man crumbled to the ground, dazed.

Red and I stared in disbelief.

"Come on," Hop said. "It isn't safe out here."

We tucked into an alley and ran in the shadows back to the rail yard.

"Where did you learn to fight like that?" I asked.

"Life. Everywhere you go, someone is out to get you. The only thing I have to protect myself are these." He held up his fists. "And this right here." He pointed to his head.

Red slipped her hands in her pockets and shrugged. "A gun works better."

Hop stopped walking and stared. He opened his mouth to speak, then shut it.

At the edge of the rail yard, we hid behind trees and watched. The place crawled with bulls, long black sticks bouncing against their thighs.

"They'll take her for sure," I said. "They're offering a reward now, it sounds like."

Red slipped the paper out of my hands.

"No, Red. Don't read it."

"The Jilted Jezebel." She exhaled. "They're right about one thing. I did kill that man."

I stifled a gasp. I didn't want to react. Neither did Hop.

Honesty kept Red teetering between a little girl and a young woman too wise for her age.

"We can't get out there." Hop glanced at the end of the tracks. "They're lined up, waiting for us."

"Warm Springs is only a few hours away." I slumped into the dirt. "We're so close."

"I know. But if we're caught, they'll arrest Red and throw us to another state."

"What do you mean?"

"Hobos and kids get arrested all the time. Usually they don't bother with prison, they just ship you off to the state line. Who knows where they'd send us."

We ducked back into a thicket of cedars. The trains whistled into the hot, steamy afternoon.

Hop sat against a tree. "We can rest here tonight. Try in the morning."

"We'll still be us in the morning," Red said. "And the bulls will still be waving their guns."

"Do you think we'll make it?" I pulled the newspaper out of my bag and stared at the image of Mrs. Roosevelt. "And if we do make it by Thanksgiving, will she see us?"

"We'll only find out by trying," Hop said.

The article on the First Lady talked about the letters she'd received. Little kids asking for coats and wives desperate for work for their husbands. And some angry as can be. I read on to see that many people despised her attempts to help women and put a stop to lynching. Some told her to shut up and be a good wife. Start acting like a respectable lady and let her husband do the talking.

I looked up from the paper. "Why are people so afraid of a woman with a voice?"

Hop ran his fingers through his hair. "Why would anyone be afraid unless women are so powerful, they could change the world?"

It was so simple, but that sentence showed me that Hop wasn't your average man. He saw the world in possibilities.

"There's something in her voice when I hear it on the radio," I said. "It's warm and soft, but underneath is a fire raging. I wonder who else can hear that."

"I hear men talk about her on the trains and in the jungles," Hop said. "Bless her poor heart, some say. Poor ugly thing. Last year I met a man in Ohio who complained that the bucked-tooth ogre was ruining our country. A few months later, who showed up at his coal mine but Eleanor Roosevelt herself."

I sat up. "She did?"

"She strode in with her white dress and shook their soot-covered hands. I heard about it later at a job milling buckwheat in the next county. That man had to put his groceries on company credit for three times the normal price. Mrs. Roosevelt demanded the mining companies allow the workers to buy groceries elsewhere. Unions came in and negotiated because of her. That man died in an explosion, but I hear Mrs. Roosevelt took the issue to Washington, DC."

"She said her place isn't in the White House. It's in the rural towns and farms where families struggle."

Red sat up. "My father hated her. Called her a socialist who gave our money to degenerates." Her teeth bit together so hard I saw her jaw muscles twitch. "Makes me want to meet her."

"I got a day job at a farm in Tennessee. Patching up their fence," Hop said. "The little girl wore a blue coat. Much too nice for that dusty old farm. She said she wrote to Mrs. Roosevelt and asked for a warm coat for winter. A few months later, a box arrived with a note. It said, 'We all deserve comfort. Signed Mrs. Eleanor Roosevelt.' That stuck with me."

"We have to find her," I said. "She can help us. I know she can."

Red stood and straightened her overalls, pulled down her cap, and started walking.

"What are you doing?" Hop asked.

"I'm walking to Warm Springs. We have to catch her."

"It will take all night," he said.

"Better than sitting here like targets. You coming?" She threw her hands up.

"Yeah." Hop shrugged. "We're coming."

We scrambled after her. We walked the line of the tracks, far enough away to hide from sight but close enough to feel the rumble of the trains.

Orange streaks faded into a soft purple, like the phlox that grew out of the lava rock back home. It spilled out of crevices in the spring, purple flowers spread out like spilled paint. Just like the clouds in the Georgia sky.

We crossed the base of Pine Mountain. The air cooled, settled somewhere between daylight and moonlight. As we turned, a crowd of people appeared through the trees, walking the same direction as us. I nudged Red to tuck her hair in her cap.

The harvest moon lit a path. We narrowed together, Hop reaching to hold my hand.

"What are they all doing?" I whispered.

"No idea." The group of men, some women, and even families walked through the forest, eyes set ahead.

A light voice piped up behind me. "Are you also headed for the spirit of Warm Springs?"

I turned to see a mother cradling a toddler in her arms. The child's feet dangled, ankles skinny and tight. It made me think of Johnny's twisted legs.

"Pardon me?" I asked.

"The healing water. Are you headed for it?"

"No, just passing through." I tightened my grip on Hop's hand.

"Some want to meet the President," the mother said. "Others, like myself, hope to find a cure in the warm water, just like Mr. Roosevelt did."

A gurgle caught my attention. We walked closer to that low-hanging moon and right past a waterfall. The mist sent a chill up my arms, but the pleasing sound reminded me of home. Water that courses through the center of a place all on its own, with no help from anyone.

"My son had polio," she said. "Mr. Roosevelt built a hospital here for survivors, where the healing waters treat them. I have no money. No family." She lifted the boy, rearranged her arms with a grunt. "I hope the President will help us."

Seeing her struggle with the weight, Hop reached out his arms. The mother stopped, took a breath. Tears in her eyes, she handed the boy to Hop. "Thank you."

Hop held him, cradled him in his arms. The boy leaned his head on Hop's chest and went back to sleep. His curly hair tickled Hop's chin.

"How far have you come?" I asked.

"A few miles south of here. I just couldn't wait anymore. Little Arthur needs attention. I can't afford a wheelchair."

"I hope the Roosevelts will help."

"The healing center is my last hope. If they don't take him, I..." The words caught in her throat, and she shook her head.

Johnny could use healing waters to soften the heat and pain he'd suffered this last year. What if they sold him to a family who wouldn't fight for him, wouldn't carry him through the forest to find a miracle?

A man bumped into Red. She flinched and jumped closer to me.

"Sorry," the man said. "My eyes aren't good. All I see is shadows."

She nodded and grabbed my sleeve as the man shuffled along, holding onto a friend's arm.

"We're all out here looking for salvation." I said it more to myself than anything, but the woman turned to me.

"Life seems impossible. Breathing painful. When there's a bit of hope, it helps us open our eyes every morning. And I believe the Roosevelts might be the brightest ray of hope we've seen in quite some time."

"I know how you feel. But not everyone agrees."

"Yeah. That's the life of power. You have to be courageous and arrogant enough to believe in yourself above all else."

"Maybe we can all learn to be a bit like them," I said.

"Maybe so," she said with a smile.

"Hold up!" a man hollered.

Piled on top of each other, fallen trees had twisted together, blocking the path.

"It'll be awhile. Everyone rest," the man said.

We settled into the cover of the forest. Hop handed the boy back to his mother and joined the others to move the fallen limbs. She curled her arms around her sleeping child. The moonlight hit her face just right. There were so many wrinkles. The roundness of her cheeks long gone, her sharp cheekbones and lines in her brow didn't match the young voice I'd heard. gray strands of hair twinkled among the black, messy bun at the base of her neck.

A line of moonlight beamed on Red's face. She scooted out of it, afraid the mother would recognize her.

"My poor boy. We live in the country, and it took a doctor two days to get to us. His fever kept rising, and when his legs stopped moving, I thought he was going to die." The woman wiped a wayward hair from her eye, scraping it back with the rest.

"Can he be cured?" I asked.

"I don't know. But Mr. Roosevelt is our best chance."

The woman looked at Red quizzically. Red moved closer until her arm touched mine.

"Aren't you just as pretty as a daisy."

Red bit her lip.

"She doesn't talk much, my sister."

"Yeah, you probably sit back and watch," she said to Red. "I can see in your eyes that you never miss a thing."

Red's breathing sped up. Her hand started tapping the dirt.

The woman kissed the boy's forehead. "I'd be lying if I said I wasn't expecting a miracle. That the healing waters will shower us both with a new life."

The woman had tears in her eyes. I understood her. When the fight settled and the world grew quiet, that's when the misery takes hold. Grabs you by the throat and doesn't let go.

"How could I let this happen?" Her face crumbled. Tears streamed down her cheeks. "I should never have been a mother."

"I can think of plenty of people who shouldn't be mothers. You aren't one of them."

"How can you tell? You don't know me."

"I know that you're here, in the middle of the forest on a cool night, carrying your child to safety. You cry for him. You don't want him to live a life of pain. I wish the world had more mothers like you."

Her weathered cheeks broke into a half smile. "Thank you." She wiped her eyes and released a loud exhale. "Looks to me like you've got your own mothering to do." She nodded at Red.

Hop returned and helped us up. "Well, path's clear. You all ready to catch a glimpse of the most famous man in America?"

Red reached for his hand.

We made our way past the waterfall and down the rocky path. The crowd of feet and wheels and sticks thumped against the earth and parted the hazy mountain air. Breaths puffed out of our mouths like pipe smoke, and we descended into Warm Springs.

The Roosevelts were here, opening their arms yet again.

CHAPTER EIGHTEEN

As the sun rose, the faces of our nighttime travelers came into focus. We joined a smiling crowd at the back of a Southern Railway train. We stood on the outskirts, watching from the trees, and just as the day grew warm, Mr. Franklin Delano Roosevelt appeared from the rear platform. He wore a straw hat and a crisp white linen suit, with the grandest smile stretched across his face. The sun seemed to shine brighter on him than the rest of us.

Applause thundered as miniature American flags shot into the air and waved in the breeze. The crowd's energy fizzled like electricity. No one even noticed Red, too preoccupied with the President of the United States.

He held the corner rails with both hands and waited for the audience to quiet.

"We are lucky to be here, back in our beloved Warm Springs, for another glorious Thanksgiving celebration. Some of you are here to experience the healing waters of this special place. I first arrived in 1924 and it was these very waters that helped me walk again. I felt the joy of standing... the joy of life again."

He paused. Took in the hush of the crowd.

"I dream that this special place will remain a treatment center for decades to come. A place where the sick can heal and families can once again find hope. It means a great deal to be here, at our Little White House, taking in this special atmosphere. I hope you all find what you came for."

He tipped his hat, and a woman hooked her arm around his as they disappeared into the parked train. People spread out on all sides, like water lapping against a boat.

"Where is Eleanor?" I asked.

Hop shrugged. "I don't know, but that was kind of special. I just stood ten feet from the President."

"Do you think these waters really heal people?"

"I think hope heals people, and the Roosevelts seem to have that in spades." He wrapped his arm around my waist. "I asked around. Their Little White House is about a mile from the polio hospital."

"Do we just knock on the door? Hide in the bushes and wait to see her?"

"We'll have to show up and find out," Hop said.

We ducked into the forest and walked the edge of the tracks, following the direction the President's car took once it left the train station. The excitement was more than I could bear. Eleanor Roosevelt, finally close enough. She would help us if she only knew we needed her. We held onto that belief with everything we had.

The Little White House columns peeked through the barren trees. Without the cover of leaves, we could see the grounds and cottages, open to anyone standing at the fence line. Pristine white, the buildings shone in the sunlight.

"That's probably the Secret Service." Hop pointed to a guard booth barely large enough to hold the man inside.

"We'll never get past them," I said.

"No, I don't suppose we will."

Doors opened from the back of the house. Mr. Roosevelt rolled onto the curved patio in his wheelchair.

"Why isn't he walking?" Red asked.

"I don't know."

He rolled into the sunshine and lit a pipe. We crouched at the edge of the fence, watching the President of the United States at his Little White House feel the sun on his face just as we did. A woman appeared from the doorway. I held my breath, anticipating a glimpse of Eleanor.

A younger woman in a pink dress and curled hair brought him a cup of coffee.

"A secretary?" I said.

The woman read from a pile of notes. He nodded, and she fussed over his coffee cup. She turned to walk away, but stopped to lay her hand on his shoulder. Mr. Roosevelt rested his cheek on the woman's hand.

"Looks to be more than a secretary," Hop said.

Of course. Men need to be needed, and Eleanor needed no one. I remembered her words on the river that day, the string of people she loves disappointing her.

How lonely her life must be.

"What now?" Red asked.

"We could just ask to speak with her," Hop said.

"They'll say no. People came to the Pilot Butte Inn to glimpse Mrs. Roosevelt and they kicked them all out."

Hop shook his head. "We can't outsmart the Secret Service."

"The servant's quarters," I said. "That's probably our only way in."

We crawled along the fence line near the cottage above the garage where we watched and waited for several hours. We were losing hope when several trucks arrived. They rolled through as the gates opened. A woman shuffled out, her face flushed with panic.

"Hurry. Hurry." She directed them. "It's getting late, and I'm behind. Come now." She swatted at them as they unloaded boxes.

Red stood from behind the fence.

"Red, sit down. They'll see you." I pulled at her pant leg.

Without hesitation, she walked to the open gate and headed straight for the trucks.

"What the hell is she doing?" Hop said.

"I don't know. But I guess we're following." We caught her just as she approached the woman.

To our shock, Red led the charge. "Ma'am, do you need help? We'll work in exchange for a meal."

The woman put her hands on her hips. She scanned our clothes and our dirty faces. "Well, you certainly are brave, coming in here. You know I could call for the Secret Service to arrest you?"

"Some things are worth the risk," I said.

"My assistant is out sick. And I'm quite behind on dinner preparations." She looked at the boxes stacked outside the kitchen door. "Do you peel potatoes?"

"We can help with anything you need," I said.

"Well, come on. The name's Daisy."

"I'm Magnolia. And this is Hop and Red."

"The Roosevelts believe in helping the needy. If the missus hears I turned children away, I'll never hear the end of it." She threw a glance at the doorway. "I'll put you to work and you'll get yourself a fine meal when you're done."

We nodded.

"Wash up there," Daisy said. "I'll find you plenty to do."

We scrubbed our hands and faces clean and looked around in awe. It wasn't much more than a country cottage, but Eleanor's touches were everywhere. On a desk, a letterhead just like the note she sent me. A brass plate engraved letter opener. A pearl hairpin. Meggie, their Scottish terrier, tore through the yard.

We set to work on all the things Daisy asked us to do. I folded linens, Hop peeled potatoes and Red polished the silverware.

"Do you think they know how lucky they are?" Hop asked.

I opened my mouth to respond, but a voice appeared behind me. "Yes."

I turned to see the housekeeper, a young woman, dabbing her brow with a handkerchief.

"I've worked for them for several years. They're exactly who they seem. They let you in here, didn't they?"

"Well, Daisy did," Hop said.

"They encourage it. Mr. Roosevelt's polio hospital is his pride and joy. He helps hundreds of people every year and he never thinks it's enough." She leaned against the wall to catch her breath. "And the First Lady is unlike anyone I've ever met."

"She seems like one of a kind," I said.

"She is. She cares little for high society unless they can help her causes. She speaks quietly but has the loudest voice of anyone here. Every moment of her life is spent trying to make life better for the rest of us."

"I didn't mean to be rude," Hop said.

"It's all right." She sighed and straightened her apron. "I just wish more people knew how lucky we are to have them fighting for us. It's the difficulties of our small towns here that inspired them to write parts of the New Deal. We have electricity now. And food programs."

I pressed the linens together to make a sharp crease, making sure the edges lined up perfectly.

"It's a big country out there with a whole lot of struggle," Hop said.

She glanced back at the kitchen. "Breaks over." She stopped at the doorway. "See that terrier out there? Mrs. Roosevelt's constant companion. A reporter once described that dog as *possessed of plenty of nerve and fighting spirit*. Just like her owner. Who do you think writes most of the President's policy?" She winked and returned to her duties.

"She's basically the first woman president," Hop said. "Just quietly."

"Speak softly but carry a big stick," I said. Teddy Roosevelt's favorite saying. I wondered if the Roosevelts didn't have a force running through their blood, something the rest of us weren't born with and couldn't understand.

We worked for hours, washing dishes and organizing silverware.

"You've turned out to be very fine helpers," Daisy said with a smile.

"Will they be eating dinner soon?" I glanced over her shoulder to the dining room.

"No, darling. This food is for the staff. The Roosevelts celebrate Thanksgiving with a grand dinner in Georgia Hall. They invite all the patients from the hospital and their families."

"Oh." I tried to hide my disappointment.

"Don't worry. I've made you each a lovely plate. Eat up."

We sat at a round table in the kitchen, three plates of roasted turkey, mashed potatoes with butter, sausage, and cornbread stuffing. Warm gravy.

Candied yams with pecans. Ice cold milk. We ate with smiles, savoring the kind of meal none of us had ever had.

"Red, don't you think it's wild?" I whispered. "You're working right next to the Secret Service, and no one recognizes you."

"She's safer here than out there."

"Maybe we should stay here forever," I said.

Daisy returned with three plates of apple pie, each dripping with a scoop of smooth vanilla ice cream. We ate every crumb. Licked those plates dry.

"I've got one more job for you. The Secret Service and hospital staff need to eat. Come on."

"Maybe we can catch her there," I whispered.

Hop raised his eyebrows. "First, we need to get past her security detail."

We sat in the back of a truck, guarding the chafing dishes and crates of food. We bumped along the road to a building with a red-tiled roof and white pillars.

"Hey." Hop pointed. "Did you see the address? Magnolia Road." He winked and my chest nearly burst open with hope.

We drove around back, past the sleek, fancy cars that could only belong to the Roosevelts. They were here.

My heart thumped with the thought. "What do we say when we find her?"

"We tell her we need her help. Red needs protection and you need to find Johnny," Hop said.

"If we can get to her," Red added.

We unloaded the food and boxes, and helped Daisy organize the meals. The agents laughed as they ate. They discussed baseball and their families. Nothing about politics like I expected.

We snuck glances and listened to conversation, but we couldn't see the Grand Hall or the Roosevelts anywhere.

"Thank you," an older woman said to us. "You've been quite a help. You can take your leave now."

"Oh, no," I said, a little too hopeful. "We can stay. Help clean up."

"No, we have all the help we need. Here's a bag of rolls and sausage for you. Be on your way." She pushed us out the door, even as I resisted.

"But I didn't even get to see her!"

She slammed the door in our faces.

The late afternoon chirped as we kicked dirt and stared at our feet. Secret Service surrounded the hall. They paced and watched.

"What now?" I asked.

"We try," Red said.

She marched again without a thought, right up to the windows of the banquet hall. Several agents approached to block her. Hop joined them and nodded for me to move. As they created a bit of a scene, I ran to the side of the building and pressed my face against the smooth glass window.

There she was.

Smiling and regal and laughing with everyone, her husband by her side. A room full of polio patients eating a grand meal with the President and First Lady. I looked for a door. Ran my hands along the window, peering in at the different families seated around the table.

"Hey, you."

An agent neared me. I turned back to the window, looking for a way in. Just as the crowd erupted in applause, I slammed my fist against the glass, but to no avail.

I reached into my bag. Held up Eleanor's letter. "See! Mrs. Roosevelt told me to find her. Read it. Please."

"Come on, you don't belong here." The man guided me away, ignoring my pleas.

I gripped the wood planter. "No. I'm not ready."

He yanked harder, not wanting to hurt me but making sure I knew he would win.

He dragged me from the building, but not before I glimpsed the last window. At the end of the table sat the woman from the forest and her little boy. He smiled from his wheelchair, and I stopped resisting.

The agent lifted me by the waist. "Don't fight. These are just the rules."

He carried me like I was a toddler and threw me in a police car with Hop and Red.

"Did you see her?" Red asked.

I sighed, tears pushing behind my eyes. "Yes, I did." The car rumbled away from the hospital with my hands pressed to the window. My hopes of Eleanor faded with the dust kicked up from the tires.

Red's hair stayed tucked under her cap, and the policemen didn't bat an eye at another homeless kid looking for a handout. They dropped us at the rail yard. Told us to head in any direction, so long as we left Warm Springs. We sat in the dirt and watched the sun lower in the sky.

No plan. We felt farther away today than we were yesterday, even though she was so close.

"What now?" Hop said.

I rested my head on his shoulder. "You know what she says?"

"What?"

"Never allow a person to tell you no who doesn't have the power to say yes." I looked up at him. "The way I see it, she's the only one with the power, so we keep fighting. Until she tells us no."

CHAPTER NINETEEN

Most kids on the train followed rumors of jobs. We were in search of something bigger. We spent several nights sleeping in the trees and walking along the train tracks out of sight. Hop would travel into towns to beg for food or find a day's work while I kept Red hidden.

One day I brushed Red's hair for a long while to keep her from growing agitated.

"How are we going to get anywhere if we can't ride the train and we have no money?" she said.

"We keep walking, I guess. In whatever direction leads us to Eleanor Roosevelt."

"Which direction is that?" Red asked.

"I'm not sure yet."

"You really think she can help us?"

"I do. And what other hope do we have? We can't keep running from the police." I kept combing her thin red hair, long past when the tangles were out. It felt nice to watch the teeth glide through easily. "I don't know how else to find Johnny."

"We'll find him, Maggie. I promise."

"You know, Red, you have a bigger heart than you let on."

She leaned her head back and closed her eyes. "What I have is this giant hole inside of me, filled with white hot fear. It doesn't hurt as much now that I've met you and Hop."

"I'm glad we found each other."

She opened her green eyes and held my hand. "I won't stop until we find your brother." Her hands trembled. "We should save at least one kid."

Hop returned from his foraging with a swollen face. Blue-purple rings lined his left eye, his fat cheek shining in the sunlight.

"What happened to you?" I asked.

"Oh, I'm all right." He threw his bag down and sat cross-legged in the dirt. "I got us some food." He opened a brown sack and laid out fried chicken and biscuits.

We just stared at him, mouths open.

"It's fried chicken." He looked back and forth between us. "What's the problem?"

"What did you have to do to get this?" I asked.

He dabbed a drop of blood on his forehead and smeared it on his pants. "It's no big deal. I went to a few houses to ask for work. Three said no, and one met me at the back door with a shotgun. At the next place, some tough kid told me I could have his lunch if I fought him for it."

I tipped the water canteen onto a handkerchief and dabbed his forehead clear of blood.

"So, I boxed three rounds with him."

"You fought someone for our food?" Red asked.

Her shoulders twitched, and I could tell they were about to rise to her ears. Then the tapping started on her leg. Bent fingers, the tips like a claw on her thigh.

"Red, it's okay. He won't do it again."

"Like hell I won't do it again," Hop said. "I've had to fight all sorts of people in my life. I'm good at it. If I get a fat lip or a black eye, I don't care."

My hand slipped from his forehead and ran gently over the swollen cheekbone. "We don't want you to hurt yourself so we can eat."

His voice grew louder. "It's just a fistfight." He threw back from my touch, grabbed a chicken thigh, and walked off.

We stared at the food.

"We have to eat it," I said. "We're hungry, and it will kill him if we don't."

She nodded. "Okay."

Cold fried chicken holds a particular joy. We tore into it and sucked the bones clean. The biscuits, like soft pillows, freshly baked and buttery, left crumbs on our lips and fell to our laps. Hop watched us enjoy the meal from a distance.

The fire popped and cracked, filling the edges of silence. Red curled into a ball and fell asleep. Hop felt about a thousand miles away. His hands remained in his lap, signaling that he didn't want to touch me.

"Thank you for the food," I said.

"It's not like I was really hurt."

"I know. It's just that..." I scooted closer. The fire cast a warm glow, his bruise reflecting the light in a bright shine. My arms felt chained to my body, afraid to reach for him. "It scares us that you hurt yourself for us."

"I'm not trying to scare you, I'm trying to keep us alive. It's the only thing I have to offer."

I willed my arms to move. Just reach out and touch him. "It's not the only thing."

He turned to face me. "I would let someone beat me unconscious if it brought you Johnny or saved Red from another institution."

"We just want you close." I gasped unintentionally as my heart pressed into my throat. "*I* want you close."

"Then why are you afraid to touch me?"

Warm breath kissed my cheek.

"I'm afraid that if you touch me, you'll discover the rotten inside and the ugly, horrendous person I am, and you'll leave me." My chest felt like a birdcage letting in the wind through a steel frame. All open holes and a big empty cavern with wings flapping inside. Tears puddled in my eyes, but they didn't spill over. I was thankful for that.

"Why do you think that about yourself?" he said.

"It's just in there, part of me. There were happy moments a long time ago. As a child, my father would play drums on a pot and my mother would sing. She had a beautiful voice. She would close her eyes and escape somewhere. For a few minutes, I could breathe." I covered my mouth with my hands, trying to hold the words inside.

"What happened to those moments?"

"Mama had episodes. She'd scream. Pull her hair out in clumps. I had to hide the knives because once, when I was twelve, she cut her wrists in front of me. Blood smeared all over her face and the floor. I wanted my mother to die. But I stopped her."

"Why?"

"She was pregnant with my baby sister."

"You've spent your life protecting everyone else. Who protected you?"

I shook my head. "I don't deserve protection. It's my fault my father left, and my mother hated her life. It's my fault my sister died."

"What?"

The memory rolled up on me like it had a thousand times. Like lava swallowing me in a silvery-red river. I usually shut it down into blackness.

"It was all my fault," I said. "I couldn't hold us together."

He wrapped his strong arms around me, but I pulled back. He pulled tighter. It was no use. I was never strong enough.

I softened into his arms and soaked his shirt with tears of my memories as my ugly center oozed out like bile.

Hop lifted my chin, but I wouldn't look at him. His lips pressed to mine. "I won't fight anymore," he said.

The soft skin of his neck rubbed against my cheek as he hugged me, and I wanted more. I wanted every spare inch of his skin touching mine because when he did, I didn't hurt so much.

I opened my eyes. Red sat across the fire, wide awake, tears streaming down her face in the warm light. I pulled away from Hop, afraid she might start tapping or rocking.

She didn't.

"I know where we can get money," she said.

"Where?" Hop said.

"My house in Little Rock."

***

Two midnight trains and six hours into a clear, warm morning, we arrived in Arkansas. Sharecropper's cabins with tilted fireplaces and sunken roofs, hollowed logs used as chicken roosts, women barefoot with stained dresses watching us pass without expression. A general store's screen door creaked in the wind next to piles of dust gathered on a pump once used for gas. Men in torn overalls planted winter wheat on the last remaining farms, their bare arms glistening with sweat in the already seventy-degree heat.

Red walked with purpose, silent and wound tight, like a grenade with her own finger on the pin.

"Red, we don't have to do this," I said for the third time.

"Yes, I do." She stared ahead, breaking twigs into pieces.

At the start of a long dirt road, she stopped. Her breathing quickened.

An abandoned threshing machine crumbled to pieces next to the road, its wheels and chute dented and rusting under a fine layer of dirt. Red's hands pumped into fists. Tightened, released, and tightened again. Her strides elongated.

We followed behind her, watching for any sign of people. Our feet kicked the dust into brown clouds.

Across a wood bridge, a clearing of bare trees. No leaves. Just the dried, sharp branches stuck in the air like fork tines. Then, a farmhouse.

We stood on either side of Red, my shoulder touching hers. Her sleeve trembled against her skin. Not a sound but the hot wind whistling in our ears.

"It's not too late to turn around," Hop said.

Red stared at the house. A slow nod no.

I lowered my hand to her shoulder. "We're coming with you."

She stared a while longer and I wondered what kind of monster awaited us inside.

The farmland spread out into flat, smooth cakes of dry earth, shallow fissures hard as stone.

As we neared the house, a terrible stench rose with the morning heat. Rotten. Like a bucket of stone fruit in the sun, stewed in its own festering juices. I brought my hand to my nose as a gag clenched my stomach.

I wondered if a thousand rodents had died under the house, their innards seeping into the parched earth. That's all I could envision. Dead rats and decaying fruit.

At the foot of the stairs, vultures fluttered up from a dog carcass, their black wings whipping into the still air. Red looked down at the mangled flesh and kept walking. She coughed from the sour smell, so Hop handed her a handkerchief to cover her nose and mouth.

Thinned steps bowed under the weight of our feet.

Red kicked the door open, and the smell wafted out like heat from an oven. We stumbled and coughed while Hop leaned over the railing and vomited. Red shook her head, tears in her eyes, but still stepped inside.

Sleeve over my mouth, nose pinched, I willed myself to follow. Air thick as soup. Broken furniture. A dirt-filled beer bottle on the coffee table. Broken glass and sticks strewn on the floor. Every window blown out with Arkansas soil gathered in the corners. Wallpaper peeled and browned where pink roses used to be.

They say houses have souls. This one had rotted away in the dust cloud of forgotten farms for a reason.

"We shouldn't be here." Hop mumbled from under his paisley handkerchief.

Red swung a door open and instantly turned away. I reached for her, but she held her hand up. We stood frozen in the doorway to the kitchen, watching her stare into a bedroom. A layer of soil covered a brass bed with a carnation-colored blanket.

As Red crept into her old bedroom, her face twisted into silent tears. She crouched near her bed. We both stepped closer, but she held her hand out. She curled into a ball, balancing on her feet, rocking back and forth.

She sobbed and trembled. All we could do was watch and give her that moment with the pain that seemed to own her.

We covered our mouths, the smell somehow worse when we stood still.

Red finally rose, eyes puffy and face shining with tears. The look in her eyes. That angry bull had returned.

She knocked into our shoulders, pushing us apart, and we followed closely behind. The smell kicked up a notch as we neared the closed door. That old house creaked like a swaying ship.

She pushed the door open and my eyes watered. Two bare feet stuck into the air, white as skim milk. Red entered like she was walking on glass. The huge man lay splayed out on a twin sized bed, mouth open, cheeks sucked in over his missing teeth. His thinned skin shined unnaturally blue.

"Is that your father?" I choked out.

She watched his corpse like he might float up from the dead. "He must have died in his sleep." Her face twisted and writhed, the anger rolling up on her with speed.

Red stomped through the door and clanged around in the living room. I turned to Hop. "What do we do?"

"Let her have her anger. Then we get the hell out of here."

Red returned, dragging a fireplace poker. Thick metal, it scraped against the old wood floor, leaving a line in the dirt. She wrapped her two little hands around the pole and lifted it in the air.

She brought that metal rod straight down on his pale, withered face. The facial bones cracked under its weight. She brought it up again. Smashed his sternum. Cracked the poker on his face again. No blood splattered. Just crushing bones and a puff of air that stank of sour milk.

What the hell did he do to her?

She screamed with such fury that I thought she might faint. Her white face turned a bright red and her neck muscles popped out. Hop wrapped his arms around her just as she went limp. The metal rod clanged to the warped floor.

"It's over," Hop said.

He dragged her toward the back, but she gripped the door frame and locked her arms. "Wait."

She pushed off Hop and stumbled to the kitchen. She lifted a hatch in the bottom of a cupboard and reached for a beat-up can of dried beans. She popped the lid and came up with a wad of cash. Must have been two hundred dollars in there.

She shoved the money into Hop's chest. We staggered hand in hand outside, gasping for fresh air.

"Hop, we can't leave it like this. Someone will think Red killed her father."

"You're right. Make it look like a dust storm tore through?"

"No. I'll take care of it," I said.

Back in the creaking house, I imagined taking that poker to the rest of the man's bones, starting with his shins.

No time for rage.

I threw open every cupboard and collected any useable food. Cans of pork and beans, beef stew, Spam, a jar of peanut butter. Three spoons, a can opener. I stashed them in a canvas bag.

I shook each lantern I found around the house. Two empty, one shattered. Two with remaining oil reserves. I shattered one on each wall of the kitchen. Dumped a can of Crisco on the table, smeared it around with a wooden spoon. Screwed the top off a bottle of rubbing alcohol and poured it over furniture. I found a sticky bottle of vegetable oil and poured a solid line from the table, along the floor, and out to the back porch.

Bag of food around my shoulder, I pulled out a box of matches. I reached to strike a cluster of them on the box edge when a hand touched my back.

"I'll do it," Red said.

Red swiped the matches. She dropped them as a blue flame skimmed the oily path into the kitchen. We watched a slow coil of smoke and flames rattle their way around the crumbling house, Red mesmerized by the flames.

I yanked her back from the heat and we ran back to stand with Hop. We watched the flames climb the walls and swallow that wicked house, Red's memories smoking with the old wood.

We ran through the prairie, Red leading the way. Across a dried creek and through parched wheat fields. Past an old barn and down into a dried gulch.

Hop set to work building a fire. Red stared in the direction of her old house, legs to her chest, chin resting on her kneecaps. She looked so small.

Hop lowered next to me and brushed his hand over mine. We sat in silence as the day bled away. We shared a can of soup warmed over the fire, taking turns slurping up the juice.

"He never touched me," Red said.

We looked at her in disbelief. Red was about to tell her story. The story of Gracie.

"My father. He never touched me... if that's what you were thinking."

We didn't flinch.

She looked down and took a deep breath. "He never touched me at all. Never a hug or nothin'. My mother died during childbirth, so it's all I knew, me and him. We were like strangers. I cooked and cleaned. He ignored me. It was fine." Her arms braced against her sides. "And then I turned into a girl with curves. With breasts and rosy cheeks and a curvy behind."

Hop put down the food. We waited, silent.

"The farm had died. We had nothing left. One night, he introduced me to a man old enough to be my grandfather. Told me not to be afraid. I was going to help the family. He took me in my room and undressed me and covered my face with a towel while he got his money's worth."

I turned my head, trying not to cry.

"The men paid my father. He let them take me to my room so I could earn my keep. Didn't matter how I screamed or cried or lay still as death. They never cared."

"Jesus Christ, Red." Hop couldn't look at her.

"One man was rough. When I would fight, he'd hold a knife to my throat and threaten to kill me. I learned to lock down my fear real tight, shut my throat so I didn't talk or scream. Just stay silent to get through it. I fantasized about killing him. He would be on top of me with his fat, sweaty body, and I would dream up ways to tear him open and watch him bleed. And one day, that's what I did."

"You shot him."

"My father left the house when the men came to give them privacy. When the fat man with the knife held me down, I was ready. I bit his neck so hard I drew blood. I reached under the mattress and grabbed the gun I had hidden. I stole some of my father's money to buy it. Ready to wallop me good, he lunged toward me, but I pointed the gun and pulled the trigger. Blood spattered the walls. He fell to the ground and died right at my feet. Felt good to watch his face blow apart like that."

"Red, you didn't murder him. You defended yourself," Hop said.

"No one else thought that. My father turned me in to save himself. The lawyers declared me insane. That's why I seduced an old man and then shot him."

"Red, they're the monsters. Not you."

"All those drugs in the orphan asylum, they kept me from feeling anything. I locked down my voice to get through it the same way I had learned. But my fear was always there. No medicine can change that."

Hop crawled next to her. She pulled away, eyes not meeting his.

"Red, you're safe now. With us." He whispered it again. "You're safe."

She fell into his chest, then curled into a ball. He hovered his hand over her head, afraid to scare her. She reached her hand to mine. We held her and let her cry.

She wept silently, without a sniffle or wail. Hop finally lowered his hand to her hair. She winced, then softened under his touch. Eyes shut, she squeezed my hand like a sister would.

CHAPTER TWENTY

We had to get out of Arkansas. All eyes were open, searching for the Jilted Jezebel. People loved a sensation, even if it meant blaming an innocent girl. Nobody seemed to care about the truth.

"We have money. Let's just take a passenger train," Red said.

"No way," I said. "Too conspicuous."

"Best bet is to hitch a ride or catch a night train over the state line," Hop said.

"The newspapers keep writing about me. Every state probably wants to see me tied up and drugged again."

I wrapped my arm around her. "We'll just have to keep you hidden then."

"Maybe you should let me go. Get far away from me. I can fend for myself."

Grabbing her shoulders, I forced her to look at me. "We stay together. No matter what."

We'd meant to head east, toward Washington, DC, intent on catching Eleanor Roosevelt at an event or a fundraiser. But after a day battling fatigue, we jumped on the wrong train... heading west. We woke to an Oklahoma sun that lit the high plains with a clear, pale light. The loose tail of a windmill clapped in the still afternoon.

"What do we do now?" I asked.

The empty prairie stretched ahead, far as the eye could see. Once grassland, piles of dirt shivered across its surface like water ripples.

Hop grabbed my sleeve. "Come on. There's a camp near here."

The dry air stung my eyes. "What happened to this place?"

"Dust storms," Hop said. "They've flattened farms and killed animals. It's been the longest drought imaginable."

I coughed to clear my throat, but inhaled more dust than air. "The Depression wasn't enough? God conspired to choke out the air too? How can anyone survive here?"

Hop sighed. "Only the tough ones do." Soft, silky dust floated around him. "When the storms roll in, it gets so dark it blocks out the sun."

"You've seen it?" I asked.

"Yeah. Only once, but that was enough for me." He wiped the glossy sweat from his upper lip. "At a farm in Cimarron County last summer."

Red scratched at her cheek. "What happened?"

"The bulls arrested a group of us for holding boxing fights in the jungles. A bunch of policemen gathered us up, charged us with disorderly conduct, and threw chains around our ankles. They sent us to work the local farms."

"You had to work in a dust storm with a chain around your legs?" I wanted to reach out and touch him.

"It was torture. One hot August morning, a wind gust came through that looked like the end of the world. Black and thick, it rolled in like a hurricane. We all ran until our chains pulled taut. The wind blew so loud I thought it might lift me from the ground and spit me out in another state."

"That's terrifying," I said.

"They let us go after a week. I suspect we were too expensive to feed." He smacked a fly on his neck.

Drained of water and life, an unsettling humming filled the air. It fluttered from the sky and rumbled under my feet. Offset by the calm stillness, something deeply troubling crawled around on my skin.

"Can we get out of here?" I rubbed my shoulder.

"Not another train for a while. They don't stop here very often." Hop looked around the freight yard.

Torn sheets flapped in the breeze from the migrant workers' makeshift tents. A child caked in dust kicked an empty can. It reminded me of the boys in the summer.

"These people have even less than the others," Red said. "They're desperate. Wild. You can see it in their eyes."

The people dragged themselves around the jungle like a bag picked up by the wind. My stomach twisted and didn't let up.

The quiet whistle of Red's breathing caught my attention. I followed her gaze to a man leaning against a broken-down truck, fedora tipped low over his brow. He wore dirty clothes and a smug smile. He eyed Red like raw meat to tear into before it spoiled.

I pulled her behind me and stared at the man. He had a sharp scar from his lip to his cheek. I couldn't fight, not with this weak shoulder. But I would claw the man's eyes out if that's what it took.

"It's just a smile, sweetheart." He smirked, then went back to whittling a chunk of wood.

"How soon can we get out of here?" I asked Hop.

"Probably in a few hours. Don't worry." Hop held my hand. "I'm here."

We found a spot at the edge of the camp. Not a tree in sight, so we sweat and baked in the sun, watching the lost souls the world forgot. Red tapped the dirt so softly no one could hear but me.

Hop chatted with someone a few feet over. I kept my gaze on the man with the scar. His eyes remained steady on his whittling, but his attention was still on Red. I could feel it.

Hop stepped back to us. "Train's delayed until tomorrow."

I searched the man's face for motive. Did he recognize her from the papers? Or worse, a predator eyeing his target.

"Something the matter?" Hop asked.

"No, nothing."

Some of the tightness in Red's skin had softened over the past month, as a bit of fat appeared in the apples in her cheeks. She almost looked her age. She should be drinking lemonade with her friends, reading at school, learning to sew and cook. Instead, she had to keep running. Keep fighting.

Night bled into the sky. The scarred man disappeared, but I still felt him. He sent the misery into the air like smoke. I wrapped my arms around Red to keep her safe. I wanted to believe I could.

"Hop, stay close."

"Okay, I will." He wiped a stray hair from my cheek. "You're tense."

"This place. It's like there's no air to breathe."

He placed his hand on my back, just below my neck. "I'm right here."

The sounds and hidden evils popped around me like popcorn. How could Hop not feel it?

At the tent next to us, a toothless woman sliced the moldy ends off a hunk of bologna. Without looking at me, she murmured, "The man whittling the stick. Stay away from him."

"I plan to," I said.

"He's part of something. Spends his time with a group of men just as angry as him."

"What do they do?"

"Nothing you want any part of." She yawned. "That's all I know." She ducked into her tent and tied the flaps shut.

Somewhere in the middle of the night, my worry hit a wall of fatigue. I could spin myself so tight that my mind couldn't take anymore. I had been doing it my entire life.

Muffled kicks and whispers woke me with a start. I caught the tip of Hop's fingers just as the shadows yanked him away. I reached for Red, but the same thing happened. In my panic, I grabbed handfuls of dirt, hoping the cold earth would pull me from a nightmare.

But it was no dream. I was alone.

My heartbeat shook my ribs. Where were they? I narrowed my eyes and saw figures dragged toward a tent. Padding through the still camp, I walked a path lit by dwindling fires as they sparked into the dark. My stomach tightened like an orange rind squeezed of its last drop of juice.

A dim light peeked out from the front of the tent where the two flaps came together. Shuffling inside. My toes ached as I clawed the bottom of my shoes.

I heard screams. "Get off of me!"

"Red," I whispered.

Staring at the tent flaps felt like jumping off a cliff. The moment before you hit where everything goes quiet and memories rush through you. A touch of regret hooks your heart because you're out of choices, with only one thing left to do. Step inside.

Two men held Hop's hands behind his back, and a third held a hand over his mouth. He bucked and kicked, but they held tight. Red faced the door, terror-stricken, the man with the facial scar standing behind her.

"Let her go," I said.

He scratched the side of his mouth. "What's it worth to you?"

"We have no money. So just let her go." Could he smell my fear the way a wild animal would?

"I don't care about money," he said. "I want somethin' else."

His words oozed like thick oil I couldn't wipe off.

Pressing his face into Red's hair, he closed his eyes and pulled a deep inhale of her scent. Red elbowed him in the ribs, which made him laugh. Like this was a fun game.

"She's a feisty one." He circled her. Slow, deliberate. "A bit young for my taste."

Like choosing a ripe plum from a grocery bin.

"You want me to let her go?" His scarred lip twitched. "Offer me something else."

His words lifted at the end, a wind chime-like sound.

I wanted to shoot his face off and set us all free. Red's cheeks flushed a bright red that glowed against the whites of her eyes.

"Let her go."

"You offerin' me a trade?"

From the corner of my eye, I saw a deep pain on Hop's face I couldn't quite look at straight on.

"Yes," I said. "Now let them go."

"Maggie, no." Red reached for me, but the man shoved her outside.

"Come back in here and I'll slice your friend's neck clean to the bone." He straightened his hat and closed the flap of the tent. Spinning on his heels, he turned and pointed to Hop. "But you... you can watch."

I turned my head, unable to look at either of them. Maybe I could close my eyes and drift away somewhere. Let him do with me as he wanted. I was already rotten inside.

The man stepped up behind me, his hot breath on my neck. He slid my braid over my shoulder.

"I do love blond braids," he whispered.

Hop kicked and thrashed, but he couldn't fight off three men.

"Then why did you take her? Why not just go straight for me?" I swallowed, my gaze on the black stove in the corner, at a pan cooling after their supper.

"Where's the fun in that?" His eyes climbed my body from feet to my forehead. "You're a pretty little thing."

I turned, walked straight to Hop, and rested my hand on his chest. "Don't be afraid. I'll be fine. Just close your eyes."

He shook his head no, while tears gathered at his lower lids.

"It'll be over soon," I said.

The heat from the wood stove made it hard to breathe. Only one way we made it out of this.

Don't let the fear break you.

The man smiled and unbuttoned the top of my dress down to my stomach. He took his time. Let his knuckles graze my skin. I turned and closed my eyes. Tried not to vomit.

His moustache poked at my neck as he kissed it. At least I think it was a kiss. It felt like he licked me, like he wanted to taste me.

Don't cry. Hop couldn't see me cry.

He pressed his body into mine, over my clothes, just to feel me. His breath wavered. Hop wept behind me. His muffled screams fell silent underneath their hands.

I wanted to die.

The man grabbed my braid in his hand and pulled back to force my face near his. "I think you're gonna like this."

The moment swallowed me. A brief, quiet moment of one emotion— regret.

Just as his mouth grazed mine, the ground shifted. A guttural scream and a flash of red barreled through the tent. I stumbled back as a fiery stick impaled the man straight through the neck. Red's face twisted so tightly, she no longer seemed human. Like the imagined faces of those coyotes I'd heard in the forest back home. Saliva dripping from teeth, the taste for blood in their mouths.

They had underestimated her.

The man tumbled back while the stick jutted into the air. Eyes plastered wide, he felt around his bloody neck. Another man let go of Hop, leaving an arm free. Hop's elbow landed with a hard jab to one's nose, and the back of his head slammed into the other's face. One of them lunged for Red.

She backed up, knowing she couldn't fight without a weapon. I turned to the stove and threw off my jacket. Protected by the sleeve, I grabbed the handle of the cast iron pan and launched it. In the second before it hit the back of his head, I saw Red cowering in the corner, eyes shut.

I had no hesitation about crushing his skull.

The iron clanged against his head the way a watermelon sounds as it splits.

I ran to Red and swooped her up in my arms just as Hop pummeled the last man to the ground.

Blood leaked from Hop's eyebrow. I doubt he even felt it.

"Come on." He guided us into the darkness.

I glanced back to see the man debate whether to pull the stick out of his neck.

"The money," Hop said.

We ran past our section of the camp, Red's hand so wet with sweat, it almost slipped from mine. We passed the toothless grandmother, arms folded, watching us scramble.

Hop grabbed our bag on the way out of the camp.

"Shit," Hop said.

I knew from his voice that it was gone. The money, the food. All of it.

Hours passed, yet the sky remained black as a raven. I glanced behind us every so often, but no one followed us. My unease shed like a snake's skin.

Wind howled through the broken door of an abandoned farmhouse. Hop entered first and motioned us in. "We can stay here until daybreak."

He built a fire from fallen logs and furniture remnants. Red kept the matches in her pocket, so at least we had those.

Hop couldn't look at me.

"Maggie, you were going to let that man..." Her face crinkled. "You were going to let him touch you. To save me."

"Yes."

"Why?"

Different answers rolled around my head. Maybe it was bravery. Maybe it was hope that I could save us all. "I couldn't let him hurt you."

Hop cleared his throat.

Red crawled on her hands and knees closer to me. "We've all been hurt too many times. I've had about enough of that, haven't you?"

Red said it like there was an end. As if by choice alone we could stop the monsters from climbing in the windows.

"I'd like to be alone tonight," Red said. "I'm gonna sleep in the bedroom."

After she disappeared, the space between me and Hop felt like miles of unpassable ocean.

"I'm sorry I couldn't stop him," Hop choked out.

"I had no choice."

"You did have a choice. Don't you realize how that tortured me?" He said it forcefully. Loud. "When he touched you, I..." He shook his head and tightened his lips.

I waited for Red to peek her fearful eyes around the corner, but she didn't.

"No one has ever cared if I got hurt."

"What?"

"I've protected my brothers with every bit of myself, but no one ever cared what happened to me or that I'm afraid of everything."

Floorboards creaked as he shifted toward me. "I don't want you to fear me." Hop combed his fingers into the base of my hair. "Give me some of your fear."

"Is that possible?" I asked.

He reached to untie my braid, but I stopped him. "No. I need it."

He tilted his head, but let it go. Both hands cupped around my face, he brought my lips to his. His salty, tear-streaked kiss felt like freedom.

I pressed my chest to his. "Make the memory of that man's touch go away."

He kissed my neck and ran his hands along my waist, squeezing my hips with an intensity that made me gasp. He gripped my thigh as he kissed me again. "Are you afraid?"

"Only that you'll stop."

He lay me down, slid his hand along my inner thigh, pulling my underwear to the side. He rolled his fingers over me, in me. Touched me in a way that felt like I hadn't lived a day in my life. The space between my legs swelled and pulsed. Desperate for more, my body writhed with an aching need.

I reached to unbutton his pants, but he stopped me. "Not yet."

"You don't want to?"

"Oh no, I want to." He ran his lips along the space behind my ear. "I just want you to feel good. Safe. Let me do that for you."

He was right. I wasn't ready to give myself over to him. But his touch, I wanted that. I ached for it.

I let my hand slip under his shirt, my fingers spreading out over his chest and stomach. I softened my legs, spread them slightly, and abandoned the fear. His fingers touched me again, like strumming a soft tune on a guitar. His other hand cradled the back of my head, and the gnawing ache disappeared. My breathing sped up and my legs trembled, until I groaned and arched my back, by body on fire. I pressed my lips to his cheek, hungry to taste him, to feel his soft skin on my mouth.

My breathing steadied and everything went numb.

Hop stared into my eyes. "Are you scared now?"

I felt warm and calm. "No."

"Can I ask you something?" he said.

"Okay."

"If I love you hard enough, will you stop hating yourself?"

Every muscle in me tightened. "I'd like to try." It was the truest sentence I could have said.

"Good." He kissed me again. "I have something for you." He reached for his bag.

"I thought they took everything."

"All but one thing." He reached in and came up with a book. "Here. Merry Christmas."

"It's not Christmas yet."

"I know. But we can make it any day we want."

I read the title. "It's Up to the Women."

"Look at the author."

"Eleanor Roosevelt." I smiled so widely, I almost laughed.

"The day before I fought that kid for fried chicken, I built a cellar on a nearby farm. When the wife pulled me into their living room, she asked what I wanted for pay. I read through her bookshelf and pointed to this one."

"Eleanor Roosevelt really wrote this?"

Hop smiled. "She did."

I ran my fingers over the rough paper edges. Her words held such power. They filled me with that same feeling that maybe, we could all make some sort of change in the world.

"I figured no one could help you find yourself quite like she could."

I lay my head in his lap and tilted the book toward the firelight. He leaned against the wall and rubbed my arm as I consumed her words like gospel.

"Women, whether subtly or vociferously, have always been a tremendous power in the destiny of the world."

Start small. Think big.

I hear you, Mrs. Roosevelt. I hear you.

CHAPTER TWENTY-ONE

We had one plan—stay hidden and keep moving. We found ourselves outside Tulsa when an older gentleman approached. "I know that's her." He chewed on his pipe. "But I ain't in no position to judge. Stay outta sight."

Some people didn't want to turn us in. An unspoken code that life was already awful enough, no sense adding to the misery. That's the thing about the Great Depression. Living with nothing forced us all to find out who we were on the raw, fleshy inside.

Too much state to cross going south and we had to get out of Oklahoma. No choice but to head north toward Kansas. Hop would secure us a ride, and just as the truck drove off, Red would scurry out from behind a tree. Poor kid lived in the shadows.

Tucked in the back of a pickup on an eerily quiet morning, we rolled to a stop near a couple of police cars. My heart thumped into my throat. I pushed Red under a blanket and leaned back against her curled body in the corner.

The policeman spoke to the driver. "Where you headed?"

"Wichita. I've got business to attend to."

"What's in the back?"

"Guns and ammo. Selling to a shop once I get there. Picked up some kids that needed a ride."

Red grabbed the back of my dress and balled it in her fist. Hop's hand crawled over mine.

The policeman eyed the truck bed. "Where you kids from?"

"Oh, a bit of everywhere," Hop said.

"Don't be cute, son. We're looking for someone." He opened boxes and moved crates around. They scraped the metal with an awful screech.

"Who you looking for?" Hop asked.

"A girl. Fourteen, red hair. She murdered a man, escaped a nuthouse, and went on to kill two more here at a migrant camp." The policeman neared the edge of the truck bed where Red hid. "She might have killed her own father, too." He shook his head. "Sick little whore."

Red pinched the skin on my back so hard tears sprang to my eyes. The policeman looked at me and said, "Are you all right, miss?"

The tears rolled down my cheeks. "Not really, sir. I just want to go home." I'd learned that men soften when a woman cries. They needed to save us, and it clouded their wits. My father proved that.

The man removed his hat. "All right. It's okay. Is this man a friend?"

"Yes." I wiped my eyes. "He'll make sure I get home."

He nodded to Hop. "All right, then." He smacked the outside of the truck right near Red. She flinched against my back. "No more tears, all right, miss? You get on home now."

I flashed a grateful smile.

The truck pulled away, and Hop wrapped his arm around me. "That was impressive."

"I lied. I don't have a home."

"No. But you will someday." He kissed my forehead. I reached back to hold Red's hand.

***

We rolled into Wichita late in the afternoon. Red jumped out before the truck came to a stop and took off into the bushes.

We ran across plains and ducked into razed corn fields and empty ravines with tree skeletons.

"We're a long way from Washington, DC," Red said.

"We sure are." I pulled out my book.

"I promise," Hop said. "We'll find her."

At yet another makeshift camp in the trees, we gathered around a fire, snacking on dried venison from the man in the truck. Leaves rustled in the wind. Winter felt real here.

"What are we doing?" Red asked.

"Eleanor Roosevelt never stays at the White House for very long," I said. "We have to catch her on the road somewhere."

Red squirmed. "How are we gonna do that with every eye on me?"

"We just have to," I said. "We don't have a choice."

"Maybe I should go out on my own. You pretend not to want each other, but I see it."

I willed myself not to look at Hop. "We just don't want to upset you," I said.

"Well, stop!" Her eyes squeezed shut.

"It's okay, Red." I reached for her, but she slapped me away. "You can't save me, Maggie."

I froze. "I just want you to feel safe."

"I don't think I'll ever feel safe again."

"Red..."

She refused my attempted hug. "Saving me won't bring your brothers back."

She walked off into the night. Hop grabbed my arm. "Let her go."

"She can't be alone."

"That kid is tougher than any man I've met on the road. She can handle herself," he said.

"But she might run away."

"You can't hold on to her if she doesn't want to be held."

"I can't lose another one." My voice trailed off into heavy breaths. Hop held me tight and kissed my cheek.

I wondered about Johnny. If he had a mother that tucked him in at night and sang to him. Who showered him with hugs, and I love yous. I hoped so. And I wondered if Oscar remembered me, somewhere in his memories. Would he remember the sister I tried to be... or the one I turned out to be?

"Why can't I fix anyone?"

"It's not your responsibility to fix anyone, Maggie."

I looked at his dark eyes. "It's all I have."

"That's not true." His fingers ran across my cheeks like a whisper. "You have me."

My heart hurt. It squeezed and twisted, the tightness almost too much to bear. "I don't understand why you want me."

His eyes narrowed. "I've spent my life searching for ghosts. Maybe I'm meant to be alone. Unlovable. Ghosts were as close as I was going to get. Searching for the impossible kept me safe. And then this girl showed up— blond braid and big blue eyes and a gunshot through her shoulder. Determined to find the real people she loves. Would die for them." His finger traced my collarbone.

"It's fear. All of it."

"What does Eleanor Roosevelt say about fear?"

"That danger lies in refusing to face the fear. You must do the thing you think you cannot do."

"Then that is what we'll do. Together. We'll spend every day doing what we think we can't. No matter how much it scares us."

"Where do we start?"

His forehead to mine, he said, "Right here."

***

We needed to disappear. To somewhere no one knew about Red. Four train rides and six days later, we arrived in Bowman, Wyoming, on a snowy January morning. We meant to make it to Canada, but winter stopped us. We were freezing, thirsty, and running out of fight.

We made our way through farms as Hop read fenceposts. "Here, this one."

"What's it mean?" I asked.

"It means unlikely."

"Really?"

"Bad odds are better than no odds." Hop looked at our red noses and cheeks. We had our hands tucked in our pockets, and our necks wrapped in threadbare scarves from a donation pile in Lincoln, Nebraska. "We have to stop, or we'll freeze to death."

Flurries slid with the wind off the pitched roof of the two-story house. Amber light twinkled from the frost covered windows.

Hop knocked on the door and wrapped an arm around each of us.

The woman gasped when she saw three kids standing on her doorstep.

"What in God's name..." She scanned our faces.

"We're traveling through," Hop said. "We can't go on. Do you have a barn or something we can sleep in for the night?"

Hands on her hips, she clicked her tongue. "You've been walking in this weather?"

"Yes, ma'am." Hop's eyes lowered to his feet.

"You damn fools will get yourselves killed." She hesitated while she inspected me and Red. "Get on in here."

Warmth spread over me like a hug. A fireplace as tall as Red radiated heat into the living room. Jewel-toned lights the size of strawberries dangled from a spindly Christmas tree. I walked over to it and ran my fingers along the strands of tinsel.

"You like my tree?" the woman asked.

"Yes. Very much." I hadn't seen a decorated tree since before Emily died. After that, seemed like an odd thing to do, cutting down a tree to drop sap on the wood floor, drying to a crisp near the stove as we ate onions stuffed with peanut butter for Christmas dinner.

"It's frivolous, but I'm a sucker for those twinkle lights," she said.

I pulled my hand away. Tucked it back in my pocket.

"The name's Mary. Mary Littleton. Come on." She led us to the kitchen, pulled out three chairs, and motioned for us to sit.

Caught somewhere between young life and old, Mary Littleton wore high-waisted pants and men's Red Wing boots. Hair in a low ponytail, her dark brown locks framed a two-inch wide streak of gray from part to tip.

"I may not smile often, but I hold no judgement past what's in my own hands," Mary said. "Cross me, and you'll regret it. I drink whisky for breakfast and sleep with a rifle on my pillow."

"Understood," Hop said.

"Good. Names, please?"

"I'm Magnolia, but you can call me Maggie."

"Welcome, Maggie." She eyed Red.

"At one time my name was Gracie, but I'll pop you one if you call me that. They call me Red, and it suits me fine."

Mary crossed her arms and stared. Red positioned her arms like a mirror image.

"Noted. Red it is." She stepped up to Hop. "And you?"

"Hop, ma'am."

"Hop. Like over a fence?"

"Like a hop farm," he said.

"Ah, now you're talking my language. I've brewed a few hops in my day." Mary scanned her eyes over the three of us. "I didn't cook for four, but we'll make do."

We sat around the rickety table in the kitchen as Mary spooned up mashed potatoes and sliced pork chops. "Can you all work a farm?"

"We won't be here that long," I said.

"Ah. You got big plans?"

"We're looking for Eleanor Roosevelt," Red said.

Mary spit her whisky with a sputtering laugh. "What now?"

I cleared my throat. "I know it sounds crazy. But she can help us."

"Okay. Crazy ideas are the only way we get anywhere in this life. Otherwise, we drown." She pointed her finger away from her glass directly at me. "You keep thinking crazy."

We ate, mostly in silence, until our bellies were full. Red watched Mary's every move. When Mary crossed her legs, so did Red. She mimicked her pulled back shoulders, while I watched them with the slightest twinge of pain in my heart.

"Thank you, Mary." Hop stood. "We'll see our way to the barn now."

"What kind of person would I be to put three kids in a freezing barn?"

"We thought you were unlikely to help us," I said.

"Ah, the fencepost." She placed her hands on her hips. "It's dangerous out here. A woman living alone. I make sure the drifters know to fear me."

Hop looked at the baseball bat leaned against the back door. "Seems to work."

"I don't allow men in this house. Only if I invite them," she said with a wink. After straightening her pants, she stepped up close to Hop. "What do you want with these girls?"

"I'm helping Maggie find her brother and Red's running from the law. I don't have a family, and it just seems like the right thing to do."

Silence settled over them. She pointed to the staircase. "Two rooms upstairs. Only rule is don't wake me up."

Mary stayed up late listening to the Victrola. Music vibrated up through the floorboards. Red and I shared a room and Hop took the other one. I watched the shadows from the snowfall dance across the rosebud wallpaper. When you're warm and full, it gives space for other things to bubble to the surface, things you usually ignore.

Red twitched three times, indicating she'd fallen into a deep sleep. I crept out of bed and into the hallway, turning the metal knob on Hop's door for a peek inside. He sat up, shirtless. His dark olive skin and lean chest muscles took my breath away. I stepped closer to the bed with hesitation, afraid to want him too much.

"Couldn't sleep?" he said.

The bed creaked as I sat down next to him. "Do you think I'm crazy for chasing after Eleanor?"

"I think we all need a little hope. Sometimes it's the parents we've never met, and sometimes it's the First Lady of the United States."

I swallowed, flicking my eyes away from his body, then back again. "Snow's here."

"Yep," he said as his feet hit the floor.

His reflection filled the window. Tall and lean, his shirtless torso radiated heat next to me. My heart quickened.

"Which means we'll be here for a while," I said. "Too cold to risk sleeping under the stars."

He placed his hand on my thigh. "I never let myself get too comfortable anywhere."

"It's for the best. People will just let you down."

"Your mother, she taught you that?"

"I guess. Not so much in words. It was in her eyes. I was wrong and to make the world right, I had to hate myself... like she hated me."

"Look at you, you've risked your life to save your brothers and Red. How could you be wrong when you do so many good things?"

"Who hates their own child?"

He looked me straight in the eyes and I tried to pull away, but he wouldn't let me. "I can tell you every second of every day how wrong she was. But until you believe it, she will still control you."

"Things were tolerable when my father was around."

"When did he leave?" Hop asked.

"A couple of years ago. The drinking..." I shook the memory away. "He couldn't stand to look at us anymore."

"That's his problem."

"I can't go around blaming other people. My parents didn't love me, that's all."

He rubbed my hair, ran his palm down my braid. "I think they didn't know how to love, Maggie."

Tension gripped every muscle.

Hop's soft lips kissed my shoulder. They stayed there, unmoving for a long while.

"I've always dreamt of knowing my parents because I envision them as loving and kind and filling a hole inside me that has been there as long as I can remember," he said.

"Question is, will they live up to your dreams?"

He pulled me in. Held me tight against his bare chest. "Maybe I don't need to find them," he said.

"What?"

He ran a finger over the curl of my bottom lip. "That black hole? It's fading. Every time I touch you, it finds a little light."

I couldn't tell him that his touch made me want to crawl back into the dark. I fought it every second because I wanted to be good. I wanted to love him the way he loved me.

I just didn't know how.

***

One month passed with minimal snow, but the cold rushed in so intensely it felt as if the world would just freeze and disappear. Mary read stories to Red and taught her about distilling, because, as we soon realized, Mary cooked up booze in her barn. Men came from miles around for her moonshine. She held a sort of spell over her customers. Wild and tough, she made them all blush.

Red stopped wearing her hat and pulled her hair into a ponytail just like Mary's. Her posture straightened, and she stopped tapping her leg. I had to swallow my jealousy. I was supposed to fix Red. I *needed* to save her.

One day in January, Mary threw a newspaper on the kitchen table. "Maybe she heard you."

"What are you talking about?" I said.

"Mrs. Eleanor Roosevelt started a daily column. *MyDay*. Seven days a week, she records her comings and goings and inner thoughts. It's inspiring, really. No First Lady has ever dared utter a sentence of her own, and this dame has more to say than her husband. I see why you look up to her."

Mrs. Roosevelt spoke of living in a fishbowl. "Few people are so poor that they do not have an inner life which feeds the real springs of thought and action. The really important thing about anyone is what they are and what they think and feel."

I didn't miss a word of Eleanor's *MyDay* column. She didn't live behind a curtain of money and power. She showed us her heart. I hadn't known women like her existed.

Hop and I spent the days cleaning and repairing things around the house. Carried water from the well and baked bread. Mary taught me how to can fruit and vegetables. A beautiful rhythm of life pulsed through each day in this warm, safe house.

At night I'd slip into bed with Hop, and we'd kiss and touch and talk about the future. A few times I thought we might do more, but every time I tensed, Hop would hug me until I relaxed, like he could read my body for clues.

One night, I curled into his chest and tucked my cold feet under his calves. "You think we can afford a wheat farm someday?"

"We can do anything we want." He kissed the top of my head.

"But the drought, and no money. Seems like a silly dream."

"No dreams are silly," Hop said. "We need something to hold on to. It can't stay like this forever. It just can't."

"If my life has taught me anything, it's that things can always get worse," I said.

"I think you're wrong. Look at us. I have a new dream to follow. You."

When he spoke like that, I wanted to curl up like a pill bug.

As if reading my mind, he said, "It's okay, you know. That you need time."

"Time?"

"You don't see us like I do. Not yet." He brushed my arm with the back of his fingers.

"I know I like being near you." I settled my cheek back into his chest, wiggling until I found the perfect curve.

Hop ran his hand down my braid. "And maybe right now, that's enough."

CHAPTER TWENTY-TWO

We became a family that winter, protected in Mary's old farmhouse. Like water, hope fed our thirst. Without a farm to tend to, our attention settled on telling stories and laughing and dreams for the future.

After three sleepy months of clinging winter, we welcomed the sunshine. Warm air coaxed green shoots from the soil and Mary taught Hop how to till and how to scythe the stems. How to create a healthy home for crops to grow. He listened to every word, telling me at night all that he'd learned that day.

In April, the weather turned on a dime. As if winter handed itself to summer, forgetting spring existed. The heat descended on us, and we lived for the moment the sun went down.

Hop and I tended to the hardy fruit trees that somehow survived. Mary brought us a tray of lemonade and sugar cookies. "Take a rest, you two."

We sat in the dirt and enjoyed the cool, sweet drink.

"Red is doing well," Mary said.

I looked away as she spoke.

"I think she could stay safe here. I think you all could."

We lowered our glasses.

"I know you all are running from something or towards something, but if you're tired of running, you can call this place home."

She stood and wiped the dirt from her pants, nodded, and returned to the house.

"Red sure seems happy here," Hop said.

"You suggesting we leave her?"

"What if we all stay?" he asked.

"You don't set up roots, remember? Wanderlust and all that."

"I like it here." He shrugged. "Mary's kind of like a mother."

Anger rose inside me like a wave. I couldn't stop it and I didn't understand it. "I don't need a mother. What I need is to find my brother and Eleanor Roosevelt and get her to save Red from the police."

"Why do you need to do all that?"

"I just have to, okay?" I turned away toward the empty field, but Hop held my arm.

"We're safe here, Maggie," he said.

"I can't..." Tears welled in my tired eyes. "I can't let go. Not yet."

"Okay. Okay." He pulled me into an embrace and held the back of my head. "We'll find Mrs. Roosevelt. We'll track her down and ask her to help us. And we'll find Johnny. I promise."

I cried into his chest as heat bloomed between our bodies. I wanted to believe that saving them would make me worthy. But deep inside, I feared nothing would.

***

That night I couldn't sleep. The heat pressed into my chest, making it hard to breathe. I sat at the kitchen table and mixed up a glass of milk. Footsteps in the hall. They weren't soft like Red's or eager like Hop's. They were deliberate and sharp.

"Evening, Mary."

She stepped out from behind the wall. "You're a perceptive one."

"Life has taught me."

"May I join you?" she asked.

I nodded and pushed the box of powdered milk across the table.

"No, I don't touch that stuff," she said with a grimace. As she pulled a flask from the top shelf, her silk pajama pants swooshed at her ankles. She sighed and settled into the chair, taking up space like a man would.

"Do you ever get lonely out here?" I asked.

"Nah, I've made a good life for myself."

"I sometimes wonder what it would be like to live alone," I said. "Out in the woods, surrounded by pine trees and silence. Where the pain of the world can't touch me."

"That's where you've got it wrong, Maggie." She took a swig of gin. "The pain of the world isn't out there. It's inside you. And it follows you everywhere you go."

"You've had a hard life too, then."

"Shit, haven't we all?"

"Don't things get easier?" I asked, naively hopeful.

"Time helps." She rested the flask on her thigh. "Love helps."

"Love?"

"Like the kind Hop has for you. That boy's got it bad."

"I'm afraid I'm just going to disappoint him. When he finally sees the real me, he'll never want to touch me again."

"Sometimes it takes someone else to show us we're wrong."

"You don't know me," I said.

"That's the thing about this life. We can never really know what's in someone's heart. But I can tell you that underneath all the hurt, I see a little family you've created of lost souls burning to patch up each other's wounds. And it fills me with hope."

"You've got a dying farm, a few acres of wheat, and dust storms ready to level this place. How do you find hope in anything?"

"It isn't something you find. It's there." She shrugged. "If you choose to see it."

"I try not to look forward. Every moment feels like a fight to hang on."

"Yeah, that's what childhood does to you," she said.

I shot her a surprised look.

"My father beat us with a belt most nights." She propped her elbows on the table, her wild brown hair falling around her shoulders. "On the surface I see your clear blue eyes, your blond braid yanked back from your face. You're all fight and fire. But I also see that little girl you try so hard to forget."

"I've never told you anything about my childhood."

"You didn't have to. Neither did Red." She leaned back and sipped the last of her flask. "As difficult as this sounds, you'll have to forgive them someday. Your parents. The anger you hold for them will eat away at you, and you'll never understand what it means to love yourself, let alone anyone else."

"What if I don't want to love myself?"

"I know that feeling, too. But let me tell you something." She knocked her knuckles twice on the table. "That is how you get back at them. Prove they were wrong about you."

"Eleanor Roosevelt says that learning to love is an education in itself."

"She's right. And no one teaches us that. You just have to start by opening your heart."

"What about you?"

She smiled and reached for her rifle. "I've loved several men in my life. It's magnificent, being with a man you burn for." She stood, slung the strap over her shoulder. "But nothing feels as wonderful as knowing no one will ever break you again because you've decided to be whole."

"I didn't know that was possible."

"There is no greater defiance than loving yourself." Winchester rested on her back, she padded her bare feet down the hall.

I took in the silence and the words of wise women who had felt something torn from the same cloth. Mary, Nurse Franny. I thought I was the only one. Turns out, we were all traveling a similar journey.

The kind that takes a lifetime.

***

One June morning we woke to a stifling heat. It bloomed from the ground and filled the house. My skin flushed pink and Red's cheeks glowed the color of her hair.

"We really have to go work the land in this heat?" I asked.

"Let's just water the crops." Hop wiped his handkerchief across his forehead, his dark skin flushed to an auburn glow. "Let's get this done. It shouldn't be this hot in spring."

We ate biscuits with apple butter that tasted like the sweet nectar of magic, eating together on the front porch as the hot wind rushed under the eaves of the old house. Glass bottles clanked in the distance as Mary worked in the barn to prepare the latest batch of moonshine. She used to travel with a milk wagon in the warmer months to slip by anyone enforcing prohibition. When those laws ended, she kept the practice, still selling liquor in her signature milk bottles.

We carried buckets from the creek to the rows of fragile wheat stalks, the sun beating down on our necks. By ten o'clock, the air felt like an oven.

"Red, you should go inside," I said. "It's too much out here."

She shook her head no. "Mary needs this crop."

I stopped at the base of an apple tree. A few buds poked out. Inside, the slightest pink just waiting to burst open. Through the piles of dust on the branches and little water, this little straggler had survived. I nearly cried.

A buzzing drifted on the wind. I swatted my hand, looking for a bee. I saw nothing, but across the field, Hop and Red stared at the sky like they heard it too.

The buzzing worsened, flapping so loud I had to cover my ears. A rolling wave of brown barreled toward us. Were these the dust clouds? Were we about to be buried in a pile of brown ash?

The bright yellow blaze of the sun darkened, and my skin turned cold. The black dust rolling in shimmered with a thousand flecks of light. Translucent silver fluttered through the darkness.

I cupped my hands over my eyes. "Red!"

Hop ran to her, dropping his bucket of precious water in the dirt. As he ran through the crops, the swarm of dust raced up behind him with such speed, faster than any of the trains we'd been on. It rolled and climbed into the sky like steam rising.

I ran toward Red from the other side, both of us trying to reach her. I screamed her name, but she froze, eyes to the sky.

The black cloud rolled up just as we slammed against her. Hop's arms around my shoulders, mine squeezed around his waist. We held Red in a cocoon between us to protect her from the silver dust.

It didn't knock us over or swallow us. It clung to our clothes. Burrowed into our hair. Climbed in our ears and up our legs. It fluttered under my dress, along my thighs. The dust moved with a frantic flapping.

I opened my eyes. What looked like a dust cloud turned out to be an explosion of grasshoppers. Thousands of them. The silver glitter turned out to be their translucent wings reflecting the sun's light.

Ravenous, they made their way through the farm. Through the clothes on the line, tearing a sheet into threads in a matter of seconds. They covered my face like a second skin and wiping them away only brought more.

The clattering reached deafening levels, like a thousand bottle caps dumped on concrete. The swarm shifted with the wind. Their wings snapped against my cheeks and neck. The heavy weight lifted, and they were back in the sky.

Devastation.

Dead insect shells littered the dirt as far as the eye could see. Jagged remnants of wheat stuck up from the ground like ravaged carcasses.

Red wiped the bugs from her face and danced around to shake them from her body.

I did the same. "What the hell was that?"

Shells crunched under our boots as we walked the rows of dead crops. The apple tree. The pink bud was nothing but a memory. Gone.

The barn door hung off its hinges, slapping against the wall. Inside, Mary stood silent, holding a broken milk glass, the remnants of alcohol in a pool at her feet.

Red pushed off me and ran into the barn. Tough, larger-than-life Mary cried as she looked around. Piles of dried wheat depleted in a matter of minutes.

Red embraced Mary. They cried together, rocking in unison. Hop's fingers laced through mine. But I didn't care about his touch right then. I wanted to be the one that Red cried to.

"It's all gone," Mary said. "Everything."

I walked down the rows where buds once glistened in spring sunlight, full of hope and promise for a better season, and now hundreds of wayward grasshopper shells baked in the heat.

I wondered if maybe the earth was being punished—farms dry as deserts, animals starved to death, dust clouds and grasshopper storms, families ruined. We were all alone in this wasteland searching for a home.

I shook my braid, and a few grasshoppers jingled to the ground. Clack-clack. The home we had built here had died. And it wasn't coming back.

***

"How did that happen?" I asked.

We sat once again at our kitchen table. I could still feel the grasshoppers vibrating on my skin.

"It's the heat and the drought," Mary said as she poured coffee. "No fungus to kill the eggs. In the dry soil, they explode. The swarm travels through, eating everything they touch."

"You get the feeling God is punishing us?" I asked.

"God's got nothing to do with it," Mary said. "We have to leave."

Red sighed. "Can't we rebuild, plant more crops?"

Mary closed her eyes. "No, there's nothing to rebuild."

"What now?" Red asked.

"I have a friend in New York. Taught me everything I know about distilling. He won't take us in, but he'll give us jobs."

"We leave, just like that?" Red stared at her with big eyes.

"That's how life works, dear," Mary said. "No time to wallow."

"New York?" I said.

"Yes. It's fabulous there. You'll love it."

I looked at Hop with a pleading stare.

"We'll be searching for Eleanor Roosevelt," he said. "That's what Magnolia wants."

I sensed pity in his voice, and it made me want to crawl in a hole and disappear. He didn't believe she could help us.

"You're certain that's what you want?" Mary bore her eyes straight through me.

"Johnny's gone. I can't think of anyone else who has the power to find him." My eyes flicked to Hop. "I need her."

"I see." Mary unscrewed the metal knob from her flask and took a swig. "You know, you're capable of all sorts of things."

"Not this." My eyes stung. I needed to find Eleanor Roosevelt. To help me, surely. But it was something more.

Mary watched me cry. "Okay." She slapped her hands on the table. "How do we find her?"

Hop leaned back, teetering on the back legs of the chair, and grabbed a stack of papers. "Here." He lay them on the tabletop. "She tells us every day where she is."

"I'll drive you anywhere you need to go. Then I take off for New York."

"Are you humoring me?" I asked.

Hesitating, her eyes narrowed. "I wish someone would have listened to my dreams when I was young."

"Even if they were foolish?"

"*Especially* if they're foolish. It's not about the outcome, Magnolia. It's about staying true to the part of yourself that loves something with your whole heart."

My whole heart. I didn't think I had one of those. I had a thready, weak mass trying to beat hard enough to pump blood and stay alive.

***

Mary spent the next day paying visits to clients who owed her money. She returned with a few handfuls of cash in a velvet bag. "All right, Red. It's time to fix that hair. We have to change your look."

Red flicked a lock forward. "Good riddance."

Mary's concoction of peroxide and ammonia nearly knocked me out. Red squirmed and shook as the bleach settled into her scalp.

I wanted to crawl out of my skin. "Should it hurt her?" I asked, chewing on my nails like Oscar used to do.

"It will, but only momentarily." Mary tightened her gloves.

As Red's hands trembled, my heart sped up. The stress built and tightened, and I had to blink my eyes to keep them from stinging. "This seems like a bad idea."

Hop pulled me away. "Come on, she'll be fine."

I resisted, but Mary nudged him to take me away. He led me to the porch swing, creaking in the still afternoon, overlooking the wheat graveyard.

"That smell must have been getting to you." Hop took a deep breath of clear air.

I tried to ignore the thumping in my head.

"I'm sad to leave." The roughness of his hand brushed my fingers. "You started to trust me here."

There's that word. Trust. He ran his hand along my braid.

"Something about being here, about Mary, made you feel you could rest your worries. That part of you that's so afraid seemed to soften."

I wanted to smack his hand. Scream at him to run away. But I didn't. The fear of losing him felt as great as the fear of having him.

I brought my hand to my braid. "This hair. I braid it for a reason."

"Easier, I would imagine."

"Easier would be to cut it off. No, the braid pulls at my scalp to remind me of what's important."

"I don't understand."

No, he wouldn't. So why would I tell him this?

"The day Emily died. My hair betrayed me."

He shook his head in confusion. "Your hair?"

"Yes."

He wanted to reach for me and hug me, but he knew better.

The memory burrowed open a gaping hole inside me. No choice but to climb in. "I should have been home by the time Emily woke."

He tilted his head.

"I took too long. I got..." I closed my eyes. "Distracted."

"What distracted you?"

I braced for the memory that rolled down on me like a runaway boulder down a hill.

"Mama used to brush and braid my hair. She didn't care how much I cried. She yanked so hard it gave me a headache. But it was the only time she touched me."

"Oh, Maggie."

I pushed away when he tried to hug me.

"After she tried to kill herself, her world stopped. I longed for the feeling of ripping tangles. For the few minutes she felt like a mother."

"You braid your hair so tight to remember your mother?" Hop said.

"No. I started wearing my hair down. I let it fall loose around my shoulders."

"What changed?"

"One day, a boy walked me home from school. I knew I should've run straight home. But he called me pretty. My hair belonged down, he said, not back in that childish braid. It felt nice to have someone notice me."

"What happened after that?"

"I lingered. We skipped rocks in the river and talked about his family. I figured I could be selfish. Just this once. My heartbeat, the sweat on my palms, the way my breath trembled. I didn't listen to the warnings that I shouldn't be there."

"Why couldn't you talk to a boy?"

"Mama's moods were unpredictable. Papa was drunk by noon every day. The kids needed me."

"You let yourself feel good. There's nothing wrong with that."

"That was the first and last time." I turned away, stopping the nausea that threatened to take over. "I told myself it would be all right. Mama seemed quiet that morning. No twitches. No lullabies muttered under her breath."

"But it wasn't okay, was it?"

"You ever have that feeling, like the world is whispering to you, warning you? My limbs tingled as I neared the house. I didn't even go inside. I knew to walk to the water. That's when I found Emily."

"Magnolia," Hop reached for my hand, "none of that was your fault."

"After that day, I pulled my hair back into the tightest braid my fingers could manage. Tight enough to hurt."

"You're afraid that if you let yourself feel good, something bad will happen."

"Yes."

Hop kissed my cheek, so gentle it felt like eyelashes fluttering on my skin. I let myself soften for a moment. Just one glorious, peaceful moment.

He started to say something, but Mary interrupted. "Sorry to disturb you two lovebirds. Check out the new and improved... Red."

Red stepped through the door, wide-legged pants and a tucked in blouse. Her flaming-red hair stripped of its color, washed with bleach, and now glowed a bright white. It shined on her green eyes.

She smiled. A sharp, witty smirk. "How do I look?" she asked, hands on her hips.

She no longer looked like Red. She looked like Emily. Right before she died.

CHAPTER TWENTY-THREE

Mary rummaged through her house packing, and Red stared at herself from different angles in the hallway mirror. Watching Red drift away filled me with a sickening pressure that grew and pushed on my insides.

Hop found excuses to be near me. I could feel he wanted to hug away all the fear. But if he pushed me, I would harden like clay in the sun.

"Arthurdale," I said as I threw the newspaper on the table.

"What is Arthurdale?" Mary asked.

"A homestead community in West Virginia. Eleanor Roosevelt started it for coal miners and farmers. She'll be there in two days."

"To get there in two days, we'd have to drive all night."

"We can take shifts," Hop said, eyes hopeful.

She splayed out a map, traced a red line from the middle of the country to the far-right edge. "I only have enough money for gas if I go straight from here to New York. I can take you to Pittsburgh. It looks to be less than an hour from there."

"Great." My thoughts swirled with images of Johnny's smile. His big dreams of becoming a pilot. His refusal to look at anything ugly and sad. Sweet kid had all the things I could never find.

I could feel our family shift and crack. No one else seemed to notice, but to me, it felt like an earthquake.

We said goodbye to Mary's farm, the brown earth unfolding in every direction. Headed east toward Fargo. Mary sang to the radio. Red laid her head in her lap, and Mary stroked her hair like a child. I turned away to watch the scenery.

"Mary, what'll happen to the farm?" Red asked.

"Oh, the government will probably come in. Take it over and sell it."

"That's not fair," she said.

"My grandmother used to say, 'Life isn't fair. It's how you meet the challenge.'"

"I never had a grandmother," Red said.

"Mine was quite a woman." Mary released a deep sigh. "She kept me believing in life. In my own worth. I spent a lot of time with her when I'd run away."

"If we have just one person in our world to help us see clearly, it seems possible to keep living," Hop said.

Tears lined his eyes.

Mary glanced in the mirror at him. "Who was yours?"

"A man named Shorty. He ran the camp for migrant workers at the hop farms. I met him the first time I travelled back to the Willamette Valley to find my parents. He remembered them. He told me my mother was petite and quiet. My father was lean and tall, like me. He recalled my mother's name as Lucinda. Lucy for short."

He turned to watch the passing fields, all dead and gone from dust and grasshopper storms.

"You never told me that," I said.

"That little information is all I have. He knew I would never find them, but he never said that. He let me live with him to save money so I could keep traveling and search for them. Year after year, I'd come back empty and sad. He smoked his pipe and listened to me dream up stories of what my parents would be like."

I felt myself scooting closer to him. Wanting to kiss his cheek the way he kissed mine. "What happened to him?" I asked.

"He died last year. I didn't find out until I made it to harvest this fall. He left me a note. It said, *You have to accept whatever comes, and the only important thing is that you meet it with the best you have to give.*"

"His last words to you were an Eleanor Roosevelt quote?"

He nodded, holding his lips stiff, so he didn't cry.

"That's why you help me find her," I said. "Why you don't question it."

"It makes me feel closer to him, somehow. Like it's a sign."

His longing. His yearning. I understood it.

I slid my hand across the seat. My fingers curved over his palm and laced through his. He paused, then looked at me with the hint of a smile. A deep ache grabbed me. What was this feeling? It hurt in places I'd never felt before. I thought there were no more places to find pain.

I reached for his shoulders and pulled him toward me. He hesitated, then lowered his head softly onto my lap. With a thumping heart, I ran my fingers through his hair. I realized he hadn't yet trusted me enough to share his secrets.

He was too busy trying to protect me.

***

We drove all day and stopped outside Minneapolis.

Over the hours, I stole glances at Hop. His strong face had softened, his eyes less intense. That moment of honesty in the car did something. It ripped me open and left me helpless and longing.

Mary pulled up to a shabby brownstone. Women hung out the doors like vines growing from the stoop. Their breasts spilled over the top of their dresses, sleeves draped off their shoulders, and their lips like ripe raspberries.

Red tapped her finger on the window in a rapid but quiet rhythm. She was young, but she was far from naive.

"An old friend runs this place. Whatever she has, she'll share with us." Mary positioned her hat and tucked a handgun into the back of her pants. She winked and stepped out of the car.

We followed her to the back door. I kept my eyes on Red, that bull-like face taking shape with intense eyes and flared nostrils.

"Are you all right?" I asked her.

She stared ahead like she didn't hear me. On instinct, I stroked her hair, but she yanked away.

A big, busty woman came to the door. High-heeled shoes and a shining brooch pinned to her dress. "Miss Mary, as I live and breathe."

"Hi, Bess. Any room for an old friend?"

"I could never say no to a gutsy old broad like you." She pulled her into a big hug. "Who do we have here?"

Mary leaned to whisper in her ear.

"Are you?" Bess stepped back and grabbed the newspaper. "You're the group they're looking for."

My stomach tightened.

"The papers say you all killed a man in Oklahoma. Stabbed him in the neck."

"They're after all of us now," I whispered to Hop.

Bess shoved the paper under her arm. "Keep yourselves hidden. Come in."

The kitchen overflowed with bottles. Beer, gin, sherry. Bowls of fruit and loaves of bread. Dirty champagne glasses with the kiss of red plastered on the rim.

"I don't know what happened in Oklahoma, but I know Mary. And I'd do anything to protect her. So, make yourselves at home. Stay out of the bar and don't bother our guests. Two empty rooms on the top floor."

We followed Mary up the staircase. Red tightened her fists then let them go, her breath trembling on every exhale.

We entered a sitting room with three doors. One a bathroom, and the other two bedrooms.

Hop reclined on the green velvet sofa, unbothered by the pantyhose drying over his head. "Nice place."

"Bess and I go way back," Mary said. "We ran a gambling hall years ago. Before money disappeared and booze became the devil's currency. She took up this new venture, but it wasn't my taste. I needed a change and met a farmer, so I followed him to North Dakota. I think Bess made the smarter choice."

Red stared out the window. The wavy glass reflected her blond hair. "What the hell kind of place is this?" she said.

A woman burst through the door carrying a silver tray. Her pink silk robe fell open at the top, revealing a lacy bra. A cigarette balanced on her drawn-on lips and a shiny silver pin held back unruly curls near her temple.

"Bess tells us you all need some food." She placed the tray on the coffee table. Cookies and milk and a bowl of grapes. She grabbed her cigarette and watched as we dove for the food. I hadn't realized how hungry I was. Red didn't want to come near the woman.

"What's the matter, honey? Cat got your tongue?"

Red's ribs tightened. "Do...do those men hurt you?"

We stopped eating and froze, afraid to move.

The girl dropped her cigarette and cocked her head. Put out the stub in the glass dish shaped like a daisy. "Honey, come here."

Red didn't move.

"Come on, now. I don't bite."

Red stepped forward hesitantly.

"I want you to see something." She pulled up her robe to reveal a long, jagged scar along her thigh. "My husband once pushed me down a flight of stairs in a drunken stupor."

Red's face fell flat.

"Nothing was harder than trying to be a wife." She led her to the window. "These men? They're lonely. Sad. So full of shame they can't hardly breathe. They long for a soft touch, someone to make them feel like a man. They tell me about their dreams, their fears. I help them. It gives me a purpose."

"But you let them touch you."

"Yes, I do. But it doesn't hurt me. It feels good."

Red flicked her hair back from her shoulder. "It can feel good?"

The moment she said this, I nearly threw up. Red and I had spent our lives fighting the terror of touch in one way or another.

"Your body is yours, kid." The woman lit up another cigarette and fussed with her hair. "Don't let anyone decide for you what to do with it."

Mary smiled at her and nodded.

"Time for my next customer." She held Red's shoulders, bent down face to face with her. "The day you take control of your body is the day you take control of your life."

The air softened. I think we all felt it. This girl, this prostitute, cut through our fears with the ease of a hot knife through butter.

"Who's first in the bath?" Mary asked.

We took turns in the clawfoot tub, the hot water washing away the dirt and grime of travel. The memories of grasshopper carcasses and the thick air of the brothel, full of smoke and perfume and spilled gin.

I stared in the mirror and pulled my hair into the tightest braid my fingers could manage. The familiar throb started at the base of my head, and I exhaled long and slow, letting the pain settle in.

I borrowed a robe from the clothes hanging in the bathroom. Mary and Red had fallen asleep in one room. I could hear Mary's subtle snoring through the closed door. Hop lay on the sofa, his hands behind his head. Clean and warm from the bath, his smile looked even more welcoming than usual. "You can take the room. Goodnight."

Since he'd told me about his parents, he seemed afraid to be near me. "Goodnight."

I walked to the bedroom, but I felt a pull back to him, like a magnet. He didn't look at me.

I closed the door as my heart thumped. My headache ate away at my resolve, and I leaned my forehead on the door. Our worry was similar. Fear of trust—fear of ourselves. My heart raced with the thought of his smooth, dark skin. That mop of black hair, so loose and wild. How he held me every night through the winter, never asking me to give more than my kisses.

I couldn't take it anymore.

I creaked the door open, and Hop stood right in front of me, startled. "I'm sorry, I wasn't following you." He backed away, but I reached for his hand.

The tightness that surrounded me unlocked like puzzle pieces. I pulled him into the room and shut the door. He looked down at me, his chest trembling with every heartbeat.

"I didn't think you wanted to be near me, after I told you all that stuff about my parents. It makes me sound weak."

I pulled his hand to my waist. "It's *why* I want you near me."

Our chests touched as we breathed, pressed together. He kissed under my chin, brushing his lips along the curve of my neck.

"It doesn't matter where we are," he said. "As long as you're near me."

With all the courage I could muster, I opened my eyes. He pulled the robe over my shoulder, his fingers running down my arm as his kisses grazed my scar. I untied the robe and let it fall to the floor. He watched but didn't grab me like I thought he would. A soft shiver rippled through me as he trailed his fingers along my stomach.

Suddenly, I couldn't bear the throbbing in my head, so I turned my back to him. "Take it out."

"Are you sure?"

"Take it out. I can't stand it."

He removed the tie at the bottom and loosened the sections one by one. The three bands unwound, unraveling years of pain. As the braid uncoiled, my mind opened. My heart joined, and by the time he reached the top of the braid, I was so hungry for him I thought I might die.

His fingers scratched along my scalp, loosening my wet hair. My whole body went numb, but I could still feel his touch on my head. He shook out the hair as it fell to my back.

Free.

The hair tickled my skin. I let out a laugh of pleasure and his body pressed into my back, hair pulled to the side in his soft grip, his lips again on the back of my neck.

He led me to the bed. Pressed his body over mine and I wanted to disappear under it. Just fall into his strong arms and never crawl out.

He stopped and looked at me. Ran his fingers down my breastbone and down the side of my hip. "Maggie, you're the most beautiful thing I've ever seen."

A small part of me wanted to push him away, but then I looked in his eyes and I remembered the vulnerable heart he showed me today. I grabbed his thick hair and pulled him to kiss me.

His body felt warm and heavy on me, every kiss deep and hungry. He took me to a place where my past couldn't touch me. When he pushed inside, I gasped, but then he breathed my name in my ear and the tension faded. He was so strong, yet he touched me with such softness, and that knowledge made me want him even more.

We rocked and moved together in a strange, beautiful rhythm that took over our bodies. Hips pressed into mine, he thrust and moved me in different ways, discovering what felt good for both of us. With my leg wrapped around his hip, he pressed into me until I moaned. My back arched, the need for him climbing to my head and limbs, sending love into every part of me. I dug my fingers into his shoulders and stifled a groan as tears leaked from the sides of my eyelids. And the world faded into the background.

I was safe.

That night we lay in the moonlight, his hands running through my free, wild hair. Our bodies naked, close.

Drops of sweat glistened on his forehead. He wiped them with the back of his hand. "I think it's time to kick the hobo life."

"All out of wanderlust?"

"Maybe. But I dream of seeing you on that wheat farm, smiling and content. Not a care in the world. I want to give that to you. You deserve more than a migrant worker, an orphan roaming the country in search of his parents."

"I'm roaming the country in search of Eleanor Roosevelt."

"To save your brothers," he said.

"Am I though?"

My words surprised me. Being close to someone for the first time had pulled some sort of cloak from my heart.

"What do you mean?" He ran his fingers through my hair as if to stop me from tightening back into a controlled braid.

"I've lost Oscar, and maybe Johnny too. Red cares more about Mary than me. We may never find Eleanor Roosevelt. And then what?"

"Then you make a new plan. With me by your side."

"I have to prove myself."

I suddenly became very aware of my nude body. His fingers on my skin. His eyes tangled in mine.

"You don't need to prove anything," he said. "You deserve to be happy."

"I'm beginning to see that."

"My hand hurt for months. After the snakebite, I mean."

I looked at him, confused. "I'm sure it did. It was a snakebite."

"No, you don't understand. It had healed. My body didn't know that though."

"What are you talking about?"

"They did surgery. The wound had become a scar, but my arm still throbbed and stung. Venom seemed to pulse through my veins like a rapid. The fangs weren't biting me anymore, but I was certain they were."

I scanned his arm, and the tightened, scarred flesh around his wrist.

"Even after the snake was gone, I felt him," Hop said.

"Why are you telling me this?"

"Because you were just a kid. The things your parents did and said cut through you like a snake's bite. Sharp and lethal. So painful that years later, your heart still feels that sting. Even when they're long gone."

"That makes me sound pathetic."

He kissed my cheek. "It makes you sound human."

I took a deep breath and rolled my eyes to the ceiling. "How did you get your arm to stop hurting?"

"I forgave the snake. He didn't know any better."

"Forgiveness feels like a dirty word," I said.

"Then try this." He wiped my hair from my eyes with the back of his middle finger and tucked it behind my ear. "Stop treating yourself the way she treated you. You can decide right now that she will no longer control you."

My skin tingled from his touch. "You say it like it's easy."

"Simple, yes. Easy, no."

I turned my back to him, and he settled into the curves of my body. He wrapped us in a blanket and drifted to sleep. I couldn't relax with images of Johnny and Oscar thumping in my mind. What if they were helpless, and crying for me? And here I was, letting Hop's touch soothe my weary soul. I waited until I heard his breathing soften and slow, his body twitch into sleep.

And then I grabbed a fistful of hair and yanked until it hurt.

CHAPTER TWENTY-FOUR

Bright rays of sun flooded the room the next morning. My hand reached for Hop but found only crumpled sheets with the faintest scent of his soap. My heart lurched. He changed his mind and decided I wasn't worth the fight. Too damaged.

I crept out to the sitting room.

"Morning, Maggie." Mary sipped her coffee. Red played with the makeup in the bathroom, trying on red lips and hair pins.

"Where..." I took a breath. "Where's Hop?"

"I'm right here." He appeared carrying a tray with two cups of coffee, a bowl of grapes and strawberries, and an omelet.

Mary smiled and handed me the paper. "He meant to bring you breakfast in bed," Mary said.

"Breakfast in bed? Is there such a thing?"

"For young lovers there is." She sighed and let herself wander back to a happy memory.

Hop presented the breakfast with a hopeful smile, sat next to me on the couch, and poured cream in the black coffee. He pushed the cup and saucer over as his other arm slid around my back.

"Morning," he said with a soft kiss on my temple.

My heart swelled and wanted to burst open. So why did dread crawl up my limbs? Was it my nature to find the bad, even when there wasn't any?

Don't let the fear break you.

Forcing a smile, I enjoyed the most wonderful food I had ever eaten. I opened the newspaper and flipped anxiously to *MyDay*.

Reedsville, West Va. Eleanor had friends for tea. Met with rural women. Had lunch at the State University where attendees asked her any question they wished. What wouldn't I give to have been one of those people? I longed to have her all to myself, just for a few minutes, so I could ask her my burning questions. Find the answers to letting go and discovering courage.

"Well?" Hop said. "What's she up to today?"

"She's at Arthurdale."

"Then we'll head out today," he said. "You'll finally get your chance to speak with her."

A deep ache tugged at me. We would have to say goodbye to Mary today.

Red hopped out of the bathroom looking much older, with crimson lips and matching cheeks. "I'm going downstairs. Some of the girls promised to show me how to style my hair."

"Red, we leave soon for West Virginia," I said.

"Oh." She glanced at Mary. "Uh, okay."

She would be sad to leave Mary, but she needed Eleanor Roosevelt's help as much as we did.

Mary set down her mug. "I'll pack my things." She closed her bedroom door.

"Today's the day," I said. "Think she'll be able to help us?"

"I don't know, Maggie. But I hope she's everything you want her to be."

What if she doesn't remember me? Or remembers and doesn't care? She has so many more important things to manage, what's one girl's lost brother going to mean to her?

Hop ran the back of his hand along my chin. "Hey, it's going to be okay. No matter what happens today, I'll be with you."

But how long would that last? What happens after he rescues me? I'd have nothing left to give him.

A screech from downstairs. I dropped the cup, shattering on the floor. "Red."

We jumped up and followed the screams.

"Get off me!"

Hop ran so fast he glided down the stairs, Mary and I following. In the kitchen, a man held Red by the wrists. Her red lipstick had been smeared across her lips. It looked like he had kissed her, and she fought him off.

"You heard the girl. Get away from her," Hop said.

I didn't understand why Hop wasn't pouncing on the man, knocking him unconscious. Then the man turned. On the counter next to him, a kitchen knife gleamed in the morning light.

"She's mine." The man's words sloshed around in his mouth. "You can't have her."

Red crumbled to the floor, but the man held her up. The skin around her wrists went white from the pressure of his hands.

"She isn't a prostitute. We're visitors here." I calmed my voice, like I used to do with my father.

Mary whispered, "I'll get my gun. It's upstairs."

"Of course she's not a prostitute!" the man said. "You can't talk about her that way."

"My friend just went to get her gun. Bess will stop at nothing to protect her house," I said.

"I need her," the man barked. "That hair. Those red lips." He flinched. "You left me for another man. How could you?"

Hop neared them, each step slow and deliberate. "Hey man, we can talk this out. Just let her go."

The man shook his head. Sweat dripped down his temples. His cheeks glowed like red apples. "No. I need my wife. I just need to feel close to her again."

"It's not her," Hop said. "She's not your wife."

Shuffling turned to steps down the stairs.

The man looked at the floor. Then, sensing Mary approach with a pistol, he panicked, pulled Red in front of him, and grabbed the blade. He shoved it to her throat. Red let out a helpless croak, too afraid to scream.

"If I can't have her, no one can."

His breathing grew rapid, his body tensed. He wasn't just drunk—he was having an episode, just like Mama used to have. The man's haunted, dark eyes didn't quite focus.

Bess barreled through in her nightgown, shotgun in hand. The man had two guns pointed straight at him and a skilled fighter ready to attack. He didn't seem to care.

"Go ahead and kill me. I've got nothing to live for, anyhow. All it'll take is one swipe of my hand, and she's done." He leaned to smell her hair. "Why couldn't you have stayed with me?" Tears glistened on his cornflower blue eyes. The exact color of my mother's. "I'm nothing without you."

Red closed her eyes in a trance. Again, she went silent.

"I know she hurt you." I focused on the man's eyes. "I understand your pain."

"No, you don't. You women, you don't care what happens to us. We have nothing, so everyone leaves us." He tightened his grip on the handle.

"The world is mad. All of it. We're all desperate and hopeless and nothing makes sense anymore, does it?" I slid my foot forward.

He wiped away tears with his elbow, but kept the knife against her throat.

"I feel that way too," I said.

"You do?"

"Sometimes, I want to end it all, just so the pain will stop."

"Yes." Tears streamed freely down his cheeks. "I see her everywhere, and chase her down the street only to find she's a ghost. I pay for time with the girls here, so I can forget about her. But today, here she was, waiting for me."

"I know it hurts. But she's gone. And we're the ones left to pick up the pieces."

"No. She's right here. I can feel her and smell her."

Red was gone, in another world. Her blank face against her white-blond hair made my body go numb with fear. "She's not a ghost. I'm right here."

He narrowed his eyes on me.

"I'm sorry for what I did to you," I said.

"No." He squeezed his eyes shut. "Don't lie to me!"

Red didn't move a muscle. I sensed Mary and Bess nearing him, stepping in line behind me as I approached.

"I wouldn't lie to you. I need you to let her go. She's just a ghost." I stepped closer and whispered again, "She's a ghost."

He closed his eyes and cried. His elbow dropped a bit, loosening his hold on her. I reached for his arm. It's not his fault. Pain breaks people.

His arm slid away, knife still gripped in his fist. I reached for Red and gently peeled her away. I handed her to Mary, but never let my other hand slip from his arm. "It's going to be all right. We can get through this."

He nodded and dropped both hands. I exhaled. Then he bared his teeth at me with a look of pure rage. The familiar hate flooded me with a warm sensation, something like comfort. It mesmerized me.

Let him take me.

As his hand neared me, I closed my eyes and prepared. But something shoved me. I floated, eyes devoured by the darkness of my eyelids. The ground's thud hardly rattled me. Had he killed me?

Grunts and yells tumbled around above me. A gunshot. Screams. I heard them but I couldn't feel a thing. Not a damn thing. Stuck in the darkness of my mind just as I imagined happened to Red when she fell silent. It felt good to be numb.

Something slid me across the floor. When I opened my eyes, Bess hovered, shaking me. I stared at her hair. The way it curled like a pasta noodle. Why did hair hold such power over us, I wondered?

A loud crash brought me back. I felt the floor and the back of my head thumped something fierce.

"You hit your head pretty hard," Bess said. "One of our customers is a doctor. He'll be here in a minute."

Then it all came back. Pain flooded my body. I shoved Bess off me and crawled to see Hop. Motionless, with blood pooled around his stomach. The man lay still next to him, crumpled, like castoff clothing.

A man in a brown suit and loosened tie knelt next to Hop. His bald head shined under the lights of the kitchen. A barely dressed woman watched, smoking her cigarette.

He rolled Hop side to side, tore his clothing, and pressed rags into his torso. Hop's face had drained to pale white.

I couldn't lose him.

The commotion settled. Everyone slid to the floor around me, exhausted.

"What happened?" I said.

"The man slashed Hop's abdomen," Mary said. "Bess shot at the window. Enough distraction that Hop swiped back. They're both alive, but they need a hospital."

The doctor slumped. He'd been interrupted during his time with a girl upstairs and was still out of breath and flushed. Shame spread over his face, into every wrinkle and pore. I didn't trust him. Not one bit.

"No hospital," I said. "They'll call the police."

"He needs medical attention," the doctor said, hand still on Hop's stomach.

Bess stepped forward. "Take them both to the hospital. You saw this happen on the street. He was in a drunken fit of rage and attacked Hop. The boy fought him off, and you rushed over to help."

"I can't risk myself like that." The doctor's skin turned a pale shade of green. "If anyone finds out I frequent this place, I'll be ruined."

The doctor was a coward. Unwilling to sacrifice himself. Pockets of pink reappeared on Red's cheeks.

"What happens when they wake? They'll tell a different story," the doctor said.

"This one's crazy," Bess said. "They'll see that right away." She gestured to Hop. "This one won't talk. Don't worry about him."

I felt sick. Out of options. A pounding spread from my head, down my neck and through my spine. I remembered this feeling. It thumped through my bones as I ran home. Right up until I found Em face down in the water.

My body screamed to be heard. *Hold him tighter*, it said. *Don't trust them*. But my mind said otherwise.

Mary laid a hand on my shoulder. "Maggie, we need to send them. Hop will die. You understand that, right?"

Everyone stared, as if the decision rested with me.

"The police. If they find out who he is, they'll arrest him. And I'll lose him."

"You'll lose him anyway," she said.

"There's no good choice, then."

"We have to trust the doctor."

Hop hadn't moved. Not a twitch. What if he died right here, in front of me? I would be irrecoverably damaged and never recover. "Fine."

Mary and Bess set to work. The half-naked girl brought the doctor's car around back.

The doctor knelt in front of me. "That's a nasty injury you've got there. Let me take a look." He reached for me, hands covered in Hop's blood.

"I'll be fine." I waited until he dropped his arm. "Just take care of Hop. Please."

"Despite what it looks like, I'm a good man. A good doctor."

He wore a gold band on his ring finger. A child's drawing taped to his doctor's bag. "I wonder if your wife and children think so."

His belly shifted as he stood. "Put some ice on that wound."

As they lifted Hop, he grunted. It was the best sound in the world. He was still with me. My fingers grazed his as they carried him to the car. He didn't open his eyes, but I swear I felt his hand try to hold mine.

Once they drove away, Mary said, "I'll get some ice, and we'll clean you up."

I walked over to Red and placed my hand on her knee. "You're going to be okay."

"I'm tired of this," she said.

She finally sounded her age. Like a teenager angry at the world.

"What does that mean?" I asked.

"It means that Gracie is dead. I'm a new girl now. I'll carry a gun and learn to fight. Make the right friends who can protect me. No man gets to control me ever again."

I reached for her hand. "Red, I—"

She swiped it away. "I don't want to be called Red anymore. She's gone too."

"What do you want to be called?"

"My name is Athena," she said.

"Like the Greek goddess?"

"Mary's been reading Greek mythology stories. Athena's father tried to kill her, but she rose, powerful and smart."

"Okay, Athena." She didn't even want the name I gave her.

Mary led me upstairs. She cleaned my wound and handed me ice chips wrapped in a cloth.

"Red wants to change her name," I said.

"Athena, I presume?" she said with a smile.

"I'm afraid she's chasing the wrong things."

"What are the right things, Maggie?"

"Sacrifice. Helping others. That's how we heal. We prove ourselves worthy."

Mary gave me a look of such pity, it made me sick. "Maybe she already feels worthy."

"Are you saying I'm not?" I sat tall and rigid.

She handed me the newspaper. Eleanor Roosevelt's *MyDay*. "I'm saying we all heal in different ways. Let her be Athena. Let her feel powerful and free."

"Let her go, is what you're saying."

"It's not really about saving her, I think. You're afraid to lose her. And Hop. And your brothers."

"Of course, I am." Tears pressed into the back of my eyes, the deep gnawing pain of truth calling for my attention.

"You can't control life," Mary said. "People, tragedy, love. It's all out of our control."

"No, it's not." If I didn't have control, I had nothing.

She placed her hand gently on mine. "You couldn't have made her love you. She wasn't capable."

"Who, Red?"

"No, your mother."

CHAPTER TWENTY-FIVE

Mary's words had ripped me open, and I couldn't find a way to close myself back up. The lights were too bright and the sounds too loud. The world was too much.

A gnawing ache pounding through my head worse than any braid I could tie. Around midnight, I stumbled downstairs to the light in the kitchen. Bess and Mary and Red sat around the counter, bags at their feet.

"What's going on?"

"Magnolia, please sit." Mary pulled out a chair next to her.

"Is it Hop? Did he..." I couldn't find the strength to finish my sentence.

"He's fine," Bess said. "They did surgery. He'll need some time, but he'll live."

Relief washed over me. "And the crazy man?"

"He's alive too. The doctor told them the story we concocted. A fight on the street. Drunk ramblings about his wife."

"Then why do you look like something terrible has happened?"

They all diverted their eyes.

"A policeman came here today," Bess said.

"What did he want?"

She ran her tongue across her lips, buying time before she threw a grenade at me. "He asked about reports of a gunshot."

"There's still a hole in the window," I said.

"Yes. I told them a patron got unruly and grabbed a girl, so I shot the window to scare him off."

"Did he believe it?"

"No. He told me about an Italian boy in the hospital being treated for a stab wound. They suspected him of trying to kill a man brought in at the same time. Wanted to know if we intervened."

"Why do they think it was Hop's fault?"

"Because he matches the description of the Italian boy involved in a murder at a hobo camp in Oklahoma."

Memories of that day fluttered through me. The way that man touched me. How Hop had to watch. How Red saved us all by killing him.

"Now they're looking for a redhead and a blond with a braid," Bess said.

"It's only a matter of time before they put it all together and come for us," Red said.

"Okay, we'll go to West Virginia tonight. I'll find Eleanor Roosevelt. She can help us." I realized how ridiculous this sounded. But I couldn't seem to let go of her. I needed to ask for her help. To see if she would care.

"I know you need to find her... and your brother," Red said. "But I can't go with you. I'm going with Mary to New York."

"You're leaving? Hop almost died saving you." I wanted to slap her.

"No, he almost died saving *you*."

"So, you forget everything we did for you? Now you're blond and Greek and who needs the stupid orphan kids who risked their lives to help you."

"I don't think you're stupid. I think you're the bravest person I've ever met."

My face flushed hot. "You were frozen with fear. Bruised, barefoot. Afraid to speak. We brought you back from the edge of sanity after all those drugs they fed you."

"I'll never forget your kindness. But, Maggie, I brought myself back. I decided to speak and fight and trust."

"No, you can't do this." I scrambled to find words that would hold her here—close, where I could protect her.

"I'm going to New York," she said again.

"And let Hop take the fall for what you did in Oklahoma? You're selfish."

She placed her hand on mine. "Emily's death wasn't your fault, and the boys getting sent to orphanages wasn't your fault. You don't have to prove anything."

Tightness gripped my throat. I wanted to scream at her for leaving us.

"We're starting a new life in a new city. I would tell you to come with us, but I think you're meant to stay and fight for Hop."

How could this child see the world so clearly? "I can't say goodbye," I whispered.

She hugged me, tight and firm. "It's not goodbye, Maggie. It's never goodbye."

They reached for their bags. I wanted to grab them and chain them to the chairs. Force them to stay with me. Force them to love me.

But I couldn't.

Mary was right. We couldn't control life or people, and I was nearly out of the strength to try.

Mary brought me into her arms as I cried on her shoulder. Her neck warmed my cheek.

"I hope you find what you're looking for," she said. "I really, really do."

"And if I don't?"

"Then you'll come out stronger on the other side. As long as you believe in the beauty of your dreams."

She used Eleanor's words to soften my anger, and it worked. But I wasn't ready to listen.

"Here." Mary handed me an envelope.

"What's this?"

"A parting gift from both of us. But I have one request. Go find Eleanor Roosevelt. Find your idol, and then you may open this."

"Okay. I promise."

They slung their bags over their shoulders, and Mary tucked her gun in the waist of her pants.

"Goodbye, Red. I mean... Athena." The words felt heavy, like I couldn't get them out without a shove.

Red hugged me. Quickly, tightly.

"I could ask you to come with us. Save yourself and forget Hop," she said. "But something tells me you'll hang on. Until you both find yourselves in a field of golden wheat, laughing children all around you. And I'll dream that for you every day of my life."

My knees wanted to buckle.

Mary kissed my cheek. "Bess has our address if you ever need me. But I have a feeling you and Hop have your own future to build."

I watched them drive away, taillights disappearing into the night, gone forever.

Balmy air kissed my cheeks. Silence. Not like back home with the rustling pines and cicadas flicking their wings. Black, still, unending silence. I thought of Mama underground, mouth and nose filled with dirt. Stuck in the past with no way out.

I tried. I failed.

Back inside, Bess handed me a five-dollar bill. "Here. Take the train to West Virginia. One leaves at six am. Call here and I'll update you about Hop."

"Thank you, Bess."

"This is a tough world we live in," she said. "But I'd like to believe there's a woman out there able to help all you wild-eyed dreamers. I read her *MyDay* column. She strikes me as a kind woman with a tongue like a knife. Her power lies in the goodness of her heart."

"Yes, that does sound like her," I said.

"It sounds like someone else I know."

I folded the bill and placed it in my pocket. "Not yet. But I hope someday."

I started up the stairs. "Bess, how did the police know Hop was in the hospital?"

She looked down. "The doctor told them."

"I knew he would betray us."

"How did you know?"

"It was in his eyes. The sweat on his brow, his uncomfortable fidgeting."

"You certainly can read people. Makes it hard to trust, doesn't it?" she said.

"Trust is dangerous."

"Sometimes. But without it we'd have nothing to live for. Hop's alive. Now fight like hell to get him back."

***

The sun rose above the rugged mountains as we rolled south into West Virginia. Trees packed the hillsides with blue-green waves of foliage and low hanging mist. I watched the scenery from the window of a train instead of an open freight car. Men in suits read newspapers, surrounded by women with smart hats and dresses. The air didn't flow across my face and the closed windows muffled the sounds of the tracks. It didn't fill me with exhilaration like riding the rails, but I was nonetheless brimming with anticipation.

I pulled out the paper someone had tucked in the next seat. *MyDay April 8, 1936*. Eleanor went to a homesteader's dance, then a coal miner's house. "Covered in soot, no matter how much you scrubbed," she said. "But in a dishpan grew four narcissus bulbs, two in bloom." She took a picture with the little girl of the house and discussed quilting patterns with the mother.

It made me wonder how a family can live in coal soot, breathing in black dust, scraping by on government dollars, and still bother to place flowers in a dishpan.

Hidden by a brown haze, little towns popped up along the train's path. Old churches and a smattering of houses. It always seemed that wherever I headed looked the same as where I came from.

The train approached Reedsville, just a five-minute walk from Arthurdale. My heart raced as I thought about Johnny and Oscar and Hop. Here I was, so close to discovering if people truly care. What would happen when I found the answer?

The train brakes screeched as we crept into the station. People gathered on the platform, waving their hats and smiling. Quite a crowd for early morning.

I pushed through the people to see what the commotion was. A man in a black suit and sunglasses held out his hand. "Stop there, miss."

"Why? Can't I walk to Arthurdale?"

Then, out from a black car, stepped Eleanor Roosevelt. Tall, elegant. She smiled and waved as she passed.

The man kept his eyes on me, stepping to block me when I lunged forward.

"But I need to see her. Please, let me by."

"Sorry, miss."

The woman next to me seemed unaware of my frantic need to reach Mrs. Roosevelt. "Look at that floral dress," she said. "That dame sure has style."

"I don't care about her dress. When is she coming back?"

"Not sure." She waved her miniature American flag and smiled. "She's on her way back to Washington, DC. She was so lovely."

My shoulders sank. "You met her?"

"I sure did."

I bobbed side to side to watch Mrs. Roosevelt greet the crowd. I thought she might have caught my eye, so I waved and yelled her name. But so did everyone else. When she held the handle and stepped into the train car, I knew it was over.

Sharp tears poked the back of my eyes, and I slunk away as the crowd settled. At the end of the train platform, I lowered onto a bench, head in my hands.

A voice appeared. "Hey, don't be so sad. She'll be back. This entire town is because of her."

I rubbed my eyes until they hurt. "I don't live here. I traveled from... well, everywhere, just to see her."

The woman lowered her flag and sat next to me. "My little girl has dreamed of meeting her for years. And a few days ago, Eleanor Roosevelt walked into our house and took a picture with her. Miracles do happen."

"You're the one with the flower bulbs in a dishpan."

"Oh, you read that! Well, we're just tickled pink to be included in *MyDay*. We'll live on forever in her writings."

I sputtered out a pathetic, accepting laugh. What a stupid girl I'd been. "Silly as it sounds, I need her help."

"You can write to her. She answers some of her letters," the woman said hopefully.

"There's no time."

"I'm not sure what sort of trouble you're in but my mama used to always say, 'Be good. And if you can't be good, be smart.'"

"What does that mean?" I asked.

"It means you should try your damndest to do the right thing. And when that fails, use your wits to find another way. Just don't get caught." With a wink, she rose and straightened her dress.

"Ma'am?"

"Yes?"

"Why the flower bulbs? I mean, when your house is covered in black soot, what's the point?"

She sighed. "When we're past all this misery, I don't want to have forgotten what joy feels like."

She walked off as the train whistled rolled past me. I stood at the edge of the platform, watching the windows flick past. In the last car, Eleanor Roosevelt sat at the window and smiled. She caught my eye and all I could do was raise my hand, still in the air.

She returned the gesture. We held that position for a fleeting moment before the train whooshed past.

Eleanor was gone. Again.

***

At a lonely payphone booth inside the train station, I dialed Bess's number. "Hi, it's Magnolia."

"Oh, hello dear. Any luck in West Virginia?"

"No."

"Oh, I'm so sorry."

"How's Hop?" I asked.

She hesitated. "Maggie, they've arrested him."

"Oh." An ache burrowed into my belly.

"He's still in the hospital. but police are guarding the door. No one can see him."

"What's the charge?"

"The stabbing in Oklahoma," she said.

"Dammit." I held the phone to my forehead and felt the ground shift under me. "He didn't even do it. He never hurt that man."

"But he's telling the police that he did."

"What?"

"He confessed," Bess said. "Once he heals, they'll send him to Oklahoma and charge him with murder."

I couldn't speak.

Bess muttered my name a few times, and I simply hung up. The hot glass rubbed against my back as I slid to the floor. A large clock on the wall ticked down the seconds. The heat rose from the ground and sent beads of sweat down my temples.

What now?

Then I remembered Mary's envelope. I pulled it out and examined it. With a sigh, I opened the letter.

Magnolia,

I have never met a woman so determined. So unaware of her own strengths. The one thing that holds you back is forgiveness. For others, but mostly for yourself. I've been where you are. The anger, the unrelenting pain.

I know that somewhere in your future you will have a moment. A reckoning, when all your fight shows itself for the fragile veil it is.

I hope this letter follows your meeting with Eleanor Roosevelt and that it was everything you hoped it would be. In case it wasn't, I wanted to leave you with a parting gift. Something to show you how women can do amazing things when we believe in each other.

I called the orphanages in Colorado until I found the one that housed a boy with rickets named Johnny Parker. I told them I was his aunt and I've hired a lawyer to charge them with kidnapping. They adopted him out illegally with no paperwork. I threatened to remove her own children from her custody, to rip them from their family the way she had done to Johnny and countless others. She conceded. Johnny's in Dallas, Texas. 90 Primrose Ct.

So please, finish out this journey. Take help from those along the way, and never forget that Athena and I love you. For everything your family stole from you, let people like us give a little back.

-Mary

I placed Mary's letter in my bag next to Eleanor Roosevelt's as tears streamed down my cheeks.

Looks like I was headed to Texas.

CHAPTER TWENTY-SIX

It took me three days to reach Dallas. I had enough money left to buy a passenger ticket, but the thrill of riding in an open freight car called to me. I thought about how terrified I felt on that first freight train out of Bend. Now I knew how to tell if a train was traveling the right speed, where to grab the railing, and which flags indicated long distance trips.

Would Johnny really be here? What would I do if I found him? Horrible visions had crawled around inside my brain for ten months, it was hard to imagine what would be real or imaginary.

A heavy ball rolled around inside my stomach as I approached Primrose Ct. on the outskirts of the city. Pretty white fences around houses and new cars parked along the street. I was grateful Johnny wasn't on a dusty farm somewhere, forced to work the land. But even nice houses can deceive.

I walked slowly, scanning addresses and peering through windows. Then I saw it. Rocks arranged in a display of stars.

"Johnny," I whispered.

My legs crumbled, and I reached out to touch the stones, trying to feel the memory of my brother's hands. A path that swirled and danced. I imagined flecks of starlight glinting off them, floating golden sparks into the sky, beckoning for me. Johnny lit my way home, just as he did on Mama's grave.

I sat on my knees until they were numb, wondering what to do. A tall boy stepped out the front door.

Johnny.

His round cheeks had thinned to angular features and on his nose, a dusting of freckles like mine. Blond hair in a clean cut, and nearly straight legs. He jumped off the step like a regular kid, gliding a toy airplane through the air. He took my breath away.

I'd dreamt of how to save him. How to rescue him from the misery of adoption. I hadn't imagined he would be *happy*.

I considered walking away. Drifting into the hot afternoon like a dust cloud. But I needed him to know that I loved him and that I tried. It took everything in me. I rose slowly, grasping the fence posts to prevent my knees from faltering.

"Johnny."

He lowered the plane to his side. Waiting to see if his imagination had played tricks, his head tilted, and he waited for another word.

"It's me," I choked out.

He turned around and froze, staring at a ghost. Maybe he had forgotten me like Oscar. Maybe he hated me.

He stepped hesitantly to the fence and examined my face. Tears rested on my lower lids, and I couldn't find words.

"Maggie?"

Yes. Yes, it's me, I wanted to shout. But my throat wouldn't move, my lips frozen. The tears though, those rolled freely down my cheeks.

"They told me you were dead."

"What?" I managed to say.

"The orphanage. I asked when you would come for me, and they told me you had died."

I gripped the fence with both hands, feeling like I might faint. He waited for me. He had to grieve my death. Alone.

I wanted to tell him they lied to me too, but I swallowed that need and held tight to protect his fragile heart.

"No, I didn't die. I fought to find you. I'm sorry it took so long, but I'm here now."

He turned to look at his house.

"I can take you away. We can find a new home and..."

"Oscar?" he asked.

I nodded and collected myself. "Oscar. He's... well, he's in a nice place with friends who can help him feel safe."

"I guess that's good." His gaze trailed to his feet. "I miss him."

"I miss him too, buddy."

"You never came for me." His eyes rimmed red.

"I'm so sorry." I inhaled a shaky breath. "I tried so hard to find you."

"It was easier when I thought you were dead." He met my eyes. "Maybe that's why they told me that."

I wanted to die—a painful, torturous death for what I put them through. "That's all over now."

He bent down to move a rock back into place at the point of a star. "I believed you would save us."

"I rode freight trains and threatened the orphanage and stole food just to find you. I need you to know that I tried. With everything in me, I tried."

He stood, rubbing the back of his neck. "And now you're here."

Thoughts sprang to my mind of promises I could make and hugs I could smother him with. I could teach him to hop freights and travel the country. He was right here, close enough to hold. But I asked him the only question that mattered. "Are you happy here?"

"Yes, I am. My father is a lawyer. He reads me books and teaches me about airplanes. My mother bakes the best pies."

My insides burned like a slow bleed. He had a life and was better off without me. "Your legs. They're healed."

"Mostly. Malnutrition, they called it. My parents had me see a doctor. They stuffed me with food and had me do lots of exercise. I can run now."

"That's great. I'm so happy for you."

"I have a little sister. She's annoying, but I love her."

I released a teary laugh. "Yeah, well, us sisters mean well. Even when we disappoint you."

He didn't return the laugh. "It was awful, you know. Living in that orphanage," he said.

I rolled my eyes to the sky. "I'm so sorry."

"They were so mean. They shaved our heads and made me stand for hours, even when my legs hurt. They locked me in a room alone when I'd cry."

I reached for him, but he pulled away. "I hated you for leaving me."

"I'll never forgive myself." I wanted to hug him so badly it hurt. I knew I did everything I could have, but in the end none of that mattered.

The door opened, and a smiling woman emerged. Curled hair and rosy, pink cheeks. Johnny's mother.

"Hello," she said as she wrapped her arm around Johnny. "Can I help you?"

"Oh, I was just... admiring these rock stars."

"Yes, our little John just loves them. Draws them everywhere."

I broke into a mess of tears. I couldn't stop it.

"Oh, darling, are you all right?"

I waved her away. "I'm fine. It just reminds me of my brother. I lost him recently."

Her eyes softened, pity stretching across her face. "I'm sorry. It can be so painful to lose someone."

"I hate myself for disappointing him. For not being the sister he needed."

Johnny's bottom lip quivered and he looked to his shoes.

"Oh, well, if there is one thing I believe, it's that the heart knows love," the woman said. "I bet he knew how much you loved him."

"I hope so."

"Would you like to come inside? I made a fresh batch of cookies."

"No, thank you. I should be on my way."

Johnny wouldn't meet my eyes. He held his mother's hand.

"You have a lovely boy here," I said. "You've done a good job with him."

"Thank you. Be kind to yourself," she said. "We're all fighting some impossible times."

"Yes, we are."

I turned toward the sun hanging low in the sky, its brightness sharpening the sting in my eyes from crying. I heard his mother say to wash up for supper and that his sister needed him.

I walked past a coop in a large backyard where chickens clucked in circles. Above their heads, a board with a piece of chalk hung from a string. Under each number, tally marks, counting eggs produced by each one. Their usefulness determined if they would live another day or find their necks snapped in half.

I closed my eyes and let the grief pour through every crack.

"Maggie."

Johnny's voice could always break me. I gathered myself and turned to face him. He had followed me down the street.

We stared at each other. He cupped his hand to shade his eyes, watching a mourning dove fly overhead. He dropped his arm and looked at me. "I forgive you," he said.

I kneeled on the ground and held out my arms. He ran, crashing into me. His hair smelled of powder and soap, and I buried my face in his neck to take in his new smell.

"Johnny, the rock stars. Were they for me? Were you hoping I would come back?"

"They were for you, but not to bring you back." He wiped his eyes. "They were to bring you light so you wouldn't be so sad anymore."

He wanted to heal me.

"I know how mean Mama was to you. You never deserved it. Oscar and I looked up to you so much because of how much you loved us."

"I promise to stop being so angry. I will try to be kind to myself. Just like your mother said."

"I love you, Maggie."

"I love you to the stars and back."

"Will I ever see you again?" he asked.

"Yes. I'll tell your mother the truth of who I am and ask if I can send you letters."

"I'll tell her how much I want that."

He squeezed me one last time. I held the back of his shirt balled in my fist, pretending I'd never let go, though I knew I would.

He pulled away. "What will you do now?"

"I honestly don't know." His eyes redden so I gathered any flecks of strength I had left. "I'll figure it out, Johnny. I always do."

"Bye, Mags."

"Goodbye, Pilot Parker."

Everything ended up as it should be.

He ran to his yard. To his baby sister and his new life.

We had a lifetime of heartache to overcome. At least now Johnny had a fighting chance. Letting him go was the most loving, motherly thing I could have done.

And it hurt like hell.

***

I'd lost the boys. Failed everyone. What a fool I'd been to think Eleanor Roosevelt could save us. No one could.

I sat on a rock near the freight yard, watching the sunset. Another state. Another splash of color. This one glistened a blue gray with streaks of purple.

I could kill myself. Leave the world and stop the pain. But I didn't have it in me. Too much anger, maybe.

Hop was in custody. Oscar was in an orphan asylum with no memory of me, and Johnny could finally walk because in his world, I had died. Everyone would be better off if walked into the darkness alone. If I stopped letting people in, I would stop hurting them. It would stop hurting me.

So, on that rock, I decided to spend my life watching sunsets. No home, no wheat fields, no laughing children. Just myself and my memories, far away from the pain of the world.

Mama, you win. I'm worthless.

A strange relief rippled through me. I tightened my braid so hard it pulled my eyes back. The pain felt good. Tangible. Reliable.

I hopped on the first freight car. I didn't know where it was going, and I didn't care.

My feet dangled off the car as the train rumbled, preparing to fly me away. Relief set in when I thought about my empty future. The joy of never loving anyone again.

The train rolled forward as the whistle screamed into the warm amber light. The fields glowed soft and dreamy through my teary eyes.

As the train rolled out of the yard, a few men jumped from the bushes and ran along the tracks. They probably all had families that tugged at their heartstrings. Filled them with shame and regret. I pitied them.

One grabbed the rail and landed his thick black boots on the metal floor inside my car. He removed his hat and stared at me.

Shock gripped my entire body.

"Papa?"

CHAPTER TWENTY-SEVEN

The train rattled my father side to side. He shuffled his feet to steady himself, but his face remained frozen.

"Papa, it's me." I stood and pulled my braid over my shoulder.

"No," he muttered. "Couldn't be."

The tall, smiling father from my youth had withered into a hardened migrant worker. Worn away to a rigid, thinned skeleton. Wrinkles puckered his eyes.

"I never thought I'd see you again." I wanted him to throw his arms around me, weep, and declare himself a father again. "It's been nearly three years." I remembered a missed birthday. "I guess I'm eighteen now."

"Magnolia?" he squeaked out.

"Yes, Papa. It's me."

"Why aren't you home, taking care of your mother?"

I braced myself on the wall of the car. I hadn't thought I would ever have to explain myself. He was supposed to remain a memory forever. "She died."

His face broke out of shock, disappointment setting in. I wondered if he would jump off that moving train.

"She... died? How?"

I didn't want to talk about this. I wanted to hurl those memories off a cliff and watch them shatter into a thousand pieces. The view was pretty. A drizzle of rain had turned the world to color again, lighting the plains with a touch of green.

"Magnolia, please tell me."

I kept my eyes on the flat slope of land whirring past us. "After you left, she cried and yelled every night. She laid in bed so long her skin broke open into sores. Then the cough and fever set in."

"Oh my God." He sounded like he was going to cry.

It filled me with rage. I turned to face him so I could see his shame. "She just... stayed in bed?"

"You betrayed us. The pain tore her apart, starting with her heart and ending at her skin."

He removed his hat and rubbed his eyes to stop the tears. "Oh, sweetheart."

He wasn't referring to me.

"Johnny had rickets. His bones twisted like oak branches, and Oscar finally became the emotional mess Mama made him to be. If you care to know what happened to them after you abandoned us."

"I did what I had to do."

"All these years I dreamed of you coming back. I imagined the apologies. The pleading. But you aren't sorry at all, are you?"

"That's why I left. You needed me to be a different father. One I could never be."

"It's my fault you left? Because I needed a parent?" My stomach thumped.

"You didn't need shit. You knew how to hunt and fish and cook. You sang the kids lullabies. I knew the family would be better under your care than mine."

"You made me that way. I had to be responsible because you were never home and when you were you were so drunk, you'd piss yourself." My rage was too strong for sympathy.

His face turned red. "I stopped drinking."

"I don't care. You left us with that hateful woman." I realized just how much anger I carried for them. How much I wanted to scream it.

"She wasn't always that way." He slumped against the wall, slid to the ground, and rested his head in his hand.

"My first memory is her throwing a can of beans at my face."

"I mean... before you."

Few things in my life had the power to level me. Papa did it in two words. "I turned her evil?"

"It wasn't you. It was what you represented."

"I was a baby that never asked to be born."

"Sit. Please."

I had to talk to my legs. Tell them not to throw my body onto the tracks. I just wanted the pain to stop. But I lowered myself to the edge and dangled my feet out. It reminded me of Hop, and I ached for him.

"Your mother used to sing and smile. Those laugh lines were there for a reason. She had fits of rage sometimes. And days when she couldn't stop crying. I could always hold her and tell her I loved her, and she would come out of it. I liked feeling needed." He closed his eyes.

"She hated me."

"When she was a child, her mother took her to an orphanage, but kept her baby brother."

"What?" I sifted through my memories. "I don't remember hearing that."

"She tried to forget it ever happened. They had no money, so she dropped her off at the steps of an orphanage when she was ten. When your mother begged her to stay, the woman shoved her to the ground. Told her it was better that way."

A little egg cracked open inside me. Something I had never once felt for my mother—pity.

"Her mother never came back, and I married her when she was seventeen. She was a runaway, singing in saloons with strange men grabbing at her. It pained me to see this beautiful young girl so hurt and broken."

"You tried to save her."

"The fits and temper got worse after you were born. My little Magnolia, blond, willful. A force to be reckoned with. It hurt her too much to look at you."

"She said that?"

"No. She didn't have to."

"That's why she loved the boys," I said. "They were the brother taken from her. The little boy she could finally love."

"I always had a soft spot for you, my beautiful, brave daughter. I thought there was enough to go around, but she didn't agree."

My whole body shook in a tightened tremble. "You let her hate me."

"I'm sorry, Maggie. With your steel-blue eyes and tough demeanor, I thought you were stronger than I was."

"I was a kid."

"I see that now. I was so desperate and drunk all the time. All I could see was how much better you'd be without me. I failed everyone."

"No. You don't get to feel sorry for yourself. I had to feed the family with whatever I could shoot. I cleaned Mama's bed sores and stopped her from banging her head against the wall. I stroked Oscar's hand after the nightmares. Mama died because I couldn't save her. And the house burned down, and the boys got sent to an orphanage, and I killed Emily!"

My body collapsed into a tight ball.

"You didn't kill Emily," Papa said.

"Yes, I did." Tears gripped me so tightly I had trouble breathing. "I left her alone with Mama when I knew I shouldn't have. I stayed too long because a boy flirted with me. It was all *me*."

"Magnolia, she went down to the water to look for rocks. They found them in her pocket. It was an accident."

"An accident I could have prevented! I should have seen it coming. Mama couldn't handle her, and I missed the signs. There were always signs."

"Your mother didn't let her out of her crib. Oscar did."

I scraped my fingers through my hair, from my forehead back through the top of my braid, loosening strands and letting them fall to my face. "Oscar?"

"Yes," Papa said. "He let her out and told her to go play. Your mother was sleeping. He told me later he thought he was helping."

My brain struggled to put it all together. "His nightmares started after that."

"He was so delicate. We repeated the same story to soothe him. Mama lost her."

"That's why he doesn't trust himself. Afraid he'll hurt another kid."

"It was a terrible mistake," Papa said. "But it was never your fault."

One false truth had defined my entire life.

"After Em died, your Mama started seeing things. Hearing things that weren't there. She was sick, Maggie." He sighed, like someone had let the air out of a balloon. "I left because I was trying to protect you."

"It wasn't about us at all. You left because *she* stopped needing you."

Papa picked up a wheat straw and split it in two. Broke those into halves again, and again, until he clapped the dust from his hands.

"What have you done for the past two years?" I asked.

"This, mostly. Worked the harvests across the country. Slept under the stars."

I smiled. "That's the life I'm starting now. One where I'm free and wild."

He cocked his head to the side and tightened his brow. "Mags, no. You aren't meant for this life. It's dangerous."

"You said it yourself. I'm the strongest person you know. I can handle myself."

"I know you can. What you can't handle is the loneliness."

The light fell across his face in an amber glow. The lines on his cheeks showed his years. How tired he'd been.

"You're meant to love and care for someone," he said. "Be someone's wife and mother."

I let out a laugh that even surprised me. "So I can disappoint everyone who needs me? No way."

My heart hurt so badly I cringed. I couldn't imagine it was possible to love someone else and have them love me back. Hop tried. I wouldn't let him.

"What if inside, I'm nothing more than a rotten, hateful girl?" My chest tightened. "What if I'm her?"

His eyes bloomed red and swollen. He almost cried, but never quite got there. "I don't know what to say to that, Mags. I think her own hate put a lie inside you."

"I hated you for leaving."

"I know."

I thought of Johnny. How he forgave me.

"You have a big, thumping heart just begging to share love with someone," Papa said. "I hope you find that."

I lowered my head to my hands and blocked out the light with my palms. A soft hand landed on my shoulder. I didn't pull away this time.

"What happened to your arm?" he asked.

I peeked out from behind my hands. "Oscar shot me."

"What?"

"It was an accident. He's in an orphan asylum. He doesn't remember me."

His hand slid from my shoulder. "And Johnny?"

I smiled, remembering his big twinkling eyes and his warm hug. "He's gonna be fine. A nice family adopted him."

Papa stared forward. I didn't expect a reaction.

"And where does that leave you?" he asked.

He didn't care about the boys, not really. Nothing mattered after the words, *Mama died.* I watched the fields flash by. Flicks of orange and yellow light bounced off the freight car. "It leaves me right here."

"One day, Maggie, you'll have to face your fear."

A thunderous sound rolled up on us. A pack of wild horses running alongside the train. Their muscular legs flashed through the golden prairie. I thought back to that day in Bend when I started this journey. The day I decided to put my family back together. Franny told me that we are all broken children, until we're not.

Maybe this journey was never about getting the boys back. Maybe, it was about me.

CHAPTER TWENTY-EIGHT

I woke to a still car, noting beads of sweat that had formed on my temples. I sat up and looked around to emptiness.

Papa was gone.

He showed himself to be the same man he always was. He didn't want me, and maybe, I didn't want him. I took all the want and smothered the boys with it. Asked them to fill my empty spots. I no longer had siblings to care for. I had me.

I picked up a rock and threw it with my injured shoulder as far as I could. I screamed so loud my throat stung, and I collapsed onto all fours, gasping for air through tears. He looked his only daughter in the eyes, and he left without a goodbye. Again.

My head throbbed.

I rubbed my eyes and scooted to the edge of the car. My feet hit the pebbles. Men with slumped shoulders and desperate eyes shuffled through the freight yard. Workers with thready muscles and bony frames. I wanted to help them all. Cook them food and send them home to their families.

I was lonely. And it knocked all the air out of me. My heart hurt because I realized Papa was right. I lived on fear and drank it like water. Afraid of love and trust and living.

I knew right then that a solitary life would break me just the same. If I didn't feed that part of myself that needed to love someone, I would die a slow death from the loneliness of my own making, just like my mother.

I looked around to the parched land and knew exactly where I was. Oklahoma.

I found a payphone about half a mile from the freight yard in a town I didn't know the name of and dialed Bess.

"Magnolia, how are you, sweetheart?"

"I found Johnny. He's happy, with a kind family. I had to let him go."

"I'm so sorry," she said.

"It's better this way." The words landed on my skin like a bee sting.

"You know, letting go is one of the hardest things in life."

"That seems to be all I do lately."

"And Eleanor Roosevelt?" she asked.

"A stupid dream. She's gone too. How's Hop?"

"He's gone, sweetheart. They took him back to Oklahoma to stand trial. I tried to pay his bail, but the police wouldn't budge. Said it was for Harper County to deal with."

"I left him."

"You went to find your brother."

"I let him down, Bess. He needed me and I left. The way he loved me, it terrified me."

"Yes, well, learning to love is an education in itself, is it not?"

Papa said that Mama put a lie inside me. "I want to trust. I just don't know how."

"There are no guarantees in life, Maggie. But maybe, if you trust your own heart, that is the only thing you need."

I wanted that more than anything in the world. I closed my eyes. The hot afternoon sat on my cheeks and neck. "How do I do that, Bess?"

She sighed. "Magnolia, do you love anyone?"

"What kind of question is that? Of course I do."

"Name them."

"Oscar. Johnny. Athena, Mary... Hop."

"That sounds like a full heart to me," Bess said.

I traced a crack in the glass wall of the phone booth. Bottom to top and back down again, then picked at it with my fingernail. "Why does it hurt so much?"

"Now that, you'll have to ask God."

"I took all the blame for my family. My sister's death. Truth is, I don't think I could have tried any harder."

"You can't stop people from disappointing you, sweetheart," she said.

"My father proved that." I puffed out my lips, lowering my shoulders from my ears. "I'm tired, Bess."

"I bet you are."

"I told Mrs. Roosevelt that I was running out of fight. That worried her. But maybe that is exactly what I needed. To stop fighting."

"Maggie, the only person you need to stop fighting is yourself."

A chill blew through me, and the ache in my chest flew away like a breath. My hands didn't burn. My tears didn't sting.

A woman's voice clicked in. Told me to place another coin in to keep talking.

"I don't have another coin," I said frantically.

"You don't need it," she said. "You already have everything you need."

Click.

I felt light. Free. Except for one thing.

Behind the payphone was a pharmacy. I walked to the counter. "Excuse me, I need something."

"We don't give handouts. Try the soup kitchen."

"I don't need a handout. I just need to borrow your scissors. Please."

Under the hot Oklahoma sun, I took in the warmth and started to cut. As the scissors sliced through the thick braid, the thumping in my head quieted. Pieces slipped free into the wind, and, with each strand, a little more of myself let go. The last snip sent the long blonde braid to the dusty ground. I stared at my hair coiled at my feet and I wept.

I shook my head from side to side and smiled at the lightness of it. The way it brushed my cheeks. The way it didn't hurt me.

I'd lost everything. Now it was time to get it back.

***

A quick trip on the local train took me north to the jungle where Red had slashed through that man's neck. Cold sweat dripped down my back when I thought of that night. How I almost let that man touch me with Hop watching.

My short hair bounced. My eyes were focused and my vision clear.

When I arrived, I asked around if anyone remembered that night. I pushed everyone to tell me what they knew.

"The Jilted Jezebel," one said.

"I hear it was the Italian kid. Killed someone in Philly, too."

"They were also looking for some girl with a blond braid."

The toothless old woman sat in front of her tent, like she hadn't moved since that night. "You again?" She said. "You look older without that braid."

"I'm surprised you remember me."

"I never forget a face." Her mouth puckered like a forgotten apple.

"I need information on the man that died."

"Better leave it be, child," she said.

"You told me that night that he belonged to a group."

"I want no part of it." She waved me away. "Besides, they arrested that Italian kid for the murder. It's done."

"Please." I paused, not knowing what to call her.

"The name's Eleanor."

"Of course it is," I mumbled to myself with a laugh. "I need to know about these groups. Who are they? Where can I find them?"

"Oh no." She crossed her arms and shook her head. "I want no trouble."

"Eleanor, I need to know. It's very important."

"You trying to get yourself killed?"

"I'm trying to save the Italian boy. He didn't kill that man." I looked into her smoky gray eyes. "What would you do for someone you love?"

"Oh, dammit. I'm a sucker for a love story." She leaned her head back and exhaled. "They meet at an old barn twenty minutes south of here. It's next to an abandoned house. The one with a red handkerchief hanging on the line. They're planning something. I don't know what, so don't ask me."

"Thanks." I stood and rubbed the dirt off my palms onto my dress. "When I first met you, you seemed a little..."

"Crazy?" she said with a grin.

"Well, yes."

She leaned in and whispered, "I let 'em all think that. It keeps me safe. A woman must protect herself. It's a dangerous world out there."

"Yes, it certainly is."

"Hey, you need to be careful." She pointed at me. "These people are angry."

"I don't know any other way to help Hop."

She grunted and teetered off to her tent, and came back holding a handkerchief wrapped around something. "Here." She peeled back an edge to reveal a pistol. "Only use it if you have to."

"I can't take this."

"Yes, you can. I don't need it. At least you'll have a fighting chance."

"Thank you, Eleanor."

"If anything goes wrong, I never met you." She flicked her hand to indicate she was done with me.

I tucked the handgun in my bra between my breasts. The cool metal against my skin made me feel powerful. I'd never shot a pistol, but I could handle a shotgun with the best of them.

I waited for sunset and lurked down the road as the terra cotta sky folded out over the prairie. In the distance, I eyed the abandoned house and barn, the red handkerchief on the line.

I smoothed my skirt. With the few dollars I had left, I bought a simple red cotton dress with a skinny belt at the waist. The worn, faded clothes of yesterday found their way to the jungle, for another girl desperate for a little hope.

I slunk along the wall toward the closed doors where light spilled from between splintered boards. Voices roared from inside, loud and unafraid.

The muffled sounds were hard to make out. I held my ear to the door and heard the words government, fed up, fight back, our America.

They were communists.

Without time to think of a plan, hands suddenly grabbed me and shoved me inside. A trash can fire in the center of the barn flickered light along the bare walls. Men and women held lanterns that cast shadows over their angry faces.

"I found her outside," the man said.

"Let her go." A man hopped down from a ladder. He chewed on a toothpick. His brimmed hat shadowed his long, angular face. He wore a brown suit and a perfectly situated tie and his black shoes reflected the light. "What's your name?"

I said the first name that came to mind. "Red."

"Isn't that a coincidence." He smiled, toothpick still in his teeth. "That's our favorite color. Do you know what it represents?"

"No."

"The blood of workers who died in the fight for fairness. Have you bled for a cause?" He removed his hat and smoothed his hair.

"I believe I have, yes."

"So, Red. What are you doing here?"

I searched the faces of the crowd. All stoic, but anger bubbled below the surface. So strong I could taste it. I needed them, and it made my heart race.

"I'm angry." I tightened my fists and pulled from every memory. Every heartache. "I'm tired of being poor and hungry and helpless."

Their faces changed. Their eyes aglow with excitement.

"That's right. We're all tired of that," he said.

He stepped closer and puffed out his lips. The look in his eyes reminded me of the man from the jungle that night, how he wanted to tear into me like a feast.

I reached my hand down my dress and came up with the pistol. Aimed it right at the toothpick in his mouth. "Touch me and I'll blow your face right off."

"You even know how to use that thing?"

Eyes still on him, I said, "Take one step closer and find out."

Hands up, he stepped back with a smug smile. Then what sounded like one hundred clicks, and at least a dozen guns were pointed straight at me.

"Your move, Red," he said.

"I don't want to shoot you. But if you touch me, I'll fight back." I didn't move my hand, not a twitch. All I could think of was Hop, sitting alone in a jail cell with a stab wound to his stomach.

"You aren't afraid?" he asked.

"I've been through worse. None of you scare me. It's life, out there." I nodded toward the door. "That's what scares the living shit out of me."

He raised his hand, eyes still on me. They all lowered their guns. "You're just the kind of person we need."

As he stepped toward me, I straightened my elbow, leaned my shoulder into the gun, and narrowed my vision. "I meant what I said."

"Noted. Now put down the gun. We don't want to hurt you."

Longing to hold that barrel right between his eyes, I wanted to tell him I was done being a victim. The woman from Arthurdale's words rang in my ears. *Be good. And if you can't be good, be smart.*

"I don't trust anyone," I said. "I just want freedom, and payback for the poverty I grew up in. The dirt floors and the ramshackle cabin. The father who left and the mother who died. The children who had nothing and the big sister who had no way to fix them."

Their faces softened. Everyone understood.

"You out here for yourself?" he asked.

"I'm out here for someone I couldn't help. It's payback time."

"We're all here for the memory of someone. I see you, Red. We all see you."

If eyes are the window to someone's soul, this man's held an entire universe. His crystal blue irises reflected the light, nearly drugging me.

A woman stepped forward with a plate of food. "Sit with me. Have a bite."

I lowered the gun and took a breath. The man put out his hand. "You can have it back when you leave."

I handed him the gun and walked with the woman to a hay bale. The hunger gripped my stomach. I devoured the plate of sliced roast beef, cold potatoes, and a hard roll.

"We're all tired, sweetheart," she said.

I understood them. Years of sacrifice and need bloomed a fear under a thin shell, like a bubble about to pop. What if America wasn't the promised land we all thought it was? If you lost it all, would you fight? These people bet on Americans as fighters.

I sipped down an entire bottle of Coca-Cola without a breath.

The man stood on the bed of a truck. He spoke with such conviction and unwavering confidence. "We've been patient. We've sacrificed our farms and our jobs and our security. For what? So the wealthy can feast while we beg for crumbs?"

The crowd erupted in cheers.

"We are America! Us." He punched his fist into his chest. "Haven't we had enough?"

"Yes!" the crowd shouted. The woman next to me wiped her eyes.

"What are we going to do about it? Will we stand in the bread line and beg?"

"No!" The voices reverberated across the barn.

"Will we take a government handout, stay silent and passive?"

More voices rattled the walls.

"Or will we fight to the death for what is ours?"

Thunderous applause and shouts rumbled the ground.

"Who is he?" I asked the woman.

With stars in her eyes, she said, "We call him Earl. He's our hope. The reason we believe things can change."

I leaned forward and lowered my voice. "We can, you know. Change things. If we do it together and fight with everything we have."

"Yes, dear. We sure can."

"But how?" I asked.

She looked around and hesitated before locking eyes with me again.

"You can trust me," I said. "Us women need to stick together."

She nodded with a knowing smile. "We blow up the system. Oh, I shouldn't say anything. I get so excited with the prospect of taking back our country and our freedom."

"The devastation of the last few years is enough to make anyone hungry for power."

"Yes," she said, her eyes aglow. "Are you prepared to fight?"

"I've spent my life preparing for this moment. I'm more ready than I've ever been."

"You really are one of us." She trembled with a chill of excitement. "Earl's planning something big, and it starts right here in this town."

"Why this town?"

"This has seen the worst of it. The dead farms, the dust clouds. This place represents the failure of our government. These people need us."

This was my moment. My only hope to save Hop. "I want in."

She nodded to Earl.

I approached as he polished the shiny green door of his pickup with a soft cloth. I dropped my wall of heightened instincts that told me to run from him as fast as I could.

"Your words," I said. "They did something to me."

He smiled. Shining white teeth like pearls. "Did they, now?"

"You have such strength. Such power."

"You're full of power too," Earl said. "Every one of us is."

"I don't feel powerful. Just angry."

He rubbed the back of his neck as he scanned my red dress. My hips. "Angry is good. It means you're a fighter."

I neared him. Not close enough to touch, but enough that he could see my chest thumping in rhythm with my heartbeat. "You make me want to fight."

His eyes lit up with excitement.

"Can we really do it?" I said. "Take it all back, I mean?"

"We can if we have each other. Are you ready to give over to the cause and trust us? Trust me?"

Breathy, I said, "I'm ready. What do you want?"

He hesitated. Looked in my eyes. He needed to protect his secrets, but he wanted me. He wanted me to need him. "I don't know if I can trust you."

"No, I suppose you don't." I slid my hand down the curve of my waist, trying to catch my breath. Something about his low, whistling voice captivated me. My chest touched his. I peeked through the top of my eyes at his pink lips.

He leaned close, breath on my cheek. "I promised I wouldn't touch you."

"So don't."

"The beauty of a young woman reclaiming her rightful place in the world. The fight, the hunger." He licked his lips. "It holds a power over me."

"I need to take control and fight back." Leaned into his ear, I whispered, "Tell me how to make them pay."

He closed his eyes like he wanted to kiss me. "Friday night. We're planning something. Something big."

"I want to help."

"I can't tell you much more, it's too dangerous." He reached to my collarbone, almost grazed his fingertips across my skin.

"You promised."

He pulled back. "I know you've been hurt. But we can make it better. *I* can make it better." He reached into the truck bed and handed back my gun. "Come early tomorrow. I'll be here."

"We taking this truck to town? Driving through some buildings?"

"No," he said with horror in his voice. "This is mine. I use it as a platform to speak to my people. I keep it shiny and new so they know that this life will lead to good things. That there is hope."

I ran my hand along the ridge of the bed and grazed my fingers on the smooth metal. "You have a gift. You give power to the voiceless."

He blushed, his chest puffed out. "Red, you're the most beautiful thing I've ever seen."

I smiled. Slid my gun in the space between my breasts. "Good night."

He placed his hat back on and nodded.

As I walked away, I could feel him watching me, tracing the outline of my backside with his eyes. At the door I peered back with a smile, face near my hand on the wood. He placed his hands in his pockets and returned the gesture.

I slid the doors shut and walked away. Then I ran. If he had touched me, I really would have blown his face off.

CHAPTER TWENTY-NINE

The bright sun sizzled the concrete on the doorstep of the police station. After several hours, a man arrived to unlock the door.

"Move along, miss," he said.

I stood, rubbing my eyes. "I need to speak with you."

"I've got nothing, now go on. Young women like you shouldn't be out on the road. Go home."

"There's a man in your custody. Hop. I'm here to get him out."

He jangled his keys and fiddled until he found the right one. "Nothing doing. He murdered a man."

"No, he didn't. I did."

He turned to me, softened his shoulders. "I'm not buying it. Pretty young thing like you? You're probably in love with the boy and want to save him from a murder sentence. No way you murdered anyone."

"You have no idea what I'm capable of."

He looked at me quizzically. "You telling me you killed that man?"

"Yes. And I'll tell you everything and confess. But you need to release him."

"That's not how it works, lady."

"The communists. They're coming for you."

He stared at me. Rolled the idea around in his head a bit. Then he pushed the door open. "My name's Officer Davis. You can call me Davis for short. Why don't you come in for a cup of coffee."

The small building had sparse walls with cracks in them. It smelled of burnt coffee and sweat. I searched around, expecting to see a jail cell. "Where is he?"

"He's in the county jail. This is the police station. Now sit here in my office."

The clock on his desk ticked the seconds away. They had their guy, and they didn't want to believe a girl could kill a man.

He returned with a fellow policeman, a young man with thick eyebrows who placed a mug in front of me. "I'm the police chief."

I sipped the coffee nervously.

The chief cleared his throat. "You say you have information?"

"I do."

The men glanced at each other. The chief lowered his hands to the desk. "How do you know that?"

"Because the man I killed was a communist."

"How did you kill him?" he asked.

"He wanted me." I swallowed and looked at my knees. Placed my hands on them to stop the shaking.

The men looked at each other, then lowered their eyes.

"Go on," Davis said.

"I met Hop on the train heading east. I'm an orphan and he took me in and protected me. That night in the jungle, we slept close because I was scared. I woke to men dragging us away. They pulled me into the tent where that man waited. He told me he had a thing for blondes. They held Hop down and made him watch the man touch me."

Tears caught in my eyes. They stung like acid.

"What did he do to you?" Davis asked.

"He unbuttoned my dress. He didn't care that I cried. I think he wanted me scared. A metal rod heated in the embers of a stove in the corner. I presumed they wanted to torture someone. Maybe it was going to be me. At one point, Hop went out of his mind with anger and kicked the men off him. They started fighting, and I wasn't strong enough. So, I grabbed the hot metal stick and rammed it through the man's neck."

"And the redhead?" the young man said.

"The redhead made a run for it. She disappeared before those men could grab her. She didn't speak, so I didn't catch her name."

"The boy didn't stab the man?"

"No. He's never hurt anybody."

"Why did he say he did?" Davis asked.

"To protect me."

The young man scratched his head. "He would go to jail for murder to protect you?"

"Haven't you ever loved somebody?" I looked up with hopeful eyes.

"And the communists," Davis said, "what do they have planned?"

"I'll tell you if you let Hop go."

The chief grimaced and crossed his arms. "Young lady, this is not a game we're playing."

"I know that. Nothing about this is fun for me. If you need to arrest me, then fine. I'm the one who killed that man. I was defending myself. But Hop did nothing wrong and deserves to be free."

Seconds ticked by while the men stepped outside the office to talk. I sipped the coffee and thought of Hop. His smile. How much I wanted to hold and kiss him.

The door creaked open. Davis sat at his desk opposite me. "All right. You've got a deal. Tell me what you know."

I shook my head. "Hop."

He placed a paper in the typewriter and started typing, his keyboard clacking feverishly. After a few minutes, he rolled the paper out and slid it to the chief, who signed it then turned it around to me.

He opened his mouth to talk, but I flew my hand up, palm to his face before he could speak. "Yes, I can read."

I scanned the document. I'd gone on record detailing how I murdered the man at the migrant camp. The document explained how I would offer my information in exchange for no charges to be filed in this self-defense case. At the end, it said that Hop will be released after I work with authorities to gain information on the communist party. Signed, the police chief.

"How do I know I can trust you?" I asked.

"This document protects us and you."

The tightness closed in on my throat. He could wrong me, just like everyone else. Trust could be the end of us both.

Davis motioned for the chief to leave. The door latched shut. Davis removed his hat and sat on the edge of his desk.

"Listen, I know you're scared. You have little reason to trust me. Truth is, the man you murdered was a terrible human being. He's wanted in several states for attempted murder and burglary. This world is a safer place without him. I have no interest in pressing charges against you."

"But you're fine to use me."

"I want to bring down these commie bastards. They've preyed on the weakest and most vulnerable, convinced them that violence will solve their problems. It won't. It will only take desperate people and make them do something they can't come back from."

"What do you want me to do?" I asked.

"We know they use the jungle to spread information. We've heard the rumors. A young girl with big blue eyes could gain their trust easily."

I stood and wiped my palms on my dress. "Sir, you have kind eyes. You don't twitch or shake or fiddle when you talk. You remove your hat when you speak to me. I can tell you mean well. But I don't trust anyone."

"I understand. Thing is, I have a daughter about your age. She's... well, she's not with us right now. She's sick and needs someone to look out for her." He choked on the words. "I treat others how I want her to be treated."

"Where is she?"

He wrung his hands together. "I don't think that's relevant."

"No, maybe not."

He paused and examined my face for a long while. "She's in an asylum in Tennessee. I couldn't help her. I never could."

"It's the worst feeling in the world, isn't it?"

"Yes," Davis said. "I believe it is."

I signed the paper and slid it back to him. "The followers seem innocent. They just want a better life. They're led by a man named Earl who needs to be a savior. He's a powerful speaker, mesmerizing even. Because Earl needs the power so much, he's blind. He can be manipulated."

Davis crossed his arms. "You read people."

"Like a book."

"What are they planning and when?"

"Friday. I don't know the specifics. They want complete mayhem."

The chair creaked when he leaned his weight back and crossed his arms, taking in the information. "What made you trust me?"

"I'm kind of out of options, aren't I?"

"You're a sharp young woman," he said.

"You might wrong me, but I can't live in fear anymore. I've had enough of that."

"Get us the information and I'll make sure Hop goes free. My boss wants the communists gone. He'll agree to anything that rids us of their trouble."

I scanned his desk and settled on a newspaper open to a story about Eleanor Roosevelt. She wasn't going to save me. I had to do this myself. "Okay. I'll do it."

"I'll be close. If there's any trouble, I'll bring in my guys to protect you."

I stood and straightened my skirt. "And then I get Hop?"

"Yeah. You have my word." He stood, cocked his head to the side. "Their promises didn't sway you. Why?"

"I guess I believe there are good people watching out for us. Trying their best to get us out of this. Besides, people like Earl are all the same. They don't do it for us, they do it for themselves."

"Come on, I'll buy lunch. We have some planning to do."

***

Evening set in, the air hot and still. Not a breeze to ruffle my hair or cool my skin. Davis's wife put makeup on me. Pink cheeks and rouged lips. She curled my hair into big bouncing curls. My heart thumped when I stared at that barn door, at the quiet stillness inside. Not quite sunset, I watched the giant orange sun float toward the flat stretch of earth around me.

I stepped inside to find Earl dangling his feet off the truck bed. He jumped down when he saw me, eyes lit up. "You came."

"I promised I would."

"I thought about you all day," he said.

I stepped hesitantly toward him. "I haven't been able to stop thinking about your speech."

"Our message resonates with you."

I locked my elbows tight to stop my hands from fidgeting with my dress. "Your passion speaks to me. I want to follow you."

"No need to follow. We can walk side by side."

He smelled so clean. Fresh soap with a splash of aftershave.

I pulled my shoulders back. "I don't trust men. Not after what happened in San Francisco."

He stepped back, interest piqued. "What happened there?"

"I met a man. Quite like you, actually. He promised me freedom from poverty. I wanted to make a difference and he took advantage of that."

"Who was he?"

I crossed my arms over my shoulders.

"Tell me. I'll rip his head off if he hurt you. I know a few guys in the city. A few important men."

"He was important, all right. Had a stash of money and guns around him all the time. He had big plans."

"What did he do to you?"

His fingers gingerly wrapped around mine as an ice-cold shot flashed through my center. I let him hold my hand and forced my cheeks still to hold back a grimace. "He hurt me."

"Son of a bitch."

"I can't tell you anymore. He'll find me."

Earl grabbed me and pulled me into his chest, buried my head against his shoulder. I wanted to pull away and knee him right between the legs, but I breathed and remembered my purpose. "Please, I'm too frightened."

"Of course, I understand." He rolled his eyes up, collecting himself.

He reached for my hair, barely touching a curl. "You look beautiful."

"Thank you." My stomach ached.

"This is a lonely life," he said. "I have to be strong for everyone else."

"You don't need to be strong for me."

"I can see that. It's in your eyes."

I ducked from his hand as it neared my cheek. "I've had to be strong too. Those men in San Francisco can be tough."

"Some of our leaders are misguided. If I ran things, I'd bring everyone in. Make them feel safe."

I ran my finger along the shining door of his truck and slipped my gaze up toward his, widening my girlish eyes. "He held me captive. I believed he would save me, but all he ever did was hurt me."

"It was Munchin, wasn't it?" He shook his head. "That German is known for being a brute."

I shook my head no.

"Brewster?"

No, I shook my head again. "Higher up than him."

He looked around then whispered, "Charlie?"

I covered my face and forced tears.

"Charlie Foster, of course." He shook his head. "That monster."

I turned from him. He laid his hand on my shoulder, but recoiled when he felt my mangled flesh. "Did he do that to you?"

"I told you, I don't trust men."

"Foster. I'll kill him."

"His friend is no better. They're planning something big. I ran, too afraid to be with them for one more day."

"Yeah," he said. "The train plan."

"Think they'll make it happen?" I glanced over my shoulder.

"We're waiting for them. As soon as they make a move, we'll follow. Blow up everything we can."

"They terrified me."

"I'm not like that," Earl said. "I want to hold you. Make you feel safe."

A bird fluttered through the rafters. I watched it flap feverishly into the dark corner. "I'll feel safe when I burn this country to the ground."

His eyes lit up. "We'll set it on fire. Together."

He pulled me close and leaned his lips near mine.

"We start here," I said. "This town. Tonight."

Breathy, he said, "Yes. My friends in Oklahoma City, they'll protect us. Keep us hidden while we plan another attack."

"Go into hiding?"

"We'll be together. This is crazy. We just met. But I feel something with you, Red."

"These friends of yours, is it safe?"

"Don't worry. One's a policeman. No one would ever suspect him." His breath warmed my palm.

I placed my finger on his chin. "So much destruction. Why?"

"They won't listen to us. It's the only way."

"It's not the only way." I ran my hand through his hair, then grabbed a fistful and yanked his head back. "Hurting people won't bring back my family."

"Red..." His eyes widened.

I squeezed until my hand hurt. "And you won't fix me." I shoved him into the truck.

"Hey, I told you. I don't want to hurt you."

I reached into my dress and pulled out my pistol. Aimed it straight at his face. "Back up."

"Red, please."

"No. I know who to trust and it isn't you." I backed away but held that gun steady as stone. "You're the worst kind of human. You think you're doing good, but all you're doing is hurting people."

"What is this?"

I shot the back tire. Then the front one. Air hissed out and the truck bounced lower to the ground.

Earl grabbed his hair with both hands. "What are you doing?"

"Righting a wrong." I shot at the ground near his feet.

He squealed and climbed onto the edge of the truck bed. "What the hell, Red?"

"Red's gone." One more shot through his front windshield and the glass shattered in a glorious crackle, raining to the ground as Earl huddled in a ball, hands covering his face. "Are you frightened, Earl?" I held the gun pointed at his face and neared slowly. "I've had enough of people like you."

He cowered, the fluid, dazzling blue of his eyes clouded by fear. "It will never get better," he said. "You'll stay poor and hungry."

"I've learned that people are kind. They'll help you and love you… if you let them. It's a shame you never learned that."

The doors slid open. Policemen rushed in and grabbed Earl by the arms. Cuffed his hands behind his back.

"Why did you do this?" Earl asked.

"There are people I admire in government. I won't allow you to hurt them. Not for anything."

Eleanor Roosevelt might be a ghost, but her effect on me will remain on my heart forever.

They carted Earl off, and Davis stepped up next to me. "Did you get anything?"

"San Francisco. Munchin, Brewster. Charlie Foster. He's the big guy. They're waiting to blow up the trains. Once the guys in San Francisco move, they all will. Earl had friends in Oklahoma City ready to protect him. One's a policeman."

He removed a pad of paper from his pocket and wrote the names. "You did good, Magnolia."

"I meant what I said. There are good people out there trying to do the right thing."

His upper lip quivered. "I try to live up to the man I am in my daughter's eyes."

"I think you're doing her proud."

"What do you say, should we go get your Hop?"

"Yeah. But before we do, can you tell me more about this asylum in Tennessee? I need to find a good place for my brother Oscar."

He led me to the police car and opened the passenger door for me. "Get in. We'll talk on the way back to the jail."

***

I stood anxiously with Davis under the starry sky, staring at the door. I willed it to open. Finally, the chief appeared, and out came Hop. He was thinner with short hair and angular lines to his face.

He rushed to me, wrapped his arms around my shoulders, and cried into my neck. When he eventually pulled back, he examined my short hair. "Your braid's gone."

"Yeah. I didn't need it anymore."

He held his forehead to mine. "How did you get me out?"

"With a little help from a friend."

Davis smiled and before he shut the door, said, "Head down to the diner. I told them to have a few plates waiting for you."

"Thanks. For everything."

He nodded slowly and tipped his hat before closing the door.

Hop held his hand to my cheek. "I thought I'd never see you again."

"Me too. I almost lost you at Bess's, then at the hospital, and again here." I held his shirt in my hands and pulled tight. "I don't want to lose you again."

"And Eleanor Roosevelt, did she help you?"

"No. I did this myself."

"Maggie, I'm so lucky to have met you. I love you."

"I love you too." I ran my hand along his soft, olive skin. "Nothing went to plan. I lost everything, but I found myself."

"That's all I've ever wanted for you." He ran his fingers through my curls in a soft touch that sent a thrill through my body.

"Everyone's gone. It's just you and me," I said.

"Well, that means we get to write our own future. What should we do with it?"

"I know exactly what I want."

He pulled me into a kiss. A soft, deeply loving kiss that softened every muscle in my body. I knew right then that I'd found home.

CHAPTER THIRTY

It's been over twenty years since my life fell apart. Since I lost my brothers and set out on an adventure that would change me from the inside. The people I met along the way taught me to love, to hope, to face my fears. Turns out that falling apart is how we rearrange the pieces how they should have been from the start.

My daughters are grown. They know little about my past. Their Uncle Johnny is a pilot in the US Airforce. Uncle Oscar comes to visit sometimes with his caretaker. We keep the house quiet when he's here. He disrupts easily, but he loves larger than life. He smiles and hugs the girls, but often forgets their names. Sometimes he tells them stories of his youth in Bend, Oregon.

In the winter of 1938, Hop and I married at the courthouse in Knoxville. We scrimped and saved for two years. At a local diner, I waitressed and Hop washed dishes. We bought a small parcel of land for next to nothing. It was dry and parched, just like the rest of the country. But we had each other, and I was expecting our first child.

As fully as I loved Hop, I give credit to Lucinda, my baby girl, for finally showing me I deserved love. It was her presence in my arms that pulled the last thread of loneliness that had been woven into my life. We called her Lucy for short, just like Hop's lost mother.

That spring, the rains came. It was glorious, and we danced under the downpour, "Over the Rainbow" playing on the radio from the front porch.

We planted our first rows of wheat that year. And we spent the next twenty years living out our dream. I drank my coffee in the wheat fields and watched the sun rise and set in the golden waves that clattered around our home. Children laughed in the distance. It was here I let my mind wander to Red and Mary and Bess and Franny. The women who'd molded me, who changed me.

Hop never did find his parents. It bothered me more than him. "You are my family," he always said. I guess it was enough for him.

I tracked Eleanor Roosevelt's life closely. I read all her books and listened to her radio programs. She became even more important and influential after the war years. After her husband died, she came into her own. Grew more outspoken on civil rights and women's rights. She pushed harder and louder, unintimidated by her critics.

I applauded when she resigned from the Daughters of the American Revolution. They refused a Black opera singer at their auditorium, and she made a spectacle of their racism. I cheered when she became the first woman to represent the US as a United Nations delegate and wrote policy for the Human Rights Commission. I smiled when President Truman kept her on as an advisor. And I stayed up late reading every word of her published books and magazine articles.

One morning, we rocked on the porch, the lonely house free of children and laughter, enjoying the rare stillness of farm life.

"Put on a nice dress, Mags," Hop said. "I have a surprise for you."

Hop never lost that hopeful dreamer inside. He was always surprising me, reminding me not to take life too seriously.

"Okay," I said.

We drove west into the farmland, talking about Lucy's pregnancy, expecting our first grandchild in a few months, and how our youngest Emily, would graduate from the University of Tennessee, Knoxville. How life had been good to us.

Hop pulled up to the Nashville airport. He parked the car and smiled.

"What are we doing here?" I asked. "Are we flying off on a secret vacation?"

"No, darling. This is your moment. Yours alone."

"I don't understand."

"I know, but you will. Go on inside."

As strange as this was, I trusted him.

Night had settled. I had no idea what I was looking for. I wandered the empty terminal, dotted with only a few colorful stewardesses and lounge music softly floating from the speakers.

At one of the gates, I noticed an elderly woman. Dressed sharply, back tall, eyes on the window. I recognized her as our neighbor's mother, who had supper with him every Sunday.

"Hello, Margaret," I said.

"Oh, hello Magnolia. It seems we're the only ones awake." She smiled and patted the seat. "I've been waiting for you."

I lowered next to her and admired her white suit and perfectly curled hair. She always did want her son to join her in politics, but he loved the farm life.

"Margaret, what are we doing here?"

"That husband of yours sure does love you."

"Yes." I smiled widely.

"Hop's been good to my son," Margaret said. "He brings coffee every morning. But I'm sure you know that. Since my daughter-in-law passed, well... he's been so lonely. I do believe Hop has saved his life."

"He's saved mine every day for twenty years."

She smiled and smoothed her skirt.

"So, what then am I doing here?" I asked.

We watched a plane roll near the terminal, its lights flickering into the windows.

"Ah. The mystery has arrived." Margaret secured her purse over her forearm and waited for the door to open.

And then, through the darkness of the Nashville night strode a tall, imposing figure. I recognized her smile first.

"Mrs. Roosevelt," Margaret said. "Pleasure to see you again."

They hugged, a warm, friendly embrace.

No Secret Service. No bodyguards. This woman who taught me how to love and live and discover courage stood before me as a living, breathing

thing. I suppose I had memorialized her in my mind. Too spectacular, too bold, and too daring to be a real woman. Yet here I stood, smelling her perfume. Lilacs. Just like twenty-two years ago.

She held Margaret's shoulders, and with a grand smile turned to face me.

"Hello," Eleanor said. "Who might you be?"

"I... I'm..." I collected myself and cleared my throat. "My name is Magnolia. You may call me Maggie, if you'd like."

"Hello, Maggie. What brings you here tonight?"

"You," I said.

"Well, I'm flattered."

"Where's your Secret Service?" I asked.

"No need for them tonight." She linked arms with Margaret. "We have pressing business in the mountains, don't we?"

"Yes, ma'am, we certainly do," Margaret said.

Eleanor smiled at me. "And you, Maggie, are you here to join us in our secret quest tonight?"

I thought of Hop, and how much adventure he gave up for me, for our family. How it's been years since I'd dared to embrace a wild dream. "It looks like I am," I said.

"Splendid." She balanced her beaded handbag on her forearm. "You realize it's quite dangerous."

"Yes."

What could this seventy-four-year-old human rights advocate and her elderly friend possibly be doing at night in the mountains of Tennessee? I knew one thing, this risk seemed like magic. Serendipity. I had to answer the call.

We walked to Margaret's car parked just outside the terminal. Again, no police. Just Eleanor Roosevelt and a couple of friends heading to the mountains. Exhilaration pounded through me. I hadn't felt this alive since we were ragged orphans screaming along in an open freight car.

Mrs. Roosevelt unclasped her bag and removed a revolver, which I could only assume to be loaded. She placed it on the seat between them.

What the hell kind of trouble were these ladies getting into?

We bumped along the road, the two laughing and catching up.

"Maggie, don't be frightened when we drive past the crowd," Eleanor said. "They're angry, and they want to intimidate me. If you don't take a stand, you leave the impression that you're cowardly. But I've made a commitment that I intend to keep."

I didn't want to let on that I had no idea where we were going. She thought I was part of whatever uprising we were heading toward. "Who'll be in the crowd, ma'am?" I asked.

"The Klan."

"As in Ku Klux?"

"The very same."

Margaret spoke up. "The KKK placed a twenty-five-thousand-dollar bounty on her head. Threatened to kill her if she followed through with this civil rights presentation."

"The FBI tried to stop me. As if they ever could before. They have a file on me three decades long. I've lived with screaming protestors and conservative newspapers calling me a communist. Un-American. The death of civility." She dismissed it with a small laugh. "I've learned to thrive in controversy. I've found a purpose, and it gives me great joy to know that no one can take it from me."

"That is a strength few women possess," I said.

"It's what comes about when you look fear in the face. When you decide to pursue what's in your heart." She turned to face me, arm propped over the seat. "When you have decided what you believe, what you feel must be done, have the courage to stand alone and be counted."

Chills skittered up my arms. Her words. Her strength. Her eyes staring right through me. All these years following her accomplishments, and I had no idea she would stand down the Klan with only a pistol and a relentless belief that goodness wins.

I remembered the day I came across the newspaper article in the alley all those years ago. Hungry. Terrified. Lost as a stray sheep. Even then, her words had the power to lift me to a place of hope.

We drove past a smattering of scowling men who seemed unaware that the longest serving First Lady, the woman whom they wanted to hang from a tree, sat inside this tan station wagon. They assumed there would be a cavalcade. A dozen cars of men around to protect her. They couldn't imagine how fearless she really was.

High in the mountains, we arrived at the Highlander Folk School. Two women greeted us, both elderly. It seemed to me that the changemakers, the fearless, were led by aging women who decided they'd had about enough of the way things were. They wanted the way things should be.

We drank fruit punch and waited for sunrise, my head buzzing with excitement. Eleanor discussed her work at the United Nations and her husband's legacy. She greeted young students from the school. Black and white, women and men.

I learned this school was established in 1932. I didn't need to know much more than that, as I remembered the bleak years so vividly, they felt like a whisper on my skin. We were so desperate and scared, the entire country had suffered a crisis of faith. We trusted the American ideals of work and patriotism. And then it all fell apart. That sort of devastation was a breeding ground for resistance.

I could see why this place was important to her. Education as a tool for social change. It was at the heart of every speech she ever gave.

I stood in the back of the crowd, leaned against a black gum tree, watching Eleanor Roosevelt prepare for her speech. She stood on the porch in the sticky Tennessee morning, a matronly grandmother with a pillbox hat, a tailored dress, two strings of pearls, and a microphone.

"Highlander school has been doing excellent labor education, which has been proving day by day that colored people and white people can live, work, and play together and grow in a Christian spirit of understanding and charity." She paused and looked around. I sensed she read the crowd, feeling how far she could take her statements.

"In 1933 alone, white mobs lynched twenty-eight Black Americans. I fought tirelessly to put an end to it, but I was up against a society that didn't want to see its ugly parts. The next year, I joined the NAACP. We presented an anti-lynching bill to Congress, but it was struck down. But I have not, not for one single day, stopped believing that we are better than this. I will continue to fight for the rights of all our citizens. For justice and equal opportunity."

The crowd hushed. Mesmerized by her soft voice and her powerful words. She spoke to the hearts of people. She certainly spoke to mine.

She shook hands and laughed with the students after her speech. These young men and women were so hungry for change. It wasn't much different from my youth. We needed someone to look up to. To show us that change is worth fighting for.

"She's quite a speaker, isn't she," Margaret said.

"She really is."

We collected ourselves and drove away from the school. The sun blared into my eyes, scratchy from lack of sleep. It did little to dampen the feeling of pure euphoria.

"Well, Maggie, how did you enjoy our meeting?" Eleanor Roosevelt asked.

"I found it inspiring. I always find your words inspiring."

"Tell me, how did you get involved in the civil rights movement?" she asked.

I felt myself blush. I searched for some explanation and found myself stuttering. Luckily, Margaret interrupted. "Ma'am, will you be needing to stop anywhere before your flight home?"

"No, thank you. I have much work to attend to in New York."

As we neared the airport, I grew sad at the prospect of leaving her and this unexpected night. When we arrived, I offered to carry Mrs. Roosevelt's bag to the terminal.

"Yes, that would be lovely," she said.

Margaret hugged Eleanor goodbye and whispered in my ear, "Hop left you something in your purse."

I opened my bag to find Eleanor Roosevelt's letter. I'd kept it all these years.

"Thank you, Margaret."

"Join us for supper this Sunday?"

"We wouldn't miss it," I said.

Margaret situated her big black sunglasses and drove off.

Inside the airport, there appeared to be a wait while staff cleaned her plane.

"Mrs. Roosevelt," I said, "can I tell you something?"

"Of course, dear."

"I'm not part of the civil rights movement. Although I support your cause, that is not why I came here last night."

"Oh?"

"I'm a wheat farmer from Knoxville. I came here to meet you."

She cocked her head in surprise. "Well, it has been lovely to make your acquaintance. Was there something you wish to speak with me about?"

"Actually, we've met before."

"We have? You aren't familiar to me, I'm afraid."

"1935. You were on a tour of the Pacific Northwest. I was a maid at the Pilot Butte Inn. We spoke on the porch and walked along the river discussing family and responsibility."

Her face turned serious. "I've met so many people over the years."

"Of course." My heart sank. I reached into my purse and handed her the faded envelope.

She unfolded it and read her own writing from a time long gone. She placed her hand at her heart. "Yes. You took care of your brothers. I remember."

"Yes. My parents were both gone, so I tried to raise them."

"I bet you did a splendid job."

"No, I didn't." I said it with a nervous laugh and had to fight the tears I had long since swallowed. "You remember how desperate those times were?"

She nodded with heavy eyes. "It kept me up at night. How hunger and longing gripped the nation. How much I wanted to save everyone."

"You saved me."

She arched her eyebrows. A hint of a smile.

"You did. I read an article about you one day when I was searching the trash for moldy food. Your message of hope and determination. It turned a light on inside me. I lost my brothers shortly after that. They took them when they had medical needs. I'm embarrassed to tell you that I chased you across the country, believing that you could help me get them back. It was your promise in this letter that kept me going."

She swallowed and took a pause. I suspect not many things turned her speechless. "You never caught up with me, then."

"Almost at Warm Springs on Thanksgiving, but Secret Service busted us."

"Yes!" Her eyes lit up. "I heard they removed some kids. That was you?"

"Yes. Then I went to Arthurdale. Missed you by a few minutes. I did see you leave on the train, though."

"Well, I'm so sorry you had to go through all that. I wish I would have known. I would have made certain you had an audience with me."

"It was a painful time. A lot of loss. But it's in those times that we discover who we are. I met many inspiring people on that adventure, including my husband."

"Wonderful. I thought about you many times after our meeting by the river."

My heart leapt. "You did?"

"Yes. You were so young and beautiful and courageous. But I could see how much you struggled. How deep your wounds were."

"You could see all that from one conversation?"

"When you've travelled as much as I have, you learn to read people's faces. Their body language. You held a lot of anger."

"Yes, I did. It took losing everything to finally let it go."

"That takes courage."

"I've followed you, read every *MyDay* column, and listened to every broadcast. Watched every television program. But it was your words to me at the river all those years ago that I still hold close. How strong and capable we really are."

A man came through the door. "Mrs. Roosevelt, your plane is ready."

She nodded. "Yes. Thank you." She placed her hand on my arm. "It is my deepest held belief that women have been at the center of every ounce of change and progress this country has seen. Power in the world starts with power in your heart."

She turned to walk away, and I had to ask the question that had burned inside me for all these years. "Does it still hurt you, the way your mother treated you?"

She stopped and took a few steps back. "Yes."

"Oh." I'd hoped she would tell me it all disappears. That you hit a certain age and all the hurt floats away like dandelion fluff.

"Maybe that's why I remembered your face. Your anger. I recognized it."

"I hated myself for years the way she hated me. I've grown. But flashes of her eyes, her words, they still find their way to me. It still hurts."

"Yes, it does. Because the one person in the world we should have been able to count on told us we were worthless. Ugly. A mistake."

Tears pooled in my scratchy eyes.

She told the attendant to hold the plane. "I need one more minute." She led me to a chair and sat down. After a pause she said, "I have one regret in life."

"Just one?"

"Well, only one having to do with things I could control." She glanced outside at the blue skies and giant silver planes taking off and landing. "I was not a good mother."

"That can't be true."

"It is. I've been unable to show emotions, though I wish I could. There's a strange feeling inside that tells me I can't. If I showed vulnerability to my children, my husband, then I might die."

"I know that feeling well. We learned it early on. Trust is dangerous."

"Yes. I still struggle. I love all mankind, but I do not know how to let my children love me. I have lived with a deep desire to connect with people and a strange fear of intimacy."

"Is that why you fight for women? So you may heal yourself along the way?"

"I suppose that's part of it. But don't you want to prove them wrong? Our terrible mothers, that is. I strive to make a difference because I cannot accept that I am meant to be forgotten."

We sat in silence, a moment of connection that I'd spent my life dreaming of. I'd been chasing the dream of a perfect mother who could teach me and guide me. As it turns out, being a mother was her one true fault. On this, I had surpassed her. It was the only thing I was truly proud of. I'd found the love for my daughters that I hadn't had for myself.

"Possibly, it is time we both grieve for those little girls. For the mother they never had," she said.

"And forgiveness?"

"That, perhaps, is for another day."

A warm flood washed over me. It burst out from the inside. It took me two decades, but I finally did get my moment with Eleanor Roosevelt. She helped me see that I was never broken.

She squeezed my hand and stood, nodded to the impatient attendant. "It's time for me to go. What a pleasure it has been to spend this time with you, Magnolia."

"It's been everything I dreamed it would be. Thank you, Mrs. Roosevelt."

"Call me Eleanor." She winked, and with a twinkle in her eye, she boarded her plane for New York.

Outside the terminal, I took a breath of humid air and smiled when the breeze skimmed my cheek. I had to stop and take in this life-changing moment. And by that, I'm not talking about meeting Eleanor. Although that was pretty special in itself. I'm talking of the moment where you decide to let go. I'd been approaching this for decades, I now realized. But now, in one moment, I finally felt it. It was time.

I walked through the parking lot and found our Ford parked under the shade of a sugar maple, Hop asleep in the driver's seat.

I knocked on the half-open window. He smiled in his sleepy haze. I sat in the passenger seat and kissed him softly on the cheek.

"Well, was it everything you dreamed of?" he said.

"More."

"I'm so glad, Maggie. You deserve it." He kissed my temple.

"You're a very special man, Hop."

"You look different," he said. "Happy."

"Yes. I feel happy. And tired. Let's go home."

"Okay. But where have you been all night?"

"Oh nothing, just took on the KKK."

He caught a sharp inhale and shook his head. "No, I don't want to know. Margaret assured me you'd be safe."

"I wasn't scared for a moment."

I thought of how I would write to her in New York, and what a dream it was for the young Magnolia to sit and discuss matters of the heart with the most impressive woman in the world. How lucky I really was.

"Hop, I'd like to take a trip."

***

One week after I met Eleanor Roosevelt, I stood at the end of a dusty road next to the Deschutes River, near the house that had haunted my dreams for nearly thirty years. Hop waited at the edge of the forest, hands in his pockets and tears glistening in his eyes. I had to do this myself.

It was greener than I remembered. Those years were dry and dusty. I hadn't imagined that the trees would keep growing and the rain would eventually return, expecting my hometown to stay as it was in my memory.

I kicked rocks as I walked down the road, with no idea what awaited me. I expected a burnt house and ravaged land. As I neared the house, memories crawled around me, but I stopped, took a deep breath, and let them settle.

The lush land overflowed with life, every crack filled with moss and wildflowers. I had forgotten how beautiful this place could be in the late spring. The river rushed in the background. The smell of pine and the thin cloud of yellow pollen that floated in the air.

A few logs in the shape of a square, a wood stove, and one step. That's all that remained. I guess the grocery man never found a use for this place. I'm grateful for that. I don't know what I would have done had the pine trees we used to climb been razed to nothing.

The years of snow and wind and summer heat had taken their toll. I walked in circles, not sure exactly where the grave was. I stepped on something hard. Down on my knees, I cleared the dirt and weeds away, and there it was. Rocks, shaped into a star.

I held my hands over it and remembered Johnny with his teary eyes. The stars would bring her home.

"I've avoided coming here all these years," I whispered. "But I'm not scared anymore. The memories don't sting like they used to."

I closed my eyes and remembered the boys' hands over mine on top of this star so long ago. "I forgive myself for letting them down. Things ended up just as they should have. But now, I also forgive you, for the things you didn't understand. You were abandoned as a child. Forgotten. Angry. You couldn't be a loving mother, because your poor heart couldn't take it."

The pain inside my chest nearly took my breath away. "I'll be a grandmother soon. I've been a good mother to my girls and I'm proud of that. I often wonder if you had tried hard enough, held on longer... no, that was never possible. But you didn't leave like Papa did. I see that now. You held on in the only way you knew how."

I crawled to the other grave. The one that no longer held a cross. It was merely a depression in the ground. "Em. I will always love you. I'll never rid myself of the pain of failing you. But I can forgive myself, and I can live in your memory, to be the kind of woman you'd be proud of."

Standing at the foot of these graves, I wiped away tears, took a deep breath, and closed my eyes. "I forgive you. Not for you, but for me. I don't want your branding on my heart anymore."

I reached into my purse and took out what I came here to present. I laid the small stone in the depression over Emily. A thunder egg. Rough and grainy on the outside, brilliant blue like the ocean underneath.

I stood and said goodbye to the burnt house by the river. The fear of being touched and loved. The belief that I was a failure. The Magnolia who thought she could control the world or prevent another tragedy. She can rest here, with Mama and Emily.

I've discovered that we are resilient creatures, capable of smoothing all kinds of scars. The worst are sometimes the ones you can't see, like a hidden lashing never allowed to heal.

As a wise woman once said, "To handle yourself, use your head. To handle others, use your heart."

And that is what I plan to do from here forward.

Thank you, Eleanor.

THE END

ACKNOWLEDGEMENTS

Authors put their heart into every story, but some push us to our limits, and force us to look deep inside to a place we've spent years protecting. When I started writing *Chasing Eleanor*, I had no idea that I would go through so much. I didn't expect it to break me and put me back together again. Magnolia taught me that sometimes, we need to write to heal ourselves.

I've always been fascinated by the Great Depression, and knew I'd need the perfect story to tell if I was going to attempt writing in this era. Magnolia gave me that in spades. Her complicated toughness kept me going when I wanted to quit.

To Lisa and Brigette and Naomi, who saw me through a full rewrite and lots of tears to get this story where it needed to be, and to Jen for supporting me every step of the way in this wild world of writing and publishing. To Sayword, whose friendship has kept me afloat, and who is as quick to cheer for me as she is to pick me up when I'm having trouble doing that myself.

I'm beyond thankful for my husband Mike and my sister Heather, and stepdaughter Chelsea, who celebrate my successes with as much enthusiasm as I hold for this journey.

My two daughters keep me showing up every day to write. They make me want to leave this world a little better for them.

And lastly, I must thank Eleanor Roosevelt. My lifelong idol. I've always looked up to her and admired her gentle strength. Her commitments to our world are unmatched, and her support of women's voices is still sorely needed. I took a few liberties with the dates she said particular quotes, as I wanted her powerful words to make it in this story as much as possible.

In 2020, I started writing about a teenager named Magnolia, who was trying to survive for her brothers, when my research led me to a story that Eleanor Roosevelt visited the Pilot Butte Inn at the exact month and year that I set this story in. I took that as a sign. Through every early morning writing session, I held tight onto Eleanor Roosevelt's teachings. Her words carried me through this emotional process, as I was hungry to find forgiveness in my own life. In only the way Magnolia could, her deep strength helped me find the empathy I've been in search of for years.

Thank you once again to Black Rose Writing for the support and allowing my love letter to Eleanor Roosevelt to get to print.

And thank you to every reader who took this emotional journey with me.

Start small. Think big.

~Sip Coffee. Savor Books.

-Kerry

ABOUT THE AUTHOR

Kerry Chaput is an award-winning historical fiction author. She believes in the power of stories that highlight young women and found families. Born and raised in California, she now lives in the beautiful Pacific Northwest, where she can be found on hiking trails and in coffee shops. Connect with her at www.kerrywrites.com.

NOTE FROM THE AUTHOR

Word-of-mouth is crucial for any author to succeed. If you enjoyed *Chasing Eleanor*, please leave a review online—anywhere you are able. Even if it's just a sentence or two. It would make all the difference and would be very much appreciated.

Thanks!
Kerry Chaput

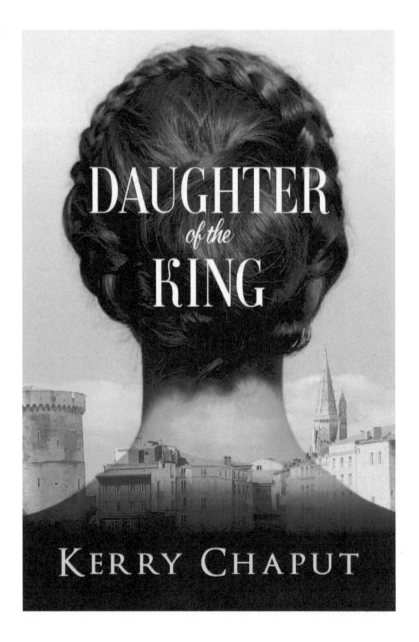